THE
NEXUS

MYSTICS BOOK THREE

KIM RICHARDSON

FABLEPRINT

FablePrint

The Nexus; Mystics Book Three

Copyright © 2014 by Kim Richardson

All rights reserved, including the right of reproduction in whole or in any form.

Cover by Kim Richardson

Text in this book was set in Garamond.

Printed in the United States of America

Summary: When Mrs. Dupont used Zoey to set The Great Junction in motion: the event that occurs when two portals from different worlds align and make a permanent doorway, with it came disaster.

ISBN-13: 978-1720997870

ISBN-10: 172099787X

[1. Supernatural—Fiction. 2. Science-Fiction—Fiction. 3. Magic—Fiction].

BOOKS BY KIM RICHARDSON

SOUL GUARDIANS SERIES

Marked

Elemental

Horizon

Netherworld

Seirs

Mortal

Reapers

Seals

THE HORIZON CHRONICLES

The Soul Thief

The Helm of Darkness

The City of Flame and Shadow

The Lord of Darkness

DIVIDED REALMS

Steel Maiden

Witch Queen

Blood Magic

MYSTICS SERIES

The Seventh Sense

The Alpha Nation

The Nexus

THE
NEXUS

MYSTICS BOOK THREE

KIM RICHARDSON

CHAPTER 1

A GIANT PAIN IN THE

NECK

The giant's grin revealed a mouthful of rotten teeth.

"You die. Me eat girl."

Its rough, scratchy voice rasped like wind through rock.

Zoey raised her boomerang.

"And I thought giants were supposed to be big and dumb. Clearly, the agency was wrong about you, weren't they big guy? You're not a brainless fridge after all, are you? No, you're practically a genius."

The giant's wet, pink eyes gave no indication that it understood.

It stood about twelve feet high and was as large and thick as a redwood tree. A mass of wiry straw-colored hair decorated with jewels and precious stones fell from the top of his small, flat head. It looked like a very ugly Christmas tree. More jewels were tied around his muscular bare arms, and he wore thick rings around his three fingers and three toes. He was naked except for a kilt-like fur skirt. Skulls and bones hung from his belt, and his skin was dark green and rough like tree bark. If trees could have offspring, Zoey figured this giant would be a pretty close match.

"Me eat girl," repeated the giant.

Zoey rolled her eyes. "I heard you the first time—"

"Zoey, *seriously?*"

Simon's tousled blonde head appeared from behind a rock.

"We're not here to chat, you know."

Simon emerged clumsily from behind the large boulder. He wore a simple black jacket, a white t-shirt, and jeans. He looked even more lanky and goofy than usual because he had grown over the holidays and still wasn't in total control of his limbs.

"How long are you going to stand here and wait for it to smash your brains in? They have a reputation for being ruthless and unpredictable . . . and they *kill* for *fun*. I'd also like to point out that these mystics are *meat* eaters . . . ."

He glanced over his shoulder. "Besides, the Mutes are starting to notice the giant. We have to hurry and get out of here. Let's fry this birdbrain and split."

Zoey narrowed her eyes. "I wonder how the Mutes see him? You think they see him as like a big tree?"

"Who cares? Zoey, come on! Enough small talk; we need to get a move on."

"I know. I know," muttered Zoey.

She looked out over the beaches of Houghton Bay, Wellington, New Zealand. The ocean breeze smelled like the fish market near one of her foster homes. But the spectacular view couldn't lift her spirits.

Mrs. Dupont had successfully completed the Great Junction, and the Agencies around the world were in a panic. What was worse, Zoey's mother was still imprisoned in the Nexus.

Zoey had tried to transport herself directly to her mother, but she couldn't open a doorway to the Nexus. Other than the fact that Mrs. Dupont had used Zoey's blood, Zoey didn't know how the horrible Mrs. Dupont had opened the portal.

In the end, Zoey realized her only hope to reach her mother was to *use* the portal Mrs. Dupont had created. She thought of nothing else.

After Mrs. Dupont's escape, the Operative programs had gone into overdrive, and the entire year's schooling had been crammed into four excruciating weeks, without *any* breaks. Then Operatives had been sent on assignments on their *own*, without supervision. Things were *that* bad.

They had been elevated to OSC, Operative Special Clearance, and given a golden badge with the letters OSC embroidered in red thread to wear so that other agents would see that they were officially agents. And while Zoey did not wear the Shield of Valor she had been awarded, Simon wore his OSC badge proudly on his chest. The little piece of cloth gave him extra courage, like an adrenaline shot.

Zoey had been saddened when she was paired with Simon and not Tristan. Although Simon was her best friend, and she was glad to be paired with him—he *wasn't* Tristan.

She did her best to hide her disappointment.

She smiled in spite of herself and turned her attention back to the giant.

"You've got two choices, Mr. Giant. You either come with us willingly, or we take you by force. Your choice. What'll it be?"

The giant licked its lips, and strings of yellow spit flew from the corners of his mouth. "You red like tomato. I love tomato! Me eat tomato now!"

Zoey glowered and flattened her hair with her left hand. "Who you callin' tomato, tree bark—"

"Move over *tomato*," interrupted Simon, "I've got this."

He stepped in beside Zoey and faced the giant. He puffed out his chest and said, "See this badge, giant? That's OSC—Operative Special Clearance. You know what that means?"

He didn't wait for the giant to answer and continued, "That means *we*, me and Zoey, have the *authority* to bring you in. By the Code, Section 3052."

"There's *no* such code," whispered Zoey.

Simon leaned towards Zoey and whispered back, "But *he* doesn't know that."

He raised his voice. "Giants trespassing on Earth without letting *us* know first," he tapped his badge, "and endangering the lives of the humans are breaking the code. Which means we're here to arrest you, big guy. Hands up!"

Zoey lowered her voice. "Aren't you supposed to say, *you're in violation of the Mystic Treaty* first? It was the first thing Agent Vargas made us learn after we got our OSC badges. Remember, Simon?"

Simon shrugged. "Right, I forgot that part."

He pointed to the giant, "Who cares, it's not like *he* knows the rules."

The giant bared its teeth and started to laugh a deep, guttural laugh.

"You funny. I eat you, too . . . after I eat tomato."

The tomato references were *really* starting to annoy Zoey, but she kept her agent cool.

"This is your *last* warning giant," she said confidently. "Come with us quietly, or we'll have to use force, and that means things are going to get messy."

The giant grinned and watched them like they were scrumptious cupcakes. A loud rumble came from his belly.

"I don't think he intends to cooperate," said Zoey.

"Nope," agreed Simon. "Which leaves us with only one option."

Zoey raised her boomerang again—

CRACK!

Wind buffeted Zoey's back with a roar, like a bomb had just exploded beside her. She turned around and held her breath.

A twelve-foot blue hole had ripped through the atmosphere. It shimmered and churned like a ring of rolling water. Then a large green three-fingered hand decorated with rings reached out from the surface. Another giant climbed out of the portal.

"Great, now there are *two* of them," whined Simon.

The new giant stumbled out from the portal stinking of rotten eggs. It seemed genuinely astonished to be here, almost as though stepping through the portal had been *unintentional*. But how could that be?

It had the same wet pink eyes, small flat head, and rough, forest-green skin as the first giant, but it was shorter and nearly twice as thick. It looked like it had just swallowed another giant. It wore a crown of human skulls on its head and had the same tangle of jewel-encrusted straw-like hair. A hand-stitched leather cape draped over its square shoulders, and a sharp spear hung by its side.

Although Zoey had seen mystics cross over into her world with the help of the interloper devices, she had never seen a mystic step from this small of a portal before. It was like it had just stepped out of a doorway. This portal was like the mirrors they used at the agency.

While the portal was open, she could see the world beyond the portal clearly. It was that same red world of deserts, smoke, and ash that she had seen twice before. It was the Nexus.

And then with another *crack*, the portal vanished.

Zoey sensed that something was off. Why did the giant look so surprised?

As the new giant looked around, it stared at Simon and Zoey, and then it finally noticed the other giant. The two mystics studied each other. The shorter, fat giant grabbed its oversized belly and bounced it up and down like a basketball.

It looked at Zoey and rasped, "Agent tasty. Me hungry *now!*"

It pointed its spear towards them.

One giant was a big enough challenge—two giants was a *significant* problem.

And then, without warning, the fat giant sprang towards Zoey and Simon like an angry rhinoceros, roaring and snarling. Yellow spit flew from its mouth, and its pink eyes were wild as it swung its spear like a sword.

But Zoey was ready.

She hurled her boomerang as hard as she could. It sped in the air so fast it looked like gold pixie dust and hit the giant on the side of the head with a powerful *thump*.

But the giant didn't even flinch. It charged at Zoey.

She hesitated for a moment, shocked that her boomerang had *zero* effect on the giant. The spear's tip came towards her head—

"Zoey! Move!"

Simon pushed Zoey out of the way, and the spear missed her scalp by an inch. They rolled on the ground and came up facing both giants. Zoey spit the sand from her mouth and reached up to grab her returning weapon.

Simon saw the shock on her face and said, "I had a feeling this would happen."

Zoey glared at the giants. It was clear by their laughs that they did not consider Zoey and Simon to be a serious threat. They were going to kill them easily and then *eat* them.

"What feeling?" she asked finally.

". . . That your precious boomerang wouldn't work on them," Simon answered. "Giants have skin as tough as steel, and their heads are as thick as rocks. Your boomerang won't even get their attention."

Zoey clipped her weapon back onto her golden bracelet.

"Okay, so how do you plan on neutralizing them if our weapons don't work? With your charming good looks?"

Simon smiled sheepishly. "I knew you'd come around one day."

Another rumbling sound came from the bigger giant's belly. "Hungry," it said and pulled a curved blade smeared with maroon stains from its belt. It brought the knife to its face, licked the blade, and grinned at them like a mad butcher.

The other giant gave Zoey and Simon a toothy grin and raised its spear. It snarled and spat like a wild boar ready to charge.

Zoey shifted uneasily. The giants were ripped with muscles. She was sure they could crush their bones like eggshells. But then she remembered something.

"Didn't the mystic manual say that giants could be neutralized if we knocked them out?" she said. "I think I remember reading something like that."

"It did," answered Simon, "But it would take all day for us to do it. I thought we'd try something new—"

The giants circled around them and started to jab at them with their weapons.

Quickly, Simon reached inside his jacket and pulled out two metal batons.

"Maybe we can get their attention with these babies." He pressed on a knob, and the small baton extended to the size of a baseball bat.

He grinned when he saw Zoey's expression.

"Here's yours."

He tossed a baton to Zoey. It was cool and surprisingly light. Following Simon's lead, she found the button and pressed it. Immediately her baton extended. On the sides, written in bold red letters were the words:

Giant Pro Beater
Your One Hit Wonder!
(Batteries sold separately)

Zoey stifled a laugh. "Is this for real? Who's in charge of naming our weapons?"

"Who do you think?" said Simon. "Agent Franken, who else?"

"Of course," said Zoey smiling. "It all makes sense in some really *strange* way."

She took a few swings with her right hand, getting a feel for its weight.

"I've already added the batteries, so we're good to go," said Simon happily. He gave a test swing of his bat like he was about to hit a homerun.

"So we just hit them with these, and it should knock them out—?"

Movement appeared in the corner of Zoey's eye. She had been so preoccupied with her new giant beater that she had temporarily forgotten all about the giants. Big mistake.

The mystics launched their attack. With horrible rasping battle cries, they sprung at the young operatives and slashed their weapons like huntsmen about to butcher two small wild rabbits.

The giant with the spear came for Zoey. As it neared, she could distinctly see black and brown stains on its tip. Her instincts kicked in, and she ducked and spun just as the tip of the spear crashed into the ground where she had stood a second ago. The giant growled in displeasure and yanked its spear free. When it turned to face Zoey, she could see that its pink eyes had darkened and were almost red. It looked angrier than ever.

"You've got to hit it with the bat!" bellowed Simon as he dodged a massive fist from the other giant.

"Yeah, thanks for the tip," said Zoey angrily.

Simon cursed as he whacked his *Giant Pro Beater* at the mystic's legs, torso, and neck—but he missed with every strike, like an uncoordinated kid who could never quite hit the baseball. For creatures so thick and big, they moved with the suppleness of cats. It was almost as though the giants could anticipate their moves. Were these creatures mind readers as well?

"*Where* do we have to hit them? On their heads?" cried Zoey, but Simon was too busy trying to save his own skin to answer. She would just have to figure this one out fast, before she ended up as a splat of tomato juice.

The giant with the spear snarled furiously at Zoey. It leaned forward, brought its spear in front of its chest like a knight with a lance in a jousting tournament, and then charged at her. When the tip of the spear came close to her chest, she blocked it with a hit of her bat. But the force she needed to deflect the giants charge sent her to her knees. Her teeth clattered, and she was surprised to see she hadn't broken any bones in her hand or arm. The giant's strength was extraordinary. It was like hitting a mountain of rock. How would she ever get a clear shot? And *where* was she supposed to hit it?

Zoey heard a grunt and turned around—

She howled in pain as white exploded behind her eyes. For a second she felt her feet leave the ground, and then she crashed to the earth hard and her bat slipped from her grip. It was like she was pinned under a truck. She heard something crack inside her chest. She raised her head off the ground.

The giant sat on her, so close that she could smell the rancid vinegar and rotten meat on its breath. The last of her air escaped under the pressure of the creature's weight on her chest. Then it leaned forward, wrapped its hands around her throat, and squeezed.

She blinked at the snarling mouth and the yellow spittle that flew into her face. The giant's eyes burned red with hunger.

She couldn't breathe. She was going to die.

CHAPTER 2

PORTALS

As the giant tried to squeeze the life out of her, Zoey could only think about what Tristan would say when he found out that a giant had killed her on her very first OSC job.

And then something inside her stirred.

She grabbed handfuls of sand and threw them in the giant's face. The effect was instantaneous.

The mystic let go of her neck, and Zoey coughed and gagged for free air. She crawled away from the howling creature and began to search for the bat. She saw it in a soft clump of wispy grass ten feet away. Although every breath was like a thousand knives carving the inside of her chest and sweat trickled down her face, she struggled towards the bat.

Heavy footsteps shook the ground behind her.

She grabbed the bat and crept up onto a three-foot boulder.

She could almost feel the giant's breathing on the back of her neck.

She waited until the very last moment, crouched, and spun. She leaped into the air and swung her bat as hard as she could.

CRUNCH!

The bat smashed into the giant's head, but the mystic hardly even moved.

A series of strange silver bubbles circled the giant's head for a moment, and then they popped and disappeared so fast that Zoey thought she must have imagined them.

She came back to her senses quickly and leaped off the boulder. It exploded in gray dust as the giant skewered it with its spear.

Zoey landed softly in the sand and watched the giant.

She began to panic. She had only made the creature angrier when she had hit it across the head.

"Die!" It snarled. Thick droplets of yellow-green spit flew out of its mouth.

But then as the giant whirled towards her, it stopped. It looked confused, as though it had forgotten something important. It staggered forward and dropped its spear. Then the mystic's eyes rolled into the back of its head, and it fell face first onto the ground like a dead tree.

Zoey couldn't believe her luck. She walked over to the giant and kicked it. Nothing happened. She kicked it again, just to be safe. The giant didn't respond.

She raised her bat and examined it more closely. "Not bad for just a *bat*. And all these years I sucked at softball . . . if they could see me now. Remind me to have a chat with Agent Franken later—"

"Zoey! A little help here!"

Zoey turned around. Simon dangled from the other giant's grip like a child's toy.

"Help me!" he screeched. His face was beet red, and his bat lay near the giant's feet like a twig.

"It's going to eat me! Help!" He punched at the giant's hands with his fists.

Taking a deep breath, Zoey gripped her bat firmly and sprinted towards Simon.

"Hey ugly!" she bellowed between breaths. "Put my friend down, or you'll end up like your friend over there. I said let him *go!*"

The giant ignored her and squeezed Simon's throat.

"—ELP!" was all Simon could manage. Sweat covered his red face and his eyes watered. The mystic was crushing his throat.

With an angry swing, Zoey whacked her bat against the beast's back so hard that the force sent a ripple through her fingers that went all the way up her arm.

But it was like hitting a brick wall. The giant took no notice of her or her bat.

Again, small silver bubbles emanated from the bat and then popped and disappeared.

In a rage, she rained blows on the mystic's back, legs, and arms. But the giant only seemed vaguely aware of her.

She thought that the bat must be defective.

"*One hit wonder*, eh? Yeah right. I want a refund!"

Thinking that she wasn't hitting it hard enough for the bat to work, she gave the giant another volley of whacks.

When she was out of breath, the giant finally turned its head around. It looked at Zoey like she was an irritating mosquito.

"Put my friend down," said Zoey boldly.

She inched forward and faced the creature. "Let him go! This is your *last* warning."

She squared her shoulders and raised herself on her toes, trying to make herself taller.

The mystic's laugh sounded like the rumble of an earthquake.

"He die. You die. Agents *all die!*"

"Nobody's dying, giant," she hissed. "At least not *us*! I can't say the same about you or your buddy over there."

The mystic looked at the motionless giant on the ground behind Zoey. It looked back at her, frowned severely, and growled deep inside its throat like a lion about to tear apart its prey. Its cold pink eyes sent a chill down Zoey's back. If she didn't come up with a plan soon, the giant was going to rip her apart like a well-done turkey.

With great effort, Simon raised one of his arms and pointed to his own head. "Hit. Head," he croaked.

And then Zoey understood.

The giant lunged at her with its free hand.

Zoey ducked, jumped to the side, and came up over the other side of the great creature. She tried to jump and hit it in the head, but she could only reach its upper back. She held her weapon with her right hand and leaped in the air as if she was going for a basketball slam dunk, but the mystic was too tall.

"ZOEY! WATCH OUT!"

A massive fist came hurtling towards her head.

She jumped backwards, tripped, and fell, but miraculously still held onto the bat. She rolled on the ground and then scrambled to her feet. If she stopped moving, the giant would crush her. The mystic wailed furiously, thrashing Simon's body around like a ragdoll as it went for her again.

Zoey winced at the pain on her friend's face. His eyes were slowly closing. His skin had gone from red to a scary purple-blue. He couldn't breathe. She *had* to do something or she would lose him.

And then it hit her.

Just as the great brute charged at her again, she balanced the bat in her right hand like a harpoon, aimed, and fired.

Maybe it was the practice she'd had using the boomerang for months, or maybe it was luck, but the bat soared in the air like a fat arrow and hit the giant smack in the forehead with an echoing *thump*.

The giant looked surprised that she had actually hit it. It wavered like a great tree in the wind as the same mysterious silver bubbles popped around its head. Whatever was affecting the creature, Zoey could tell it was fighting it. The giant's body shook, and sweat trickled down its horrid face. It took in rapid breaths in an attempt to overcome whatever was attacking it. It seemed stronger than the other giant, and for a horrible moment, Zoey thought they were doomed and that the bat hadn't worked. But then Simon slipped from the beast's grip, and the great beast froze mid-step, toppled over, and landed on the ground in a cloud of dust.

"Simon!" Zoey cried out in relief. Simon staggered to his feet on his own, his head still attached to his body.

He smiled weakly as he rubbed his sore neck. "I'm still breathing."

Zoey grabbed Simon in a bear hug. "I'm so glad you're okay," she squeezed him tightly and then let him go.

"You had me worried for a minute there. I thought you were a goner. Your face had turned blue. I don't know what I would have done if the giant had killed you."

Simon's face reddened, and he pulled away from Zoey awkwardly.

"I'm not that easily killed," he said as he wiped the giant's disgusting yellow spit from his face. "Yuck! Besides, we're almost like *real* agents. We know how to defend ourselves, don't we? I think we did a pretty awesome job, all things considered."

"Right," laughed Zoey. Simon always had a way of putting a smile on her face. "Of course we did."

"Why are you laughing?" said Simon. "I almost had him you know . . . he just . . . he just *surprised* me. And I dropped my bat, that's all. I could've taken him, easily. I've been working out—check these out."

He rolled up his sleeve and flexed his raisin-sized bicep muscle. "I've got killer arms. Girls dig that."

Zoey covered her eyes and laughed harder.

"Go ahead, laugh, but you know I'm cut like Bruce Lee."

Simon kicked the giant. "That's for choking me, stinker. Told you that you were going to get it. And now it's nap time, big guy."

Zoey inspected the giant a little closer and made a face. "They smell like they've been rolling around in garbage and then washed in sewer water. No, I take that back. I don't think they've ever bathed. EVER."

"I don't think bathing is a requirement with giants," informed Simon as he fought unsuccessfully with the yellow snot that stuck to his jacket.

"In fact, I think the more they smell the better in a giant's world. Maybe that's how they attract the females . . . the *more* they stink, the more they *get*."

"Eww, that's nasty." When Zoey laughed, she cried out and held her rib cage gently.

Simon frowned. "What's wrong?"

"I think I've might have broken a few ribs—"

Suddenly, Zoey felt the ground shake beneath her sneakers. Thunder boomed in the bay, and she heard shouts and cries. Her first thought was *another giant*.

Zoey and Simon shared a worried look and then turned towards the sudden commotion. Down by the beach people had gathered and were pointing at something. Zoey rushed over to the edge of the small rise to get a better look.

An oval-shaped, blue shimmering light hovered above the tan-colored beach and wavered like an upside-down pool of water.

Zoey's heart thumped against her broken ribs. "Simon, are my eyes playing tricks on me or is *that* another portal?"

"Yup, that's a portal all right."

"And am I going mad or can the Mutes *see* it?"

Simon stood by her side. "Uh . . . I think they can. Yes, they most definitely can. This is bad, Zoey. This is really, *really* bad."

Zoey's chest tightened. Any second now a mystic would cross over, and there was no telling *which* mystic or how *many* of them. It could be more giants, but it could also be something a lot more evil and sinister.

Two guys and a girl circled the portal as they inspected it. They seemed to think this was some kind of joke, like the portal was the result of some sort of visual effects stunt. They laughed and shoved one another playfully, inching closer and closer to the wavering light of the portal.

"But how can that be?" asked Zoey, feeling more and more nervous as the Mutes ventured closer to the portal. "Unless I missed something on the memo, I thought only Sevenths could see portals. How is this even possible? It doesn't make any sense."

"Beats me," answered Simon as he pulled a strand of yellow mucous from his hair. "It's the first time I've heard of this. I mean, everything is a little out of whack since feline-face did the Great Jointing—"

"Great Junction."

"Yeah, that thing," said Simon. He inspected a strange brown clump on his jacket that might have been pudding but definitely *wasn't*.

"I think you're right." Zoey shifted uneasily.

The portal had attracted nearly twenty people now. The curious teenagers moved closer and closer to it. Her heart beat faster and faster. She felt like she was going to jump out of her skin.

"When the second giant appeared—that portal—it *closed* right away," noted Zoey. "How long do you think this portal is going to stay open?"

Simon shook his head. "No idea. Each portal is unique. Think of them as different doors. Some are small while some are huge. Some stay open longer than others."

"Is there a way to close them?"

Simon shrugged. "I don't know. When you think about it, the portals are *forced* open, right? Then it only makes sense we should be able to *close* them."

He glanced over his shoulder. "We should get back soon. I don't know how long the giants are going to stay down."

"But what about the portal and all those people?" asked Zoey, "We can't just leave them!"

"We can't do anything about it now. The best thing we *can* do is get back to the agency as soon as possible and let them know. I'm sure *they'll* know what to do."

Zoey knew he was right. Both giants were unconscious, but she knew that hauling them back was going to prove difficult. There was nothing they could do about the portal now besides telling the agency about it as soon as possible. She hoped they could close it somehow. But what about all the people who could see it? How were the agents going to explain or fix that? She would have to worry about it later.

"I have a bad feeling about this," said Zoey as she turned around and started to make her way back to the comatose giants. "Let's go—"

"Uh-oh."

Zoey halted and then rushed back beside Simon. Her heart sank.

The group of teenagers was dangerously close to the portal, so close that if one of them decided to reach out now they would *touch* it.

"No," said Zoey, exasperated. "Oh God, no."

"Don't do it, man," said Simon. His face had gone from red to white in a flash. "*Don't* do it."

The curious teens laughed and shoved one another, all trying to get to the front as though they stood in front of a large mirror. And then before anyone could stop him, one of the teens reached out and touched the portal with his fingers. The tips of his fingers grazed the surface of the portal, and he withdrew them quickly.

Even from a distance Zoey could see his hand was unscathed. The teen gave his friends a cocky smile and stepped closer—

"NO!" shouted Zoey at the top of her lungs. But she was too far away, and her voice was drowned by the sound of the waves.

It was like watching a horror movie when one of the actors went into the room where the murderer waited, hidden behind the door. Even if you shouted *no, don't go in*, at the screen, they always went it.

Zoey tore down the hill, forgetting the giants and Simon, and raced towards the portal on the beach.

"No! Get back! Don't go near it!" she bellowed between gasps of air. "Stop! Get back!"

The teens halted and looked back at her, and for a moment, she felt relief. But then they laughed and turned back towards the portal. Maybe they thought she was part of the performance?

"This isn't some practical joke!" Zoey's thighs burned as she tried to run faster in the loose sand.

Too late.

Zoey watched helpless and horrified as the three teens walked right into the portal. They smiled as though they were in a circus performance—as though it *wasn't* real, so it couldn't harm them.

And then the portal swallowed them. It shimmered one last time and vanished with a *crack*.

CHAPTER 3

OLD ENEMIES

Zoey and Simon returned to the Hive and secured the giants in a *Maximum-Security Holding Cell*. Then they hurried to Room 1D to report back to Agent Vargas. He confirmed that the portal incident on the beach in Houghton Bay, New Zealand was not an isolated case.

"So far, we've gathered accounts of at least *three hundred* of these portals opening all over the world," said the big agent as he pushed back his chair and stood.

For a human, Agent Vargas was the tallest and largest man Zoey had ever seen. He could have easily have passed as one of the Giant's distant cousins. He wore a simple V-neck shirt tucked neatly into a pair of black pants. His long blond hair was tied in a braid that hung over his large chest.

She couldn't help it, but with his bulging muscles, he always made her think of a modern-day Viking.

"And from what we've learned," continued Agent Vargas, "illegal mystics only stepped through about half of them. But the other half . . . ."

He paused for a moment. "They just appeared. But nothing came out. It was like they had opened on their own."

"Unfortunately, these new portals were visible to the curious Mutes. When the portals vanished, they took hundreds of unsuspecting people with them."

Zoey sat stunned as she listened. She didn't want to be held accountable for all the people lost in the portals. Nonetheless, she felt personally responsible.

"So do we know what's causing these portals to open?" said Simon as though he had read Zoey's mind. He sat on the desk next to her, and she felt a sting in her chest as he finished.

Agent Vargas pressed his big hands on the desk. When he looked up, his blue eyes met Zoey's, and she dropped her gaze. "There's only one thing that comes to mind—that *woman*."

"The cat woman," interrupted Simon. "I knew it! I *knew* it had something to do with her royal feline ugliness. I think if we can manage to—" Simon pressed his mouth shut.

He looked like he wanted to argue, but he remained silent when he saw Agent Vargas's scowl. His ears turned bright red.

Agent Vargas cleared his throat and continued.

"Yes, Simon, I'm afraid it *is* the only plausible explanation. But for now, you kids should concentrate on your field assignments. You still have a lot to learn and require hours of *experience* before you can truly call yourselves agents—even with your OSC badges. I'm sure we'll know more about these portals in the coming weeks."

Zoey noticed that the lines around Agent Vargas's eyes and forehead had deepened. She knew he wasn't telling them the whole truth. She was sure the Agency had discovered something far worse. But what could be worse than unexpected portals opening up and snatching people away with them?

Dread weighed Zoey down. "Agent Vargas? Can I ask you something?"

"Yes," answered the big man. "What is it?"

Zoey swallowed hard. "What happens to the people who disappeared into the portal?"

"Oh, man, that's right!" said Simon overdramatically as he pressed his hands on his head. "I hadn't even *thought* of that."

Agent Vargas stared at them both without speaking for a moment, as though he either didn't *want* to tell them or simply didn't *know* what happened.

"I'm afraid their fate is not a very good one," he said finally. "I fear most of those poor souls are probably already dead—killed by mystics. And if by some miracle some survived, then they probably wished that they were dead already."

"What do you mean?" asked Zoey. "What's going to happen to them?"

She suppressed a shiver as she imagined the teens she had seen on the beach being ripped apart by eyeless, black-winged Duyen demons.

There would be nothing left of them but piles of clothes stained in their blood.

Agent Vargas sighed. "Once the Mutes cross over into the Nexus the veil will be lifted. They'll be able to *see* every mystic, as we do here, but only in that other world. The mystics won't understand the difference and will think the Mutes are agents. They'll kill some and take others as prisoners. They will torture them to get back at us. They will die the most horrific and painful deaths. It saddens me to think we can't stop it from happening."

Zoey and Simon stared at each other without speaking. She thought of the teenagers on the beach again and felt a stabbing pain in her heart. They had thought it was a joke. They didn't deserve to die. She prayed that some had survived and hid somehow. She remembered seeing vast red mountains. Maybe there were places to hide in the Nexus?

"So you think they're all dead?" Zoey's throat was very dry. "We can never get them back?"

The big agent looked at Zoey, his lips pressed together in a hard line, but he didn't reply. He wasn't sure what to answer.

"That really sucks," said Simon gloomily. "I mean, how *can* they survive? They don't even have weapons or the proper training to defend themselves against the mystics. They'll probably die of fright when they realize the monsters from their childhood nightmares are *real*."

Zoey's heart raced.

"You think no one can survive there? Not even an *agent*?"

Simon's head snapped in her direction.

Zoey's insides twisted as she thought about her mother trapped somewhere in that other world. She knew she had to be extra careful about how much she was willing to tell Agent Vargas. He was clever and could very easily read between the lines. If the Agency knew what she was planning to do, they would most definitely lock her up.

Agent Vargas watched Zoey carefully.

"What have you heard?" There was something strange in his expression, like she had discovered some secret.

"What if an agent *accidentally* crossed into the Nexus," said Zoey, with tension in her voice. "Surely they *could* survive. I mean, like Simon said, they would have the necessary skills, right? They could defend themselves, right? So it's possible?"

"Yes," answered Agent Vargas, and excitement fluttered in Zoey. "What are you getting at with this? Zoey, I get the feeling there's something you're not telling me?"

Zoey had gotten her answer, and she wasn't going to tell him anything else.

Agent Vargas was about to drill her when the door opened, and Tristan and Stuart strolled in.

Tristan's dark almond eyes caught hers, and her heart did a somersault. As much as she tried to ignore the feeling, it always crept up on her whenever Tristan was near. She hated herself for being so sensitive. There was no getting away from it—Tristan was her weakness.

He was dressed all in black except for a tight blue t-shirt. Although he wasn't yet fifteen, he was built like a professional athlete. His thick brown hair framed his chiseled face and high cheekbones.

Zoey remembered how vibrant he had looked the first time she had seen him at the abandoned theatre. He looked taller now, thinner and a little more worn, like he was taking on too many assignments and getting too little rest. His dark eyes looked older too, somehow, full of concern and responsibility.

Simon hadn't changed much. He seemed more comfortable in his own skin now. He'd always had too much hyper energy, but he seemed to handle it better. He was better at thinking things through than the rest of them.

She wondered what they thought of her now when they looked at her. She definitely didn't *feel* like the same person she had been back at the foster home. She was stronger now and more confident. She had also gained a few extra pounds of much-needed muscle, thanks to the intense training and Aria's cooking.

But when Zoey looked at Tristan's partner, she glowered.

His icy blue eyes, like a husky's or a shark's made her want to punch him every time she saw him. Stuart King's clothes were too perfect. His black hair was groomed to perfection, even his porcelain skin was annoyingly perfect—not even a hint of a pimple.

He didn't look like an OSC working out in the field—he looked like he was about to do a photo-shoot for a fashion magazine. His ruby ring in the shape of the letter O was too ostentatious. And to make matters worse, his OSC badge had been sewn on professionally. Zoey had sewn hers herself and had added glue just to be safe, but the edges had a tendency to curl upwards.

"Agent Vargas," said Tristan as he reached the front of the big man's desk. "We secured the Sagamite in Riverside, California. It's locked up now in cell block #412—"

"Pfft. A Sagamite?" mocked Simon as he strolled around Tristan. "Those puny little critters that look like monkeys with antlers? That's nothing. Me and Zoey caught—not one—but *two* giants single handedly. It was awesome. *I* was awesome. You and your *superstar* missed quite a show."

Stuart glared at Simon, but Simon blew him a kiss.

Tristan turned and smiled at Zoey. "Two giants? Really? That's impressive."

Zoey nodded. "Two nasty and very *smelly* giants. I feel like having a shower just remembering their smell."

Simon clasped his hands behind his back and circled Stuart, eyeing him suspiciously.

"And did his *highness* participate in catching the Sagamite—or did he watch safely from a distance?"

Stuart's scowl deepened, but he kept his cool, which only added fuel to Simon's insults. If it had been her, Zoey would have punched Simon already. But Stuart was his usual, calm, unreadable, and ice-cold self.

"Figures. You didn't want to get your *precious* hands or expensive clothes dirty," said Simon. ". . . So you made Tristan do all the work, and you hoped to get the credit, too? Well, your royal stuck-up-ness, I've got news for you, that's not how it works here."

Simon was dangerously close to Stuart's face. If he leaned forward an inch, their noses would touch.

"Get lost, Brown!" A large vein throbbed on Stuart's forehead. "Or I'll do to you what *I* did to the Sagamite."

Simon shot his arms in the air. "Wait a minute!"

He leaned closer and examined Stuart's hands. "I see a bit of dirt under *that* fingernail. Hurry, call your manicurist—"

Stuart shoved Simon so hard that he crashed into a row of desks.

Simon recovered quickly.

"Off with his head!" he shouted and charged for Stuart like an angry bull.

"Enough!" bellowed Agent Vargas. Simon skidded to a stop but kept glaring at Stuart who sneered at him triumphantly.

"Are you little *children* or are you *OSC*?" Agent Vargas's voice boomed against the walls like thunder.

Zoey cowered back. The room was suddenly very still and quiet. She could hear her heart drumming in her ears.

"Because right now you're acting like spoiled, idiotic kids." The agent's expression darkened as he measured them each individually, and for a second, Zoey thought she and the others were about to join the giants and the Sagamite down in the basement.

31

"We're about to live through *very* hard times—worse than anything this world has ever faced. This is *no* time for immature, childish games."

He raised a large finger and pointed to Simon and Stuart.

"And you two better start behaving like agents or there'll be trouble, I can promise you that."

"Yes, sir," said Simon. "Sorry, sir."

Stuart remained quiet, but Zoey could see a smile on his lips. It was almost as though he felt that even Agent Vargas couldn't touch him.

Agent Vargas crossed his arms over his chest. "Now, I want you two to shake hands."

"What?" said Simon, and he nearly coughed out his own tongue. With his eyes bulging, he stood and pointed.

"You can't be serious? No way. I'm not shaking *his* hand. He's got cooties. Besides, *he* pushed me *first*. Let's face it, we're *all* thinking it—the guy's a jerk."

"You'll shake his hand if you want to *stay* in this program," warned Agent Vargas, his voice etched with irritation. Zoey knew Agent Vargas wasn't a man to be trifled with, and she hoped Simon knew it too. If Agent Vargas wasn't going to make Simon shake Stuart's hand, she was *going* to make him do it. He was her partner, after all. She needed him.

Stuart jeered and raised his hand. "Come on, Brown. Don't be such a baby. We're all agents here, aren't we? Or are you in a class of your own?"

"I'm not a baby," growled Simon curling his hands into fists. "I'll show you who's a baby, you rotten sovereign wannabe—"

"Simon," cautioned Agent Vargas, and he raised an eyebrow. "Control yourself. I'm warning you—don't make me repeat myself—I *hate* having to repeat myself."

Simon had a crazed look in his eye and didn't seem to hear. He took another step closer to Stuart. "You scumbag, degenerate, deviant, dirt bag, sleaze ball, royal pain in my—"

"SIMON!"

Simon clamped his mouth shut, but Zoey could swear he whispered a few more insults.

Agent Vargas towered over him like a polar bear. "If we didn't need every able body right now, I'd throw you in the cell blocks myself! Shake his hand, or so help me *I* will *make* you do it!"

Slowly, very slowly, Simon reached out and shook Stuart's hand with a grimace on his face, like he'd just swallowed a raw onion. They didn't look at each other, and both put as much distance as they could between one another after the shake. Simon wiped his hand on his shirt as though he still had some of the giant's mucus on it.

Zoey caught Stuart's eye as he leaned calmly on one of the desks. He smiled at her coldly like he had won some sort of challenge. This wasn't over. If he wanted to play, then she was going to play hard.

"Now, can we get back to work, or do I have to send for bottled milk and blankets?" continued Agent Vargas. He eyed them dangerously, daring them to speak up.

"Good. Let us continue. I have here a handful of assignments for all of you."

He strolled over to his desk and picked up a tablet computer. He touched the screen and then looked up. "Zoey, Simon, I've got a report of a Fluegen in Mexico City. Think you can handle that?" He looked at Simon.

"No problem." Simon crossed his arms over his chest. His eyes darted in Stuart's direction.

Zoey leaned forward and whispered to Tristan, "What's a *Fluegen*?"

"They're like giant frogs. They're massive but really stupid," he said with a smile.

Zoey leaned back and made a face. "Great, more big, stinky and slimy beasts—"

"Agent Vargas! Agent Vargas!"

Agent Ward ran into the room, her face flushed like she had just run a marathon. Her chin-length gray hair bobbed up and down as she crossed the room, and her bony legs scurried under her navy skirt suit. Her usual sergeant major scowl had been replaced by an urgent expression, like she had just discovered some troubling news.

Zoey was itching to find out what it was and strained to listen.

Agent Ward made her way swiftly to the front of the class and raised her arms.

34

"I'm sorry to disrupt your class like this," she said a little out of breath as she straightened her black-rimmed glasses. "But I've just been with Director Hicks and—"

She turned and looked straight at Zoey.

Zoey felt like a fist had squeezed her heart. Whatever pressing news Agent Ward had learned, it had something to do with *her*. She wasn't sure if that was a *good* thing or a *bad* thing. She could see Stuart smirking at her on the other side of the room.

Agent Ward's face softened. "Zoey, you've been summoned to a *very* special meeting."

"What kind of meeting?" Zoey was certain everyone in the room could sense her nerves.

Agent Ward moved closer to her. She took in a shaky breath and then said, "With the National Assembly."

CHAPTER 4

THE NATIONAL ASSEMBLY

Tristan and Simon followed Zoey as she walked back towards the main hall. She had *no* idea what the National Assembly was. All that Agent Ward had said was, "It's where all the top Agents and Directors of all our nations get together and discuss matters of the utmost importance—matters which concern us all."

Refusing to go *wasn't* an option. Zoey knew this had something to do with Mrs. Dupont and the Great Junction—for which Zoey still felt that she was partly to blame. Now portals were opening up all over the world, and she knew that whatever this meeting was about, she would soon discover just how *bad* things truly were. She had a horrible feeling that somehow the Agency knew she was a *true* original. Maybe they were going to lock her up and throw away the key before she could do anymore damage . . . .

She followed Agent Ward, and they stopped in front of a large silver oval mirror with the inscription, *United Kingdom*, at the top.

"So . . . we're going to London, then?" Zoey said. "Is that where the National Assembly will be?"

She tried to sound excited, but her dread weighed on her.

Agent Ward ignored her and looked past Zoey, anxiously waiting for someone else to arrive. Perhaps more agents were going to join them on this trip? She hoped it would be either Agent Barnes or Lee. Or even better, *both*.

"Can we come too?" asked Simon as he and Tristan stood beside Zoey. "I mean . . . I'm sure we could help with . . . stuff . . . so . . . can we? Can we come?"

"Certainly not," said Agent Ward. She turned around and glared at him. "This isn't an Operative field trip, Simon Brown. This is *very* serious business—"

"And *I'm* a very *serious* guy," pressed Simon as he straightened himself. He did his best to look composed, but it just made him look goofier than before.

Agent Ward pursed her lips but didn't say anything. Zoey could tell that there was no way Simon would change the agent's mind. But he wouldn't give up. It was one of the reasons she enjoyed having him around—he was *very* persistent.

"Pretty please?" pushed Simon, and batted his eyelashes as though that was going to smooth things over with Agent Ward. "I've got loads of valuable information to share. I could—I could be of *real* service to you and the cause."

"The cause?" chortled Tristan. "Is that what you're calling this? The cause?"

After Simon elbowed him in the ribs, Tristan added. "Please, Agent Ward. I'm sure Zoey would like her friends with her. And like Simon said, I really think we could help."

"I'm afraid that's not possible, Tristan," said Agent Ward. "Only those invited and of *high* rank can attend the assembly. I'm sorry, but you can't come with Zoey. You'll see her when we get back."

Zoey looked at Tristan and gave him a grateful smile, but he set his jaw, and his distressed expression made her feel even more nervous. She bit the inside of her cheek. She didn't want to go to this assembly.

Loud footsteps sounded suddenly, and Zoey turned to see Director Hicks, and Directors Johnson, Martin and Campbell, coming towards her.

"Ah—I see you have collected Zoey, Agent Ward," said Director Hicks, smiling cheerfully. "Very good, very good."

He stroked his neatly trimmed white beard. He always seemed to wear suits that were two sizes too small. Today he wore a forest-green suit with a matching bow tie and looked like a retired professor.

He turned and smiled at Zoey. "I know this must seem very sudden to you, Zoey. Alas, we must go where we're needed, mustn't we?"

"I guess." Zoey forced a smile.

As usual, Director Johnson's expression was unreadable. His dark skin was pulled tight, and if he didn't blink every now and then, Zoey thought he could pass for a human sculpture. Zoey lost her smile and hoped her eyes conveyed enough spite for both Directors Martin and Campbell to read. She hadn't forgiven them for wanting to hand her over to Mrs. Dupont and her Alphas. In fact, she doubted that she ever would.

Director Martin's pale, thin face with lines around his dark eyes made him look older than he was. He was stiff in his tailored black suit. Director Campbell looked bored. She had curled a strand of her chin-length blond hair behind her ear, and her bold polka dot red jacket and yellow pants made Zoey dizzy. They both avoided looking at Zoey, and that was just fine by her.

"Well, now that we're all here," said Director Hicks as he looked at his vintage watch, "we really should be going. We don't want to keep the assembly waiting."

He walked up to the mirror, reached out and typed on the keypad: *Headquarters, Knightsbridge, London, England.*

The mirror swirled. The green light at the top of the mirror flicked on with a *pop*. Directors Martin and Campbell were the first to step through, then Director Johnson and Director Hicks. Zoey stood rigidly as she watched them disappear.

"Zoey, let's get a move on," said Agent Ward gently. She beckoned Zoey with her hand. Agent Ward's eyes softened. "Don't worry, I'll be right behind you."

Zoey didn't feel comforted. Simon smiled sympathetically, raised his right hand, and parted his fingers in the Vulcan salute. Tristan's face was screwed up like he was about to be sick. This was *not* helping her at all.

She forced down the panic that made her want to run, exhaled a shaky breath, and stepped into the churning surface of the mirror.

Lights flashed behind Zoey's eyelids. Her body was stretched and pulled like elastic. Just before she was actually sick, fresh air moved around her, and her feet touched firm ground. The nausea dissipated, and when she opened her eyes her jaw fell open.

She stood in a great cathedral of a hall, five times the size of the main hall in the Toronto Hive. Hundreds of glistening mirrors lined the walls like jeweled picture frames in a prestigious gallery. A giant crystal chandelier lit the room like a miniature sun, and the polished floors gleamed and sparkled. The hand-carved moldings and old-world ambiance made the room feel like a ballroom in a castle. It was a pretty *awesome* room.

The last time she had set foot in this place, bodies had smoldered in the wreckage of shattered mirrors, chunks of marble floor, and plaster. She could still remember the smell of burnt flesh and blood. The room was now restored to its former glory.

The mirrors hummed as throngs of agents and mystics stepped out and made their way through a labyrinth of passageways and stairs.

Agent Ward stepped out of the mirror and immediately noticed the expression on Zoey's face.

"Magnificent, isn't it. There isn't another Hive in this world like it; it's simply breathtaking." She straightened her jacket. "Come along now, Zoey, they're waiting for us."

With her chin in the air, Agent Ward strolled across the room towards the other directors. She moved surprisingly fast, and Zoey had to jog to keep up.

"Ah, here we are," said Director Hicks cheerfully when Agent Ward and Zoey arrived. "I've just received a message that Director Patel awaits us in the assembly hall."

"Director Johnson," he turned towards the tall dark man. "Please escort our little party. I'd like a word with Zoey first. We'll catch up with you later."

Zoey's heart thumped like a jackhammer against her rib cage. What was *that* about?

Director Hicks turned to Zoey.

"Zoey, I know this is all very untoward and sudden. It's not every day that a young girl like you gets to speak before twelve of the most powerful Sevenths in this world. It's an honor, but it can also be a burden. Do you catch my meaning?"

Zoey hesitated. "I'm not sure that I do." She shook her head. "Nope. Definitely not."

"When I was a young agent," began Director Hicks. Zoey tried to imagine him thin and young, but it wasn't working.

Director Hicks continued, "I would have given anything to be part of something so grand, so important. Whatever might be said today, I don't want you to feel *responsible*—"

"You mean the portals?"

Director Hicks nodded solemnly. "Yes . . . and no."

He looked away for a second.

Zoey thought she saw a flash of great sorrow in his eyes, as if he were escorting Zoey to her own execution. It scared her. There was something the director wasn't telling her. What was going on?

Zoey felt a slight tremor under her Converse sneakers. Were there earthquakes in London? Maybe they were close to a subway station?

Director Hicks' fingers twitched at his sides, and Zoey could see beads of sweat on his forehead as he looked around nervously. Something was definitely upsetting him. But what?

"Okay . . . I'm definitely not following you," said Zoey finally.

"Director Hicks, is there something you're not telling me? I can handle it, trust me."

Director Hicks gave her a quick smile. "I know you can, Zoey. But please listen carefully. In a few minutes, you're going to learn exactly what's been happening from the mouths of the most powerful men, women, and mystics of our society. They're going to ask you a few questions—"

"I can handle a few questions."

Director Hicks sighed. "Questions about what happened with Mrs. Dupont. More precisely, they're going to ask you about the events leading up to the Great Junction."

He saw Zoey's face fall, and he put a hand gently on her shoulder. "I just didn't want you to be taken by surprise. The assembly can be quite *intimidating*."

Zoey glanced at her sneakers. "I knew it. I'm being blamed for these portals opening all over the world . . . it's my fault, isn't it?"

"It's not that simple, Zoey," said Director Hicks, his voice gentle. "Just remember that none of this would have happened if it weren't for Mrs. Dupont. If you want to *blame* someone, I would blame her."

When Zoey looked up, she saw a smile on Director Hick's face. She felt a little better knowing at least *he* was on her side. But she knew Directors Martin and Campbell *blamed* her. She wondered if the National Assembly would have more of these types of directors—the ones that accuse without proof. With her luck, she bet there would be.

"We should be going." Zoey followed Director Hicks down a long, narrow hallway decorated with pictures of past officials. When they arrived at a great set of double wooden doors, he grasped the iron handle and pulled.

Zoey followed him in and gasped. She wasn't sure what she'd expected, but clearly, it wasn't this.

They stood in an amphitheater the size of a small indoor hockey arena. The stars peeked from an inky black sky above the giant glass roof, and at least three thousand Sevenths and mystics sat in the countless rows of seats that wrapped around the oval-shaped arena.

At first she was shocked by all the people—she had never seen so many like *her* in one place. Tristan had told her about the neighborhoods designated only for Sevenths, but she had never imagined a space filled by so many. They were like her extended family. Her seventh sense even recognized the mystics as family. She clamped her mouth shut and tried not to show how baffled and excited she really was.

A set of stairs led to a raised platform. Zoey edged closer for a better look. On the platform six serious looking faces peered over a long table covered with papers and water bottles. Two men, two women, and two humanoid mystics stared directly at Director Hicks and Zoey. The sounds of shuffling feet and people straightening in their chairs preceded an eerie silence, like before the start of a movie.

Zoey could sense the three thousand pairs of eyes staring at her, judging her. She had never felt so small and insignificant before. She thought she might pass out.

It was clear now what Director Hicks had meant by *intimidating*. But this wasn't *just* intimidating, it was worse. It was *I'm going to be sick, please pass the bucket* intimidating.

A man with coffee-colored skin and black hair leaned forward and spoke into a microphone.

"Director Hicks. Zoey St. John," a booming voice resonated around the stadium like the voice of a God. "We've been expecting you. Please have a seat."

He gestured to a row of empty chairs in front of the long table.

"Come along, Zoey," said Director Hicks as he made his way down the long staircase.

Zoey followed him down to the platform and settled in the empty chair next to him. A microphone stood on a metal stand next to her chair. She realized that she'd been holding her breath and tried to breathe normally again. She'd made fists with her hands, and she pried them open and forced herself to relax. She was an OSC, not some frightened little kid. She raised her head and looked up to the great table.

The man who spoke was probably in his late sixties. His dark skin was wrinkled, and his hair was streaked with gray. His ebony robe rippled like black water as he took a sip from his water bottle. His dark eyes were fixed on Zoey. He appeared to be the youngest at the table.

To his right sat two women and a mystic. The first woman was plump with a jovial pink face, small bright blue eyes, short white hair, and a red robe. She looked like Mrs. Santa Claus. The woman next to her was ancient and dangerously skinny, like she'd just crawled out of her grave. Her wispy white hair was pulled back into a bun, and Zoey could see traces of her scalp. Her head drooped over her purple robes, and she looked as though she were sleeping.

Next to her was a humanoid-mystic with chalk-white skin and red eyes. Her mane of purple hair drooped down the sides of her bright green robes like expensive silk drapes. She gave Zoey a smile, and instantly Zoey felt a rush of heat.

On the opposite side of the table was another man just as ancient as the walking-dead woman. He was bald, and his tired, light eyes disappeared under a heavy wrinkled brow. His light-blue robes concealed large square shoulders and a powerful chest. He could have been a great warrior when he was much younger.

Zoey lost her breath when her eyes met the mystic next to him. He had light gray-blue skin that glowed from the inside with dark tribal tattoos etched along the sides of his neck and forearms. Zoey could see traces of rippling muscles under his earth-colored robes. His angular face was handsome and rugged, and his pointy ears peeked out through his long white mane. He wore golden loops in his ears and a single golden medallion in the shape of a sun around his neck. He looked like an elf warrior from a fantasy book.

Somehow, he looked familiar . . . .

And then it hit her.

He looked like Tristan when he had changed into his *super-hero* self. Was this mystic an álfar? The more she looked at him the more she was positive that he *was*. Maybe he was a relative of Tristan's? She wiggled in her chair, uncomfortable under the gaze of his piercing blue eyes. Before she looked away, she'd swear she saw the tiniest of smiles on his lips.

The man with the dark skin cleared his throat and spoke into his microphone. "Thank you for coming, Director Hicks."

Director Hicks moved his chair-microphone near his lips. "It's a pleasure to be of service to the National Assembly, Director Patel."

His voice resonated through the stadium. "May I present to the assembly, Zoey St. John," he said and gestured towards her.

She didn't know what possessed her later when she recalled the events at the assembly, but before she knew what she was doing, she waved her hand and said, "Hey."

Director Patel raised his eyebrows, and Zoey felt her face was literally *on* fire. She knew she was as red as her hair, but there was absolutely nothing she could do about it now. Three thousand mystics and Sevenths were going to remember her as the *red girl*. She was going to be a tomato for the rest of the interrogation.

Blood pounded in her ears, and she could hardly hear anything when Director Patel moved his lips.

". . . understand what this assembly is about . . . some of the assembly leaders will ask you a series of questions which you must answer clearly into your microphone." She finally heard him say, "And you will answer them *truthfully* and to the best of your knowledge. My fellow assembly leaders and I have been deliberating since this morning. And now we are ready to hear your side of the events."

He hesitated. "Do you understand?"

"Yes," said Zoey, and then she remembered that he had to speak into the microphone. She brought her microphone to her mouth and said, "YES!" Her voice screeched like an exploding amplifier. As the members winced and unclogged their ears she made a mental note *not* to shout.

Director Patel turned to the plump woman to his left. "Director van Noort, you may ask your questions."

Santa's wife smiled at Zoey. "Hello, Zoey."

She spoke like a grandmother speaking to her grandchild. "I only have a few questions for you . . ." she said as she flipped through a long note pad. "Ah—there we are. It says here that you were brought up as an orphan, but you believe that your mother is the former Agent Elizabeth Steele. According to our information, she's been missing in action for years, but you believe she's your mother?"

Zoey leaned forward and spoke carefully into her microphone. "Yes."

Director van Noort scribbled something in her note pad. "But you don't have any actual proof that she's your *real* mother, do you? Were there any names written on your birth certificate?"

"No," said Zoey. "My papers list only the name of the St. John's orphanage where I was left as a baby."

She saw a spark of interest in the old woman's face, but she didn't say anything and she just kept writing.

"We've heard of your *special* talents," said the woman. "Can you tell the assembly what they are please?"

Zoey felt like she'd been punched in the stomach. Everyone at the great table was waiting for her to answer, and she could feel everyone in the stadium focus on her. She tried to swallow, but her throat was dry. She looked at Director Hicks who gave her an encouraging smile.

"I . . . I can manipulate the mirrors," her voice cracked.

"Can you be more *specific*? How exactly do you *do* this?"

With her heart in her throat, Zoey forced the words out of her mouth. "I can work the mirror-port matter transfers and anchors myself, just by thinking of a place or a person. I can open and close portals just by using my mind."

"A skill of a true descendant from the Originals," said Director van Noort, a hint of astonishment in her voice.

The entire stadium was silent—too silent, and Zoey wasn't so sure that was a *good* thing.

Director van Noort seemed satisfied with Zoey's answers. "Thank you, dear. That is all for me."

Director Patel turned to the corpse of a woman. "Director Aslagard, you may ask your questions."

The old lady's head snapped to attention, and she focused her wet gray eyes on Zoey.

"Zoey St. John," she said in a hoarse whisper that sounded like a stalled engine. Zoey couldn't see if she had any teeth. "Do you know what the Great Junction is?"

The stadium was so silent she could hear Director Hick's stomach rumble.

Zoey didn't know why, but the old lady made her nervous. She tried to remember how Mrs. Dupont had described the junction.

"Ah . . . it's a portal I think . . . ah . . . *two* very big portals from different worlds that align and make a permanent doorway."

Director Aslagard wiped her nose with a handkerchief.

"Very good. And do you *believe* in the Great Junction? Do you think it *exists*?"

Zoey wasn't sure where the old woman was going with her questions, but she answered anyway. "Of course I do, I saw it. So, yeah, you could say I believe in it."

The entire stadium erupted in shouts and raised voices. Zoey stiffened in her chair.

"And how is it that you *saw* it, as you put it?" questioned Director Aslagard.

"I was there."

Zoey tried to ignore the ruckus in the stadium, but it was getting hard to hear the questions.

"SILENCE!" bellowed Director Patel. The amphitheater went still.

Director Aslagard continued.

"We know that the event occurred in a remote village in Scotland, near a secret Alpha city. But I'd like to know who authorized you to go there?"

Director Aslagard flipped through a stack of papers on the table. A slip of paper slipped through her fingers.

"I don't recall seeing a transcript of that mission anywhere in our records."

Zoey felt a pressure on her chest and could hardly breathe. She wished her friends had come with her. She needed someone to tell her she wasn't a *monster*. She felt like a Salem witch waiting to be burned on a stake.

"We—no—*I* . . ." corrected Zoey.

She knew there was no point in lying. Her own Hive knew the truth.

"No one did," she said. "I went on my own, without permission."

Her reckless disregard for rules had been a result of growing up in the foster care system. But the appeal of it all wasn't there now. She had a horrible feeling she was going to pay *big time* for breaking the rules. From the corner of her eye, she saw Director Hicks's head turn towards her, but she didn't look at him. She couldn't.

Director Aslagard interlaced her skeletal hands on the table, bluish veins peeked through her paper-thin skin. "There's something we don't quite understand."

She paused as if giving Zoey time to prepare her answer.

"How is it that *you*, a Drifter as you once were, *knew* where the Great Junction would take place?"

Zoey shrugged. "I didn't know. I had never even heard of the Great Junction, I swear."

The old woman leaned back and whispered something to the mystic with the white skin.

Zoey was sure they didn't believe her. She had the terrible feeling they thought she was in it with Mrs. Dupont. She couldn't see Directors Martin and Campbell right now, but she was positive that they would be smiling triumphantly.

Director Patel cleared his throat.

"If the members will permit me to ask a few questions?" he said.

"Zoey, you say that you *didn't* know where and when the Great Junction was going to take place. If this is true, can you tell the assembly why you were *there* in the first place?"

Zoey blinked, her mind racing with answers she wasn't sure how to express. Blood pounded in her ears as she searched for something to say that would make sense.

Director Patel's face was stony.

"Zoey," whispered Director Hicks. She saw that his face was also tomato red and that sweat was trickling down his forehead. He looked like he was about to have a heart attack.

"Director Patel's asked you a question," he said. "Go on now, answer him."

Zoey swallowed hard and said, "I had a hunch."

"A hunch?" Director Patel leaned forward, his face was unreadable, but his eyes were intense. "What kind of hunch?"

"A hunch that Mrs. Dupont was responsible for the black oil that had disabled all the mirror ports. I only went there looking for a cure," said Zoey.

Director Patel waited for the voices in the stadium to cease and then continued. "I see . . . and so you mirror-ported to this Mrs. Dupont's home without any authorization. Is that correct?"

Zoey didn't like his tone. Besides, she always did things without permission—it was part of her charm.

"Yes. I went without asking . . . but I don't see what the problem is. I mean . . . after all, I was right. *She* was the one who poisoned the mirrors. She admitted it in front of everyone. Like I said, I was only trying to find the cure—"

"This *is* a problem," reproached Director Patel. "Zoey St. John, you disobeyed the most fundamentals laws of our agencies." His voice rose. "These rules and regulations were instituted for the sole purpose of protecting *us*, as well as the entire human population. We abide by them. We trust in them. And because of your insubordination, the Alpha woman took your blood and generated the Great Junction. And now we have a *serious* problem on our hands."

Zoey felt like she'd been stabbed a thousand times. She couldn't breathe. They were blaming *her*. Didn't they know she was also responsible for *saving* the mirrors and the protective borders?

But even as she tried to convince herself of her innocence, part of her knew that they were right. She *had* caused this—her blood did. She felt like a total jerk. How could she ever make up for her actions?

She could feel the rush of tears, but she forced her eyes dry. The last thing she needed was to become a hysterical, crying, red-faced, red-haired, frightened little girl. She could deal with this.

Director Patel opened his laptop computer and read from the screen.

"According to Director Hicks's prior testament, and correct me if I'm wrong," he added to the red-faced director, "We now believe Zoey St. John holds an usually high quantity of *Original* blood."

Director Patel's eyes darted over to Zoey. She felt like she was about to burst out of her own skin. "She—Mrs. Dupont—used Zoey's blood in a ritual to commence the Great Junction."

Zoey clenched her jaw, and recoiled under the director's intense stare.

"The Great Junction had always been treated as a myth," continued Director Patel, his dark eyes never leaving Zoey. "A myth fabricated by Sevenths long ago about a permanent doorway between worlds. Sounds fascinating. I would have dismissed it as a myth today if it weren't for the *catastrophic* events that are happening around the world at this very moment."

As if to reinforce his last statement, another tremor rippled through the stadium. By the looks of panic on the faces of those around the table, Zoey knew this wasn't a regular occurrence. Earthquakes weren't a regular thing in London.

Director Patel leaned back in his chair and started conversing with the other members.

For a long moment no one spoke, and Zoey shifted in her chair nervously. She kept replaying the events that had occurred when Mrs. Dupont had stolen her blood. If only she hadn't been caught. She wanted to kick or punch herself. But it was too late now. She had to figure out a way to fix this . . . but how?

Finally, Director Patel spoke into his microphone. "Thank you for your testimony today, Zoey St. John. We have no further questions for you."

Zoey sat still in her chair, unable to move or even speak, not even sure if she should move or speak. Her guilt was tormenting her.

"And now we would like to address the assembly," said Director Patel, his voice strained like he was about to announce something terrible. He cleared his voice.

"We believe that the Alpha woman, Mrs. Dupont, was successful in conjuring up the Great Junction. We have seen the effects with our own eyes, as have all of you. Hundreds of portals have appeared around the world, and many unfortunate souls have disappeared into the Nexus."

He paused, his face paled.

"There is a reason why we called a National Assembly today. Over the past month, our most celebrated scientists have gathered *disturbing* information. When the portals from both worlds aligned, the worlds *shifted* with catastrophic consequences."

He paused and sighed. "Soon our world will be cursed with earthquakes, tsunamis, hurricanes, and volcanoes. We are now confronted by a devastating force that threatens to consume everything. Billions will die, and life as we know it will expire."

Cries and shouts boomed throughout the stadium like a storm. Zoey's breath caught in her throat. She felt like she was stuck in a horrible dream. She looked at Director Hicks.

"Is . . . is this true?" she whispered to him, her voice dry and cracking.

Director Hicks stared at the floor, and when he looked up his eyes were wet. "I'm afraid it is."

Zoey felt lightheaded, and the room started to spin. She forced down the urge to throw up. This couldn't be happening; she couldn't be the *cause* of the end of the world . . . .

Director Patel stood up and raised his voice with alarm. "Neither world can survive a *permanent* portal. If we do not find a way to close it soon, both worlds will be destroyed."

CHAPTER 5

THE CONTRACT

When Zoey woke up the next morning, everything from the previous day felt like it had been a horrible dream. It *had* to have been a dream. She, the little orphaned redhead, couldn't be responsible for the end of the world, could she? It was too absurd to even think about. But there it was, as plain as rain. Zoey St. John had destroyed the world.

After unsuccessfully convincing herself that yesterday was just a bad dream, she shuffled down the stairs. She sat at her usual table and ate her breakfast like a zombie. Her limbs moved unconsciously, and she grunted now and then. When she tried to recall the morning, she didn't remember eating at all.

Zoey pushed her plate away and stared out the window. Most of the snow had melted overnight, which was very unusual for Toronto. And now the red, pink, and yellow tulips at the borders of the Wander Inn were not their usual, brightly-colored selves. They had browned and rotted, as though the snow had thawed too quickly and somehow spoiled them. Things were definitely not normal. Signs of the Great Junction were creeping up on her, and she had a bad feeling this was only the beginning.

It was the first week of April, and spring was her favorite season—but even that couldn't change her morbid mood. What were the seasons good for anyway if the world was going to end?

She opened the window, but she coughed as she inhaled a breath of what she expected to be fresh air. The air smelled strongly of sulfur, like the air itself had rotted.

She shut the window, and Aria waddled in and poured her some more orange juice.

"You hardly touched your food. Zoey? Are you listening to me?"

Zoey turned from the window. "I am."

"You need to eat," said Aria. Her yellow cat-like eyes showed her concern.

"I could make you something else if you want? How about some French toast? I know how much you love that."

"No thanks, Aria," said Zoey, and she forced a little smile. "I'm not hungry."

She turned back and stared out the window again. How could she eat when she felt like throwing up all the time? She knew Aria cared about her, a rare commodity right now at the Hive. She felt a spark of warmth inside for just a second, before it got crushed by an overwhelming feeling of dread.

Aria put a hand on her shoulder.

"Zoey?" said Aria, her voice soft and comforting. "I know what you're doing."

"Yeah? What's that?"

"You're torturing yourself. You have to stop blaming yourself for what's happening."

Zoey shook her head. "You don't get it. *I* did this—me. *I'm* responsible for all of it."

One of Aria's set of arms pressed firmly on her hips while the other two cupped Zoey's face gently in her hands.

"Now you listen to me, young lady," she began, and Zoey felt mesmerized by her yellow eyes and couldn't look away even if she wanted to. "You have to stop this nonsense. You're innocent in all of this. How can *you* be responsible for something you didn't even know *existed?* Only a cruel and wicked person would want to destroy the worlds . . . and that's not you. So stop this at once."

Zoey looked over Aria's shoulder. It seemed that every Agent in the Inn was listening in on their conversation. They all had the same look in their eyes—blame. She stared back at the table, feeling more miserable than before.

Aria let go of Zoey's face. "You need to eat before going out there on your assignments—"

"Assignments?" laughed Zoey. "Do you honestly think they're going to keep me on after all of this? Seriously? Even *I'd* get rid of myself if I could. It'll be back to the foster system for me."

Aria glared at Zoey. "Well, maybe with that *kind* of attitude they will. My mother used to say, 'The most useless of all emotions is self-pity.' Stop acting like a victim and *do* something about it."

She turned on her heel and walked away.

Zoey thought that there was something strange in Aria's tone. Was she implying something?

But just as she was about to ask Aria what she meant, Simon and Tristan walked into the Inn.

"Thought we'd find you here," said Simon as he grabbed a chair. His face was full of expectation. He waited until Tristan was seated and then said, "Are you going to tell us what happened at the assembly or do we have to *beat* it out of you?"

Zoey looked at her friends' smiling faces. She hated to disappoint them, but she recounted yesterday's events as enthusiastically as she could anyway. Her voice cracked, but she continued her story till the very end. When she was finished, she sat and waited for them to say something, anything, before she burst into tears.

Tristan was the first one to speak. His voice was soft and gentle, "I know what you're thinking, Zoey. But this isn't your fault—"

"He's right," added Simon earnestly. He tore off some pieces of Zoey's cold pancakes and ate them.

"We didn't know the crazy woman's plans," he said with his mouth full. "I mean, how could we? She's a psychopath. We're normal. See what I mean?"

"But it still *happened*," said Zoey.

She felt the tiny pieces of the breakfast that she had actually swallowed rise in her throat. She forced them back down. Her eyes burned, and she blinked repeatedly. She wouldn't let herself cry in front of her friends, even though she knew they'd understand.

For a few moments there was an uncomfortable silence, as if her friends were afraid that if they spoke she'd start crying. She decided to spare them the painful silence and tried to change the subject.

"So, why are you guys here anyway?" she asked. She tried to keep her voice steady. "Shouldn't you be reporting to Agent Vargas for today's new assignments? I'm sure there's a lot to do now with all these portals opening. Must be tons of illegal mystics that need to be caught."

Simon and Tristan shared a look, and then Simon said, "Well, we've got some news to cheer you up!"

Zoey wanted to say, *I doubt that*, but she didn't want to dampen Simon's mood. Only a true friend would want to cheer her up. So instead she said, "What news?"

Suddenly the lights flickered, and the building cracked and moaned, as though some ghostly force were squeezing it. Zoey looked outside.

The blue morning skies had become dark with angry gray clouds. Trees swayed back and forth dangerously, as if a gusts of wind would snap them in half. Little whirlwinds of last fall's leaves whipped across the grounds, chasing each other like cats and dogs. And then she saw something that made her blood turn to ice.

A sudden bolt of jagged red light flashed between the clouds like thin strands of godly hair. Red lightning. But Zoey knew there was no such thing as red lightning, so what *was* that?

She hid the terror in her face when she turned to her friends. "You were saying Simon? Simon?"

Simon tore his eyes from the window. He swallowed hard and said, "Thought you'd like to know that the Agencies are gathering special troops to try and stop the Great Jungle portal—"

"Great *Junction*," interjected Tristan. He smiled at Zoey, and she forgot all her troubles for about two seconds.

"That's what I said," continued Simon, as he jabbed Zoey's fork into a pancake and took a bite.

"They've already figured out where the portal is and they've set up a few anchor points that are close enough to it, but still hidden in case of possible threats—enter psychopath Dupont—anyway, they're taking volunteers . . . like loads of them . . . like right now as we speak."

Zoey sat up in her seat. "What are you talking about?"

Simon smiled cheekily. "Thought that'd get your attention. I might not be as good looking as pretty-boy here next to me, but Simon Brown *always* delivers the goods."

Despite herself, Zoey laughed.

"You're such a moron," she said playfully and leaned forward in her chair. "Tell me *everything* you know."

Simon looked over his shoulder and then lowered his voice. "Well, from what I've heard—"

"Overheard," said Tristan, grinning.

"Doesn't matter if it's *overheard*. I *heard* it, didn't I?"

Zoey sighed, but she felt like she was floating in her chair. "Simon, please continue before I explode. What did you hear?"

"Check this out," said Simon, clearly enjoying himself with the bit of information he possessed. "Apparently, the agencies and their scientists have been attempting to shut down the Great Hole for weeks now, but they haven't been able to. It's like, dudes as smart as Agent Franken just can't shut it down."

"Because of Mrs. Dupont," guessed Zoey.

Tristan shook his head. "Not exactly."

Zoey scowled. "Please don't tell me Mrs. Dupont has a twin?"

"No," Simon made a face, "Great! Now I have a mental image of her and her freak show of a sister. Give a nerd a break."

He shook his head and then added with a voice full of intrigue.

"You ready for it? Yeah?" He leaned over the table, "Because they figured out that the portals have to be closed on *both* sides."

Zoey raised her brows. "So one *here,* and the other in the *Nexus.*"

"Exactly." Simon drank some maple syrup like it was orange juice.

"The scientists came up with a secret weapon, but they don't have the field training that agents do," said Tristan squaring his shoulders.

"The scientists wouldn't last a minute inside the Nexus, let alone get *past* Mrs. Dupont's security on this side. Agent Barnes's has seen it. He said that there are hundreds of armed Alphas protecting the portal. The agency's trying to create teams with at least five agents accompanying each scientist. But not everyone *wants* to go—"

"Even if it means a chance to save our world before it gets sucked up by a giant black hole." Simon gulped the last of Zoey's maple syrup. "Pretty sad, isn't it?"

Zoey stared at her friends. This was her chance to kill two birds with one stone: shut down the portals and save her mother. It was perfect. What Aria had said rang in her ears, *Stop acting like a victim and do something about it.* And that was exactly what she planned to do.

But something nagged at her. "So why isn't the agency *making* agents go? Isn't that part of their duty or something? I don't get why they're *asking* for volunteers?"

Tristan drummed his fingers on the table. "Because there's no guarantee that it'll work."

"You mean because they might die."

"Yup." Simon swallowed the last of Zoey's pancakes. "Everyone is saying it's a suicide mission. I like those missions. Keeps me on my toes. You know what I mean?"

"Not really," said Tristan, as he rolled his eyes. "Under normal agency regulations, Operatives under the age of eighteen aren't allowed to volunteer for missions—"

"But since we're *not* Operatives anymore, and these aren't *normal* agency times," Simon patted Tristan on the back, "Me and hot stuff here . . . signed up."

Zoey smiled at her friends. This was what she was waiting for. She would have a chance to redeem herself and save the world in the process. Piece of cake.

Tristan flattened a piece of paper on the table. It was cream-colored and nearly completely covered in black writing. It reminded Zoey of the birth certificate she had hauled along with her for nearly fifteen years, except that this paper had a golden seal in the shape of a shield at the bottom. A long dotted line awaiting her signature was printed beside it.

With a smile that made her heart melt, Tristan said, "We're going to get your mom back."

He tossed her a pen. "All we're missing is *you.*"

CHAPTER 6

A QUEST FOR VOLUNTEERS

Zoey clipped her boomerang to her belt and followed Tristan and Simon. Her heart pounded against her chest like a jackhammer. She had gladly signed the contract, just briefly glancing at it, but now she feared the agency wouldn't let her go. She was, after all, responsible for the Great Junction. What if they *didn't* let her go? What would she do then?

She realized that she'd already made that decision. She would find a way to shut the portals down and save her mother, no matter what.

The air was unnaturally warm for early spring. It felt like summer, but there were no leaves on the trees, and the grass was yellow and brown instead of green. The smell of sulfur was even worse than she'd first thought, and she had to cover her mouth with her shirt. The dark gray skies and flashes of red lightning added to the gloom. Strong winds pushed her back, like invisible hands that didn't want her to reach the Hive. Was the storm trying to tell her something? She ignored the dread in the pit of her stomach and plowed on.

Simon swung open the doors of the Hive, and Zoey let out a breath of surprise. The grand hallway had been transformed into a campaign headquarters.

Hundreds of agents and mystics in coats and heavy boots were gathered near the reception area. They were armed for war with swords, guns, axes, and other weapons Zoey had never seen before. Some were little older than Zoey and some were middle-aged. Others looked like they belonged in a senior's home, not here preparing for battle. Shouts rang in the hall as angry agents argued with each other. She could see the fear in their eyes and sense the urgency in the room. She wasn't the only one who could feel that the Hive and the rest of the world had changed.

Long lines of agents and mystics holding forms with gold seals just like Zoey's waited by a long table. Directors Hicks, Johnson, Martin, and Campbell sat behind it.

Director Campbell took a contract from a bald man in his forties who was as tall and thick as Agent Vargas. She inspected the contract closely, and when she seemed satisfied that everything was in order, she struck the top of his hand with a heavy stamp.

"NEXT!" she called, and passed the signed contract to Director Johnson who entered the information on his laptop computer.

The next person in line, a small man with curly moss-brown hair and round glasses shuffled forward. Dressed in a dark suit and tie, he looked more like a banker than an agent. He stooped over the desk and twisted around nervously as he made up his mind whether or not to run. Zoey could sense the tension in the air.

She searched the faces in the crowd, hoping to see Agent Barnes or Lee, but they weren't there.

Zoey waited in silence. She was happy to see so many had turned up, and she was sure that volunteers in Hives around the world were enlisting, too. She wondered if they would be *enough*. Who knew what waited for them on the other side of the Nexus.

A neon sign flashed above the one operating mirror in the hall. It read: *Laggan, Scotland*. Agent Ward stood by the mirror and inspected the hands of the volunteers to make sure they had been stamped properly. She frowned at the group of volunteers who were waiting in front of her.

"Where is your science officer? No team goes without an agency science officer—"

"We don't need a science officer."

Zoey heard a man's voice. She turned around as a plump man with light brown hair, no chin, and large bushy eyebrows strolled forward. He walked as though he owned the place and everyone in it. His arrogant demeanor reminded her of Stuart, and Zoey immediately disliked him.

Agent Ward scowled at him. "What do you mean you don't *need* a science officer? Don't be foolish, man. Every team *has* to have a science officer! Those are the rules!"

The man sneered and lifted his hand for everyone to see. Zoey saw the ruby ring in the shape of the letter O around his pinky. It was just like the one Stuart and the rest of the Original wannabes wore.

"I'm a *true* Original descendant," said the man, "as was my father and mother before me—and just like that girl over there."

He smiled and pointed a fat finger at Zoey. His teeth sparkled like he had brushed with diamond toothpaste.

All eyes immediately turned on Zoey, and she wanted to melt into the wall. She disliked him even more now.

"A single drop of my *Original* blood, my fellow agents and directors," continued the man, his smile widening with every syllable, "will *close* the portal."

Volunteers crowded around to hear what the agent had to say.

Agent Ward raised her brow. "Is that so, Agent Ferguson? You think that a portal of this magnitude can be shut down by a simple *drop* of *your* blood?"

"Yes, my dear woman," answered Agent Ferguson. "Speak to your scientists. They didn't believe me either—but with enough *convincing*—and with this signed agreement—"

He flashed a piece of paper that looked like the volunteer contract but pocketed it before Zoey could see what it was.

"They all agreed that *I* didn't require the assistance of a science officer—I have my own unique skills. If *that* girl could open the portal, my fellow Originals and I know that *we* can shut it down."

A burst of applause rose in the hall, and the man bowed like he had just completed a theatrical performance. This wasn't a laughing matter, and Zoey felt the urge to rush up to him and slap him to wake him up a little.

Agent Ward grunted. She wasn't convinced either.

"Do you think he's right?" whispered Simon.

Zoey tried to remember what Mrs. Dupont had said about *why* her blood was unique, but her memory of that event was a little hazy. All she remembered was that her blood was more *potent*. Maybe she had forced herself to forget how she had been used.

"Maybe," she answered finally and shrugged. "I don't know, but I guess it won't hurt to try."

"Bet it'll *hurt* him if it fails," suggested Simon.

"I think he's making a mistake." Tristan watched Agent Ferguson shake hands with his new admirers.

"If he is a true Original, don't you think Mrs. Dupont and the Alphas would have drained his blood by now? I don't buy his performance. I think he likes the attention. I think he's full of bull."

"Maybe she didn't know about him?" offered Zoey. "Maybe she'd been so obsessed with my mother and I that she never really paid any attention to the others."

Tristan watched the man indifferently and then shook his head. "No, man, this guy is really stupid, and he's going to get himself and his team killed."

After Agent Ferguson had acquired enough new admirers and handshakes; he stepped up to the mirror and beamed at Agent Ward with his nine team members behind him.

Agent Ward typed something on the computer panel beside the mirror. There was a loud buzzing, and a green light above the mirror lit up with a *click*.

"Don't say I didn't warn you," said Agent Ward as she stepped back. "I think you're being foolish."

With a hop in his step, and ignoring Agent Ward's warning, Agent Ferguson stepped into the mirror and vanished. Zoey watched the rest of his team disappear through the mirror.

She followed Simon and Tristan to the long table and stood in line with the rest of the volunteers. The looks of surprise on the faces of the other agent volunteers stung her a little, but she forced herself to look away and pretended to read her contract thoroughly.

Before she knew it, Zoey and her friends stood before the directors. Director Martin reached out and took her contract.

"What's this?" he said as he inspected her contract.

"After everything *you've* done, you expect us to just . . . let you go? You're even more arrogant and senseless than I thought."

His accusation hit Zoey hard. She felt like she'd just been shot. She couldn't speak. She knew she had taken a chance volunteering, that the Agency might not let her go, but still she hoped.

"She's volunteering like us," said Tristan. He stepped in beside Zoey and tossed his contract in Director Martin's face. "Let's face it, the Agencies need as many volunteers as they can get, and Zoey's volunteering, just like us."

"Yeah," agreed Simon. "What he said." He slid his own contract on the table and then hid behind Tristan.

Director Martin glared at Zoey like she was a piece of gum stuck on the bottom of his shoe.

"You shouldn't even *be* here; you should have been expelled from the program—from our society. If I had my way, you'd be locked up in a high security cell forever—"

"Well it's not up to you, is it?" interrupted Tristan. His skin shimmered, and he leaned dangerously close to the director. For a horrible moment, Zoey thought he was going to punch the director. Zoey smiled; that would be awesome to see.

"You think this is funny?" Director Campbell's face was twisted in disgust.

She leaned over and grabbed Zoey's contract. "You think this little piece of paper will make us forget what you did?"

She hesitated for a moment, lifted the contract for everyone to see, and then ripped it in half.

Zoey found her voice. "Hey! What are you doing?"

Directors Martin and Campbell shared a winning look, and then Director Campbell said triumphantly, "You're *not* going anywhere."

"That's not fair!" shouted Simon, still hiding behind Tristan. "I demand a recount!"

"WHAT'S GOING ON HERE?"

Director Hicks pushed his chair back and joined them. His face was flushed.

"What's all this racket? What's going on? What are you kids all doing here?"

Zoey couldn't answer. It was as though she believed Directors Martin and Campbell were right. Perhaps this had just been a dream. Perhaps she wasn't supposed to go. She'd never win back the respect of the Agency and the Sevenths.

Simon answered for her. "These two bozos tore up her contract—ouch!" Tristan kicked him.

Director Hicks picked up the torn pieces of paper. He turned towards Directors Martin and Campbell. "And why would you do such a thing?"

Director Martin's face was severe and when he spoke spit flew from his mouth, "*She* shouldn't be allowed to go—"

"Every able agent is allowed to volunteer. That *includes* any OSC individuals who are willing to go," corrected Director Hicks. "It is up to them. Not us. Anyone can volunteer for a special mission. Anyone."

"But—" Director Campbell's face screwed up in fury. Her voice rose. "This is all *her* fault! She did this! The world's dying because of her!"

Director Hicks took Zoey's hand in his. He pressed the stamp down on the top of her hand and branded her with a red-colored *V*.

Zoey did her best not to look too pleased and waited patiently as Director Hicks stamped Tristan and Simon in turn. She did her best to avoid looking at Directors Martin and Campbell, although she could *feel* them glaring at her.

The only director who seemed indifferent to Zoey was Director Johnson. He seemed more interested in fighting with his computer than in a redheaded girl on her way to a suicide mission.

Director Hicks smiled at them encouragingly and said, "The Agency appreciates and values your commitment to help. Look out for one another and keep each other safe. Good luck to you all."

"Thank you, director." Zoey answered awkwardly and moved away from the table before he changed his mind.

Simon raised his hand and admired his new mark. He was practically drooling over it. "V for Valiant . . . V for Victorious . . . V for *Very* Awesome—"

"V for victim," said Tristan as he smacked Simon on the back of the head. But he had the tiniest of smiles on his face and looked a little smug. He wore his mark proudly, too.

They walked back towards the mirrors and faced Agent Ward when Zoey realized that they had forgotten something important.

"Uh . . . guys—"

"Where's your science officer?" barked Agent Ward as though she had read her mind. "No science officer, no mission."

"Argh!" Simon smacked his forehead. "I *knew* we forgot something."

Zoey's moment of triumph dissipated like a deflated balloon. She saw her mother's terrified face flash in her mind's eye. Was she even still alive? Every minute wasted was another minute her mother was tortured.

"But you let that guy go without a science officer," argued Tristan. "Why can't we go? We're better skilled than the last group, and you know it."

Agent Ward shook her head stubbornly. "I'm sorry, but I can't. Agent Ferguson had *special* permission—he knows what he's doing—"

"I seriously doubt that." Simon had lost his smile. He looked angrier than when Stuart King had stolen his OSC badge and flushed it down in one of the boys' bathroom toilets.

"Man, this sucks. I can't believe you won't let us go! We're OSC . . . and besides . . . you *need* volunteers! The Agency said so. You need everyone that's willing to help. That's us baby!"

"I know you kids mean well," said Agent Ward "But I just can't let you go without a science officer. I'd never forgive myself if I did. I'm sorry, kids but it's a no."

"Don't blame us when the world ends," said Simon crossly, "you'll know who to thank for that—"

"Simon Brown!" growled Agent Ward dangerously. "You're stepping dangerously close to a night locked in one of the basement cells."

Simon raised his hands in surrender. "Ooohh, I'm so scared."

Zoey grabbed Simon by the arm and whirled him around. "Simon, don't. We'll figure out a way—"

"How?" Simon's face flushed. "If the Agency wasn't so *stupid*, they'd let us go."

He raised his voice and made sure everyone in the great hall could hear him. "*We're* the ones who helped find the cure for the black oil—the three of us! You have no idea what we can do. We're a team. We're like the three musketeers—only better. You *need* us."

Another group of agent volunteers had taken their place at the table. Among them was a skinny woman who clasped a portable computer nervously to her chest, like a newborn child. Zoey knew she was that group's science officer. She looked terrified.

But Zoey wasn't terrified. She wanted to go. She *needed* to go.

Zoey pushed her way back through the volunteers towards Agent Ward. "Please Agent Ward. I know I can help."

A flash of sadness appeared on Agent Ward's face. "I know how difficult this must be for you, Zoey. But without a science officer, I'm afraid there's nothing else I can do—"

"I'm their science officer!" said a voice.

Zoey turned around. Agent Franken shuffled through the crowd in his usual silver full body HAZMAT suit, but without the hood and visor. He had two large metal tanks on his back and had rubber tubes wrapped tightly around his waist. He held a gray carry-on bag and looked like he was ready to explore the sea in in an antique diving suit. He moved slowly, and with some difficulty; finally he reached Agent Ward.

"I'm their science officer," repeated Agent Franken a little out of breath. "They're with me."

Slowly, he brushed a strand of stringy white hair from his forehead. And when he looked at Zoey, his thick glasses magnified his eyes to the size of grapefruits. He smiled.

"Sorry I'm late. I needed to make sure we had all the necessary supplies for this mission. Can't be too careful, especially with where we are going."

He adjusted his glasses, and Zoey could see a freshly stamped V marked the top of his right hand.

Zoey wanted to throw her arms around the little old man and hug him, but she was afraid she might crush him.

"Not a problem, Agent Franken," she answered. "Just glad you finally made it."

She smiled at him, and when she looked at Tristan and Simon, their grins were the size of the great hall.

"Move over!" Simon pushed the other group of volunteers back. "We were here first. Very important science officer as our teammate! Coming through, coming through! Thank you, but we'll sign autographs later."

Zoey couldn't have asked for a better team. Agent Franken was the cleverest scientist in all of the Agencies. Tristan was a brave and strong Mysterian. And the ever-resourceful Simon Brown was always an asset. It was a team made in heaven.

Simon leaned forward and whispered to Agent Franken. "So, what's the master plan?"

Agent Franken blinked his oversized eyes and said, "Just get me across to the portal alive and keep me alive while I work on the

Nexus portal on the other side. I'll need maybe twenty minutes at the most . . . if everything goes according to plan."

"That's a pretty good plan," said Simon, still beaming. "Did I ever tell you how awesome you are?"

Agent Franken stared at Simon without blinking.

"Are you ready?" commanded Agent Ward. She tapped her foot impatiently. "You're not the only team to leave today."

"Time to go, team." Zoey turned and looked at Agent Ward. She wasn't sure, but she thought that she smiled for a second. When she looked again, it was gone.

"Well now, I see that everything is in order," said Agent Ward. She typed something on the small computerized panel. "Well, then off you go and best of luck."

The green light lit up and the surface of the mirror churned and wavered like liquid water.

Zoey could hardly restrain herself from jumping to the front of the line, but she waited to let Agent Franken step through first. After all, he was a senior agent, the science officer, and he was much older than they were. It was only fair that he should go in first. She would go in after.

Agent Franken stepped forward, and with a flash of white light he disappeared.

With a last glance over at Tristan and Simon, Zoey walked through.

Beams of green and blue flashed behind her eyes as she was stretched and pulled like gum. As the sick feeling started, she thought of her mother to stop the sensation. Then she smelled the ocean and wet leaves, and her feet touched solid ground.

She grabbed her boomerang instinctively as she opened her eyes.

The early morning sun shone in a clearing surrounded by trees as tall as skyscrapers. To her right was the great stone wall outside the Alpha city. And outside the wall, at the edge of the forest loomed an enormous blue hole about two hundred feet wide. It was just as she remembered. The blue inside of the hole stirred and wavered like water, alien and imposing in the forest.

Outside the portal, the agents and science officers who had gone through the mirror before her were under attack.

CHAPTER 7

ATTACK OF THE BEARDED

BABIES

At first, Zoey thought she was hallucinating. But as her eyes focused and adjusted to the dim light around her, she knew she wasn't.

Hundreds of Alphas and monster hybrids stabbed, shot, whipped, crushed, and pulled apart any agents trying to get near the great portal like they were nothing more than mere insects. Her chest tightened as she watched a familiar science officer with puffy yellow hair make a run for the portal. He didn't make it. An Alpha woman with the legs of a lion and a lizard tail plunged a spear through him and then picked him up like he weighed no more than a child. Her distorted face gleamed as she stuck the other end of the spear into the ground and admired the dying man like a prize. Zoey wanted to throw up. It was too horrific to watch, but she couldn't look away. All around the portal, agents shrieked in a chaotic fog of panic and blood.

Agent Ferguson appeared through a break in the cluster of attacks. Zoey held her breath as he slipped unseen past the attacking Alphas and scurried over to the portal.

He drew a knife and sliced his right palm, chanting as he did so. He squeezed blood from the wound and flung some of it at the portal. She could see the strain on his face.

Why wasn't he stepping *through* to the other side? He needed to close *both* portals for the Great Junction to shut down.

"Wait!" she cried. "You need to go through to the other side!"

But Agent Ferguson didn't hear her voice over the roar of the battle.

Agent Ferguson stood back and waited. He looked triumphant. At first nothing happened, but then, like a drop of ink in water, a spot of purple appeared in the portal. He threw his fist in the air in triumph, and then lowered it very slowly. The purple blot dissolved as though it had never existed. His blood didn't work. The blood of an Original wasn't enough to close the portal.

As he inched forward again to try again, an Alpha woman with long white hair and milky skin appeared in a flash of red behind him and raised her dagger.

"NO!" cried Zoey.

The Alpha woman stabbed him repeatedly. Agent Ferguson yelped, fell to the ground, and tried to crawl away. But he wasn't fast enough. The Alpha grabbed his hair, pulled back his head, and slit his throat like she was carving a pumpkin. His eyes rolled to the back of his head, and he fell face first into the dirt, dead.

Without thinking, Zoey rushed forward and crashed into Agent Franken. His thick glasses magnified the terror in his eyes. He turned to her and whispered, "Oh dear, it's much worse than I anticipated."

Tristan and Simon appeared at her side.

"I had a feeling it wouldn't work." Tristan looked at Zoey. "He died in vain—"

"At least he tried!" Zoey turned angrily to Tristan. "He died *trying* to save us all!"

"But he also died trying the wrong side of the portal," added Simon.

He winced at the scowl on Zoey's face, and then he added quickly. "And now we know that blood alone won't do the trick."

"No, simple blood most certainly *won't*." Agent Franken adjusted his glasses with a look of grim determination. "Follow me."

The little man waddled forward as fast as his ungainly suit would allow him to go.

Zoey looked at Tristan and Simon and then followed Agent Franken. He hid behind a tree and waited. Zoey knelt down beside him. Tristan and Simon came up behind her, and she grasped her boomerang tightly. She hoped Agent Franken had a plan to get them across.

She searched the scene for a safe passage to the portal, but there wasn't one. Everywhere she looked, agents, science officers, and Alphas were in combat—and the Alphas were winning easily.

Seconds became minutes as they waited, and waited, and waited. Finally, Zoey couldn't stay quiet any longer.

"Agent Franken," she whispered, "what exactly are we waiting for?"

He raised his hand but didn't speak. She could see sweat trickling down the sides of his temples and realized he must be boiling hot in that suit. She hoped that the suit would protect him.

Nobody said anything.

"I need you to help me get across safely," said Agent Franken finally. "Once we're through, I'm going to need twenty minutes or so to shut down the portal on the Nexus side—"

"But how will we get back home?"

Simon's voice rose, and the whites of his eyes showed. "Are you planning a suicide mission? There are things I'd like to get back to, you know . . . like food and video games . . . and maybe even a first date!"

Agent Franken turned slowly towards Simon and looked at him like he had never seen him before.

"This isn't a suicide mission boy. I'd like to get back to my things as well once this is over."

He wiped his forehead with his sleeve. "But it's a very *dangerous* mission, nonetheless. In theory, once the procedure is done we should have enough time to slip back through the portal before it shuts down completely."

"Do your theories usually work?" Simon blurted out.

"Usually."

"Well, that's comforting—ouch!" Zoey knocked Simon on the head with her boomerang.

Agent Franken turned back to the portal. "Once the Nexus side is closed, I'll still need your help to keep me *breathing* while I work on *this* side of the portal."

"Got it," said Tristan. "We'll keep you safe, don't worry."

"Good." Agent Franken said. "I picked you lot because I believe in the three of you . . . and in me of course."

Agent Franken's belief in her made Zoey feel invincible. She could tackle all the Alphas singlehandedly. She caught Tristan smiling at her and felt the blood rise in her face.

Agent Franken stared at the scene in silence again. And then after a moment, he raised his hand again and said, "Now!"

Together, the three of them began to cross the grounds towards the portal. Zoey had a bad feeling that Agent Franken's slowness would get them all killed, but Tristan took over and attacked anything that came near them with his silver dagger. His skin gleamed blue as he punched and kicked a path for them. Zoey and Simon protected the back, and the team fought their way towards the portal doing their best to keep Agent Franken alive.

Simon flung homemade explosives with his S9 slingshot. He hit a rat-faced Alpha man in the face, and he exploded in a sticky pink mess.

Zoey kicked and slashed, using her boomerang like a sword. She had to keep Agent Franken safe, and the only way to do that was to get the Alphas to focus on *them* instead of him. They had to shield him until they reached the portal.

For one exciting minute, Zoey thought they were winning. She hurled her boomerang and knocked down four unsuspecting Alphas. A young Alpha panicked when he saw her and ran face-first into another Alpha, knocking them both out cold.

Another mystic with large bat wings screeched and tried to fly away, but Tristan grabbed him by the legs and sent him spiraling into the forest.

Even Simon showed skill and bravery as he knocked out two large Alpha men with an explosive shot of yellow slime.

But for every one they put down, twenty more appeared. It was an impenetrable force. They hadn't even made it halfway to the portal. The giant blue hole seemed hopelessly out of reach.

After half an hour of fighting and dodging, Zoey's blistered hands and skinny frame couldn't take much more. She wished she had Tristan's super strength. She saw the strain on Simon's face, and Tristan looked even worse. He had fought ten times more Alphas than Zoey and Simon combined and looked drained. His glowing blue skin had dimmed, like his battery was failing. He clutched his chest with his right arm, while he fought with his left. She could see blood seeping through his fingers. He was injured.

As Zoey blundered towards Tristan, an Alpha broke through behind her. She spun around and raised her weapon, but Agent Franken got there first. He swung his carry-on bag and smacked the Alpha with surprising force for someone so small. The Alpha fell unconscious.

Miraculously, Agent Franken was still safe.

Zoey could feel her hope of finding her mother washing away.

Mrs. Dupont had guarded her great portal with such enormous strength that Zoey wondered if they were fighting for a lost cause. Where was the woman anyway? Peering down at them grotesquely from her grand mansion? Just the thought of her made Zoey's blood boil.

The combat seemed to break for a moment, but Zoey's relief soon vanished when a new enemy came forward.

A group of twenty fur-covered little mystics in t-shirts and jeans came towards them. They looked like ugly children with beards. They flexed the black talons on their grubby little fingers, and their red eyes glowed with hatred and excitement. They were as cute and cuddly as hungry panthers.

Zoey exchanged a worried look with Tristan and Simon and then moved and made a protective wall in front of Agent Franken.

The hairy babies circled around them.

"I feel like I'm in a Halloween Pampers commercial," said Simon, breathing heavily.

"Does anybody know what these things are? I'm not sure whether to whack them with my sling shot or offer them milk."

Agent Franken opened his mouth, "They're—"

"Werewolves," said one of the ugly babies in a chipmunk sort of voice. He had a white tuft of fur on the top of his head like a Mohawk. "There's nothing more we hate than Agent *cubs*. And here you are . . . in *our* territory."

Zoey couldn't help herself. Maybe it was her nerves, but she started laughing.

"Werewolves? You can't possibly be *werewolves!* Werewolves are big and super strong and . . ." She looked at them again questioningly, ". . . and a lot *older*. You guys are like tiny little furry babies—"

"Babies!" said one of the miniature werewolves in that same kind of chipmunk voice, as if it had inhaled some helium balloons. "Who you callin' babies? You're the ones that look like babies. You're cubs. We could smell you a mile away."

The mystic sneered, its mouth full of sharp teeth. It wore a yellow t-shirt that said: BITE ME.

"Young meat is the most tender," said another werewolf. ". . . So juicy and warm, it melts in your mouth. I'm going to get me a piece of the blond. He looks *tasty*."

Simon looked offended. "What? No way. No one's eating me, furball."

"We'll see about that," said the werewolf with the white Mohawk.

Zoey couldn't see any females among them. And the other Alphas avoided them, like they were afraid of the werewolves or had been told by someone *not* to interfere.

"Mrs. Dupont sent you, didn't she?" pressed Zoey.

She looked up towards the big house on the hillside. "Thought she'd try and get rid of us before we reached the portal. Well, we're not giving up so easily."

"Yeah," said Simon. "We're OSC. We can take care of a few gremlins."

"This is werewolf territory," said the werewolf leader. "I've *marked* it—"

"What do you mean you've *marked* it?" asked Simon, and then made a face when he realized what the little wolf-man meant. ". . . That's disgusting and unsanitary. Do you know how many diseases you're spreading by—?"

"My pack is hungry," said the leader.

He inched forward. "I haven't fed them today, and I promised them a *special* feast of human flesh, and now here you are, ripe for the plucking."

"Come any closer, and I'll be *plucking* the fur off your head, dog," growled Tristan. He brandished his dagger, but Zoey wasn't sure that was the best thing to do.

The pack leader's red eyes flared with hatred.

"You *dare* call us dog! I'll be killing *you* first." He looked at Tristan, "but not before I rip that tongue out of your mouth!"

"Kill him boss," said a red-furred pimple-faced werewolf. "Rip his heart out. I wanna play fetch with it."

"Yeah!" agreed a werewolf with a protruding forehead. "I want to chew on his intestines—no wait—I want the one in the space suit!"

Tristan started forward, but Agent Franken held him back. "Do not be fooled by their size, young man," he whispered. "Werewolves are some of the most ferocious mystics, much worse than a pack of wild dogs. They fight to the death, and they almost always win. They are a lot stronger than they look—"

"I don't care," said Tristan. "We can beat them."

Zoey could tell he had lost some of his confidence. They all needed a breather, but it didn't look like that was going to happen.

The pack leader called out. "Looks like cub meat's back on the menu, boys!"

Suddenly the werewolves scrambled around and climbed on top of one another until they looked like furry totem poles covered with sharp claws.

Simon stifled a laugh. "What do you make of those?"

But before Zoey could answer, the totem poles attacked. The bigger werewolves on the bottom supported them, and they moved surprisingly fast.

"Agent Franken, get behind me," called Zoey.

She moved forward and shielded him with her body. Simon and Tristan formed a protective circle around him and drew their weapons.

Two werewolf-totem poles launched themselves ferociously at Tristan. Eight pairs of slashing arms lashed out at him. They hissed and growled as they cut through his clothes like they were tissue paper and tore at his skin until it bled.

"Tristan!" screamed Zoey.

But as she staggered towards him, two werewolf-totem poles boxed her in. They spit and hissed white foam like rabid dogs.

She saw Simon fire a few rounds at the last werewolf-totem pole, while Agent Franken whacked it with his bag.

Zoey cursed and raised her boomerang.

They launched their attack.

She moved on instinct. She spun and threw her boomerang. It flew ten feet, hit the middle guy of the first werewolf-totem pole in the chest, and unbalanced them for a second. For one glorious moment, Zoey thought she had toppled them, but they held on. The beasts straightened themselves, shrieked, growled, and hissed, and then charged again.

"I'm going to rip out your heart and eat it while it's still beating," growled the werewolf with the zit face. His face was almost at Zoey's level. "I'm going to taste flesh tonight!"

He shot out a claw, and Zoey hit it away with the edge of her weapon.

They were too close. She didn't have enough space for a good shot, but she had no other choice.

She could feel the hot breath of the other werewolf-totem pole on the back of her neck. It was right behind her. She reached back as far as she could, spun around, and whipped her boomerang at the head of the werewolf on top.

Crunch!

His body went limp, but he didn't fall. It was like he was glued to the other guy's shoulders.

Zoey grabbed her boomerang as it returned. She had to try again. She wasn't about to be eaten by the ugliest furry babies she'd ever seen. Breathing heavily, she crouched and readied herself—

Searing pain erupted in her back.

Zoey stumbled forward. Her arms were pinned behind her.

She screamed.

A creature raked her arm with its claws and scratched her hand.

She dropped her weapon.

Another creature landed on her back and sank its teeth into her scalp.

She shouted with pain and tried to throw him off, but she couldn't.

Little hands and claws grabbed at her. They slashed her skin and bit her, and she couldn't do anything to stop them. It was the most horrifying feeling in the world. She tried desperately not to the let dread overcome her, but she felt panic rise like a hot fever.

She blinked the blood from her eyes and saw the other werewolf-ladder approach. Their red eyes gleamed in excitement and hunger. The beasts rushed in close to her and snapped at her face. The fiends were everywhere, shrieking and biting, tearing her exposed flesh. They were going to eat her alive. She could hear Simon and Tristan screaming.

Zoey kicked out in desperation, striking as hard as she could at anything that moved.

91

It worked. The totem pole wavered, and the four werewolves tumbled to the ground.

The distraction was all that she needed.

She reached back and head-butted something behind her, a skull hopefully. Her arms were released immediately, and she collapsed to the ground. But something that smelled like dog latched itself onto her back. She reached back, grabbed it, and threw its furry form to the earth.

She ignored the pain in her back and the many bleeding and burning gashes around her arms and scrambled to her feet in search of her boomerang. She found it half buried in the ground and kicked it free.

"You cannot win," said a werewolf with scars all over its face.

"Surrender now, and maybe we'll give you a quick death."

He climbed over his brothers as they reformed their totem pole. Now two mystic ladders stood in front of her.

Zoey spit the dirt from her mouth and looked over to her friends.

Tristan moved so fast that his movements were a blur. He bellowed like an angry animal, and his daggers spun through the air so fast they hummed. Although he fought like a champion, slicing the werewolves two or three at a time, he still faced one angry werewolf-totem pole. Zoey could see that he was running only on adrenaline.

Simon wasn't so lucky. Although he was limping, and blood seeped from his shirt and jeans, he still fired his weapon. He stood protectively over a silver bundle on the ground—Agent Franken. Zoey couldn't tell if he was alive or dead.

Her blood boiled, and she let it fuel her with new vigor.

"I'll never surrender," she answered finally. If she couldn't defeat the werewolves, then she would have to come back with reinforcements. But how? What was the weakest point of a tall, narrow building?

And then it hit her. She knew what to do.

"Come get me if you can, *dogs*," taunted Zoey.

The werewolves sneered.

"Die, agent cub!" they shouted.

"Kill her!"

"Rip her apart! Make her suffer!"

"I want her hair!"

The two werewolf-ladders charged, slashing and stabbing as they hurtled forward.

Zoey took a breath, raised her right arm, angled her boomerang, and shot.

The golden weapon soared in the air like a kite caught in the wind. It soared higher and higher until it was but a yellow speck in the sky.

The werewolves couldn't help themselves. They stopped and started laughing.

"Ooops," one chuckled. "Did the little agent cub lose her weapon?"

"Why did you throw it away?" laughed the pimple-faced one. "You want to die, don't you? We'll help you along with that."

"Are you too scared to fight?" another snickered.

Zoey stood stone-faced and waited as calmly as she could. She counted in her head.

Three . . .

The two ugly totem poles wavered as they laughed. None of them paid any attention to the spinning golden boomerang shooting back down towards them at lightning speed.

Two . . . one . . .

SMACK! CLUNK!

The weapon hit the backs of both werewolves' knees.

The effect was immediate. First the mystics howled in pain, and then one by one, the totem poles collapsed.

Dust flew in the air as the werewolves toppled on top of one another, screaming, punching, and trying to pull themselves out from under the rubble of dirt and fur.

But Zoey didn't wait. She went straight to work.

She shot her boomerang again and again into the pile of werewolf cubs, until every single one of them was out cold and lay in the dirt.

But she didn't stop there. She knew her friends were in trouble.

In pain, and on the verge of collapsing, Zoey stumbled over to Simon.

The werewolves were attacking him like a pack of wild dogs. They swarmed him and sank their teeth into his hands. He yelled in pain and dropped his slingshot.

He drew a small blade from his pocket and slashed and stabbed at those he could reach. His blue eyes were wide with terror.

When he saw Zoey he screamed. "Help! Get them off! Get them off!"

Zoey leaped over Agent Franken's body, hoping that he was still alive, and grabbed on to the first werewolf's legs. She threw him ten feet into the air, and he crashed to the ground in a heap.

She kicked and whacked her boomerang on the remaining creatures. In an instant, Tristan was fighting beside her, and they hit the werewolves until Simon was free.

"No one told us about werewolves!" cried Simon exasperatedly. "How come no one ever told us how insane they were?"

He kicked an unconscious werewolf.

Zoey remembered Agent Franken.

She ran back towards the little man. He lay on his side. His eyes were closed, but when she kneeled down beside him, she saw that he was breathing.

"Thank God, you're alive," she whispered to him.

His Hazmat suit was ripped like it had been in a paper shredder, but somehow the suit had kept him alive. She looked behind her.

"I don't know how long the werewolves will stay down, but the Alphas are looking our way. It won't take long before they see us."

Tristan bent down and easily lifted the unconscious science officer into his arms.

"Let's get back to the anchor."

"So that's it then?" said Simon, looking like he'd been to hell and back. "We've failed? The world is going to end? But it *can't* end. Not now! I've never even had a date yet!"

His voice rose, and Zoey caught sight of a few Alphas turning their way.

Zoey eyes darted to the big blue hole.

"If only we could get past the Alphas somehow, then we'd have a chance to shut down the portals." *And save my mother,* she wanted to say but didn't.

She could see a tall man with dark hair and a pale face fighting among the crowd. His dark eyes were fixed on Zoey.

"Is that Director Martin over there?" she asked. She had recognized his hateful scowl instantly. But when she blinked, he was gone.

Simon followed her gaze. "I don't see him. It wasn't him. Probably just some guy who looks like him."

Zoey rubbed her eyes. "Yeah, you're probably right."

"We need a bigger army," said Tristan with conviction. "It's the only way. If we could push back the Alpha army with force, then maybe we'd have a fighting chance."

His skin was back to its original olive color, and he had a nasty purple bruise over his left eye. He held Agent Franken in his arms as if the little man weighed no more than a large house cat.

Agent Franken's face was sickly pale, and Zoey was worried about him.

"Well, whatever we do," she said urgently, "we can't stay here and think of a plan. We need to split. Agent Franken needs medical attention, and we need to go, like *now*."

She pointed to the mass of Alphas galloping towards them with weapons drawn and malicious grins on their distorted faces.

"Wish we had an invisibility cloak," said Simon miserably as he stared at the ground. "Then we'd get through for sure."

Zoey jumped on the spot, her hands on her head. "That's it!"

"That's what?" asked Simon and Tristan together.

"Simon, you're a *genius!*" A giant smile of relief spread across Zoey's face.

Simon looked puzzled and pleased at the same time.

"I am? Huh . . . right . . . of course I am . . . and can you *remind* me why I'm such a genius?" He looked at Tristan who shrugged. Both of them looked completely lost.

"I'll explain later," said Zoey hurriedly.

The Alphas were closing in fast.

"We don't have time. Let's get out of here. Hurry! Get out your DSMs."

Zoey flipped hers open. Her hands were sweaty, and she nearly dropped it. Tristan held on to the unconscious Agent Franken. She steadied her hands, and Simon and Tristan's bodies shimmered. The ground shook under her sneakers, and she could feel the oncoming army; they were so close that she could touch them—then Zoey and her team disappeared.

CHAPTER 8

UTRON ENERGY

CAPSULE

"We're all doomed!" said an agent with his head wrapped in bloody bandages.

"Our forces couldn't even make it to the portal. How are we supposed to *save* our world if we can't even *reach* it!" asked another agent on crutches.

"We're all going to die!"

"Sucked in by a giant black hole!"

"The Big Bang is upon us!"

Zoey slouched in her chair. She tried to hide from the glares she was getting from the injured and recovering agents in the medical bay. She sat on a small metal chair next to Agent Franken's bed with his carry-on on her lap. The medical bay was just as she had remembered: white walls and metal beds with white linens. The only difference was this time the room was overcrowded with patients. Agents and their science officers lay in beds, wailing. Some had missing limbs, some just cried, and some had a white sheet over them. The doctors had said that Agent Franken's injuries weren't life-threatening. He hadn't woken yet, and his dangerously pale skin made him look dead. If it weren't for the constant rise and fall of his chest, he'd look like a corpse in the morgue.

He had suffered a concussion and needed plenty of rest, and he *wasn't* to be disturbed. But Zoey couldn't leave his side. She felt partly responsible for him. They were supposed to *protect* their science officer. His hand lay limply by his side and more than once Zoey was tempted to reach out and touch it—but she couldn't, so she just twirled the handle of his carry-on bag instead.

"So . . . are you *ever* going to tell us what you meant by calling me a genius?" whispered Simon as he and Tristan shared curious looks. "Not that I mind, I mean, I really *love* that you—uh—not that I actually *love* you, love you. Know what I mean?"

"Yes. I know, Simon," said Zoey absently.

She scanned the room and focused on a rear window. Dust and debris blew against the window outside, and the skies were angry and blood red. It was almost as though it was a warning—there would be a blood bath. The group of agitated agents had lost their interest in Zoey and argued loudly among themselves.

"Good," continued Simon as he leaned on Agent Franken's bed, "'cause I just meant that I really *like* being called a genius."

His blue eyes sparkled with self-satisfaction. "I've always thought of myself as a genius, but I never say it, you know. Don't want agents to think I'm getting above myself and stuff."

Tristan let out a sigh. "You never cease to amaze me, bubblehead."

"I'm not a bubblehead," said Simon. "Haven't you heard? Your girlfriend thinks I'm a genius."

It happened so fast that Zoey wasn't sure it had happened at all. Simon hadn't just called her Tristan's *girlfriend* . . . had he?

Neither of them had ever spoken the words *girlfriend* or *boyfriend* before, so it came as a shock when Simon did, like somehow *he* made it *real*. She didn't know where to look, so she just kept looking straight at the wall like a crazy person. She thought for sure the entire room had been listening to them. Only when she realized that she had stopped breathing did she allow herself a shaky breath.

Ever since Zoey had *kissed* Tristan to thank him for bailing out her and Simon, things between them had gotten a little more *complicated*—but a *good* complicated. Even though they had never actually discussed how they felt for one another, they both knew what was there. It was undeniable, like the silent understanding that went between them—it was just *there*.

She had never had a boyfriend before, so she had absolutely no idea what to do with him. Did agents date? Where they even allowed to date?

Zoey cleared her throat. "The thing is—if we could *be* invisible, if we could be concealed somehow, we could just walk right through the portal, and they'd never see us."

Simon looked doubtful. "Okay, I get your point. But . . . we're *not* invisible. You do know that, don't you?"

"Don't be silly, of course I do," dismissed Zoey.

"So how do you suppose we become *invisible* then?" asked Tristan.

Zoey looked quickly at him and blushed. He was smiling at her. He wasn't making this easier. In fact, he looked like he was enjoying seeing her squirm.

She tried to ignore his smile and said. "By magic, by a spell or something."

"Sorry to disappoint you, Zoey," interrupted Simon as he inspected Agent Franken's fingers. "But the last I checked, agents didn't carry magic wands or pull bunnies out of their hats—"

"Those are magicians, stupid," corrected Tristan.

Simon shrugged. "Whatever, the point is, agents *don't* do magic or spells. We're not wizards—"

"I'm not talking about *agents*," said Zoey.

She noticed that some agents were slowing inching closer to them so she lowered her voice. "I'm talking about someone else. I think I know someone who can *make* us invisible."

Tristan leaned forward. "Zoey, what are you talking about?"

Zoey looked at her friends and then whispered, "Remember the story I told you about the creature that brought the recording of my mother?"

Tristan frowned. "The Minitian?"

"Yes. She's a sorceress, right?" said Zoey excitedly. "And if anyone can magic us invisible, I'm sure *she* can."

Tristan and Simon both stared at Zoey like she had just told them something that made no sense.

And then Simon whistled. "Okay, now you're talking like a *crazy* woman."

"I'm not crazy," warned Zoey. "Why are you guys staring at me like that?" she said with a slight frown. "This is our best shot to get across. I know it'll work. Don't you *want* to save our world from total annihilation?"

Simon looked confused and scratched his head. "Yes . . . but—"

"It's our *best* shot to get across the portal," said Zoey desperately. It was also her best shot to save her mother, but she didn't share that with them. She knew they could sense the panic in her voice. But it didn't matter. What mattered was to get there.

"But Zoey," began Tristan. "What if she *won't* help us? You forget that Minitians are shy creatures. They don't like agents meddling in their affairs. They spend their lives in seclusion, studying their arts and doing whatever else Minitians do. I know that Minitian your mother knew—"

"Muttab," corrected Zoey.

"Right, Muttab. I know she was your mother's friend, but she might not want to help *us*."

"He's right you know," said Simon, who was now inspecting Agent Franken's toes like he was about to decide if he needed a pedicure or not.

"She will," argued Zoey. "I know she will. Call it a hunch, but I know Muttab *will* help us."

She couldn't explain to her friends how she knew this, but she did. Muttab would help them; she was sure of it. More than a gut feeling, it was a certainty.

She leaned back in her chair conclusively, and a *clink* came from inside Agent Franken bag. It sounded like two soda cans hitting one another. What was in that bag anyway?

"Okay, so like a leap of faith then?" said Simon, but he lost his smile when he met Zoey's glare.

"But it's the *best* darn plan we've got. Isn't it, Tristan? Tristan, a little help here?"

Zoey couldn't read Tristan's expression. That bothered her.

"Okay," said Simon. He sprawled over the side of Agent Franken's bed and raised himself on his elbows. "Let's say your plan works. Let's say we get some invisible witch potion—we make it through—" he paused, his eyes widening, "How do you propose we shut the portals downs?"

"He's right," said Tristan. "You saw what happened when Agent Ferguson tried. Blood of the Originals didn't work—"

Zoey started to feel that her brilliant plan had too many holes in it.

"You'll need a UEC to do that," said a hoarse voice.

Zoey, Simon, and Tristan froze. Agent Franken's eyes were open and observing them.

Simon broke the silence.

"It's alive!" he bellowed overdramatically and jumped off the bed. All the agents in the room turned around.

Zoey glared at him, and he clamped his mouth shut.

She leaned carefully towards Agent Franken, and her face broke into a smile. "We're so happy you're all right. I was scared we'd lost you after the werewolf attacks."

She hesitated. "I'm sorry we couldn't protect you."

Agent Franken raised his brows. "You did the best you could under dire circumstances. It'll take more than a few werewolves to get the best of me."

His voice cracked, and Zoey could see the strain on his face, like every word hurt him to speak.

"The old geezer's got more in him than we thought," Simon whispered to Tristan.

Zoey ignored him.

"Agent Franken," she said carefully, "did you just insinuate that *we* can close the portal somehow?"

The old man nodded. "Yes."

"Yes?" said Tristan and Simon in unison.

Agent Franken nodded. "That's what I said. You can close your mouth now, Simon."

He looked down at himself and sighed heavily. "I'm afraid these old bones are not fit for battle. I'm in no shape to shut down the portals. I'm sorry, but I cannot be your science officer anymore." His eyes glinted with mischief, and he added in a low voice, "which is why you three *must* go on without me."

"We do?" said Simon and Tristan together.

Zoey tried hard not to smile. Her voice trembled with eagerness. "But Agent Ward will never let us go without you or without another science officer. She was pretty clear on that subject."

A hint of a smile appeared on Agent Franken's face. "She never stopped you from leaving the Hive before."

He smiled at Zoey's surprise. "Yes—I should think now, more than ever, your *special* skills are required."

There was no more controlling it, Zoey's face broke into a wide grin. She'd always suspected that Agent Franken believed in her. He knew she was capable of taking on this mission. Just the thought that he was on her side made her feel like a real agent, like she truly *belonged*. She wouldn't let him down.

Simon beamed, but Tristan wasn't smiling. He clenched his jaw. His face was drawn, and his eyes darkened with worry. Whatever Tristan was feeling, it was clear he could see the dangers that awaited them. The Nexus was unknown territory, even for the most experienced agent.

But she had no other choice. She *had* to shut the portals, and she *had* to save her mother.

Zoey moved to the edge of her seat, "What's a UEC?"

"A UEC," informed their science officer, "is a Utron Energy Capsule."

He paused for a moment, as though he was gathering his thoughts. "It's a device that was fabricated long ago with one sole purpose—to destroy portals. The UECs were built as a precaution, you might say, against just such a catastrophic event as we are facing now."

Simon sat back on Agent Franken's bed again, "You mean the Great Joining—"

"Junction," corrected Tristan. "The Great *Junction*. How many times do we have to tell you for it to sink in, genius?"

"Yeah, yeah, that." said Simon. "So, the agencies *knew* that it could happen. They knew all along, didn't they?"

Agent Franken closed his eyes for a moment. "Not everyone believed in the Great Junction, but there were a few who did, and a dozen UECs were made regardless. We've made some minor adjustments to them recently, but overall, they are the same."

"So what exactly are they?" asked Zoey.

Agent Franken took in a breath. "Weapons. Utron·is an energy source—a very powerful one. It produces explosive energy."

"So, in other words, it's a *bomb*," Simon said.

"What!" Zoey stared at Agent Franken's bag on her lap like it might explode.

Even though she couldn't see through the bag, she knew the bag had two UECs in it. She thought she might throw up.

Agent Franken saw the distress on Zoey's face. "Yes, I'd be very careful with that."

She was afraid that if she moved just an inch, the bombs would go off.

"Don't worry, my dear," said Agent Franken gently, "they're quite safe now. They will not detonate until they are opened. You have my word."

Zoey swallowed hard. "And how do we *open* them?"

She tried hard not to visualize her body blown into little red bits as the entire Hive exploded and vanished under a giant mushroom cloud.

"It's quite simple," said the scientist. "You simply twist the capsule and lift the lid . . . like opening a bottle."

It wasn't that Zoey didn't *believe* Agent Franken when he said that the UECs wouldn't detonate, it was just that she had never been so close to something so unbelievably dangerous.

After a few moments, she breathed a little easier, but she still felt uncomfortable with the bombs resting on her lap.

"I've been listening to your conversation," said Agent Franken.

He hoisted himself higher on his bed and focused on Zoey. "I believe that if there's a chance you can persuade the Minitians to help you, then you *must* try—our world depends on it."

Zoey looked away. She didn't want to be responsible for the end of the world.

"You know they can make us invisible, don't you?" said Zoey. "They have the ability to do it. They'll put a spell on us or something. Am I right?"

Agent Franken nodded feebly.

He whispered almost to himself. "Yes, the Minitians are very powerful sorceresses. They could make an entire city invisible if they choose to. But the key is to persuade them."

He looked up at Zoey again, his voice stronger.

"It'll be *much* harder than you think to convince them. They do not wish to interfere with the Sevenths."

From the way he was talking, Zoey had a feeling that Agent Franken was holding back some dark secret about the Minitians.

"Muttab will help," she said confidently, remembering the tall hooded figure with the white face. "I know she will."

"If you say so." Agent Franken didn't look convinced.

"I really do hope you are right, Zoey. And now you must leave an old man to recover. Go. The world will only last about twelve hours if we don't close the portals. Otherwise there will be nothing left."

"Twelve hours!" Simon stared at the old man like he had just confiscated his favorite video game. "But that's like *half* a day!"

"Very good, boy genius," said Tristan.

Zoey saw the fear on Agent Franken's face. "Are you sure that's all the time we have?"

"I'm afraid it is. The signs are everywhere now. Our world cannot hold on for much longer."

"Then we better get a move on," said Simon.

Zoey and Tristan eyed him angrily, and he shrugged. "What? I hate being late for anything. Even the end of the world."

The end of the world, repeated Zoey in her head. It was just too awful to think about.

Zoey scooped up Agent Franken's bag gently, like a newborn child. She felt like an idiot.

"You want me to carry the bombs, Zoey?" offered Tristan.

Zoey sighed and shook her head. "Thanks, but no thanks. This is my burden. I should be carrying them."

She hoisted the bag's single strap over her head and fitted it across her shoulder like a small messenger bag.

Tristan leaned towards her. "Don't start blaming yourself again. You have to stop. This isn't your fault—"

"Of course it is," she said stubbornly. "Well, partly."

She took in a deep breath. "I'm going to fix this, you'll see."

She sounded braver than she felt at the moment, and she hoped that her friends and Agent Franken didn't sense the panic welling inside her. Just as she was about to say goodbye to Agent Franken, she remembered something.

"Um . . . Agent Franken?"

The old man blinked up at her. "Yes?"

"Where can I find the Minitians?" asked Zoey uncomfortably. What good would their help be if she couldn't find them?

Agent Franken looked puzzled. "And therein lies the first mystery . . . ."

"Excuse me?"

The science officer rubbed his eyes. "No one knows. They live in a white-stone fortress that keeps changing shape and disappearing. It moves from village to village and never stays too long in one place. Only Minitians can see it."

"So how are we supposed to find them?" Simon's voice rose. "It's not like we have time to play the tourist. You told us yourself that we only have twelve hours. And that includes getting *their* help, and then going to the Nexus and shutting the portals."

Agent Franken looked at Zoey and smiled.

"Zoey can find them. She's the *only* one who can."

Although Tristan and Simon looked confused, Zoey knew exactly what he meant. She smiled at her friends. For once she knew something they didn't.

"Good luck," said their scientist, and then he lost his smile. "You're going to need it."

Simon laughed incredulously. "Gee thanks. Nothing like a good pep talk before an end-of-the-world battle."

Zoey turned to her friends. "Come on, let's go."

Agent Franken grabbed her wrist.

"There's something I forgot to tell you about the UECs," said Agent Franken urgently. "The bump on my head is making me forget things, but listen carefully."

Zoey leaned forward.

"Utron is lethal to us, much like radiation—"

"Great," said Simon. "It keeps getting better and better."

Agent Franken ignored him. "Once you open the first UEC— and I must insist that you open it with *extreme* caution—place it gently inside the portal. After that you'll have maybe two minutes to pass through the portal before the energy will kill you, so don't linger—"

"You don't have to tell me twice—ouch!" Tristan smacked Simon on the back of his head.

"As soon as you pass through to our side, open the second UEC quickly."

Zoey waited for Agent Franken to explain further, but he didn't. "Then what?"

Agent Franken raised his eyebrows. "Then find a safe place to hide from the blast. You won't have much time, so you better run. Anything within a two hundred foot radius will be destroyed in the blast."

Zoey nodded. "And then?"

Agent Franken let his head fall back on his pillow heavily. "And then we pray that it works, because we have nothing else."

Zoey secured the strap around her shoulder and followed the others out to the main hall. A crowd was gathering around the mirrors, but no teams were going through.

"Let's go to the Inn and get some food and drinks," said Zoey.

She pushed her way through a throng of agents.

"Good idea, I'm starving," said Simon, and he rubbed his belly. "If I don't feed this gorgeous body soon, it'll lose the two pounds of muscle mass I gained this year."

"What else is new?" laughed Tristan. "But I could use some food, too."

As Zoey made her way through the moving crowd, she felt something was off. The agents were agitated, and by the looks on their faces it wasn't because they were about to go on a dangerous quest. It was something else. But what? And where was Agent Ward?

Zoey saw Directors Hicks and Campbell flailing their arms, trying to calm them down. But the mob pushed and shoved, like crazed fans at a concert trying to get at the head of the line. Something was very wrong.

"Who could have done this?"

"What will this mean for us?"

"It's all over!"

"We're all going to die!"

All the agents were in a panic.

Zoey wasn't going anywhere until she knew what was going on.

She approached a young agent. "Excuse me, what's happened? What's going on?"

The agent trembled. "The UECs!" he cried hysterically. "They're all gone! Gone! Stolen!"

Instinctively, Zoey squeezed the strap on her shoulder. She had never let it go.

She felt the material between her fingers. But when she reached down, where the bag should have been, the strap dangled in midair. The bag was gone.

CHAPTER 9

THE WHITE FORTRESS

Zoey stared opened mouthed at the straps. Her stomach twisted until she couldn't breathe. She was having a meltdown.

Tristan grabbed her shoulders and met her eyes. "Zoey, where's the bag?"

"Oh my God, are you serious!" Simon stared at the strap in Zoey's hand like it was about to explode.

As much as she *wanted* to answer . . . she couldn't. She had *no* idea where the bag was. The bag *was* gone. It was just gone.

She'd been so careful with the bag, had held it so securely, that at first she thought her eyes were playing tricks on her.

"It's been . . . it's been cut," said Zoey.

She showed them the strap. "A sharp knife or something, I never even felt it." She felt stupid saying it, but it was the truth. She hadn't felt anything.

Who took her bag and why?

Tristan frowned as he surveyed the hall. "It could have been anyone in here."

Zoey knew that anyone could have taken it without her knowing, but they had to have been stealthy. Neither Tristan nor Simon had noticed anyone coming near her.

Simon shared a quick conversation with a nearby agent and hurried back towards them.

"Apparently, *all* the UECs are gone," he said in a low voice. "Every single one of them has been stolen from the science officers. And get this—no one saw what happened. They just disappeared. No one else has any idea who took them either. What are we supposed to do now?"

Zoey caught a few agents looking their way. Their cold and accusing eyes focused on the strap she held in her hands. And before she knew it, a mob of agents was whispering and pointing reproachfully at Zoey.

"Yeah, that's her," she heard one man say.

". . . Bet *she* took them," said a woman with short auburn hair. "Look at her. She *looks* guilty!"

"She's in on it. She's working for that Mrs. Dupont, I know she is . . . ."

Here we go again, thought Zoey. *Would they ever accept her?*

She scanned the hall. The *real* traitor had been here moments ago, but they were probably long gone.

Suddenly, someone grabbed Zoey from behind and spun her around. A fat finger pointed at her face.

"YOU!" hissed a large woman in tight outfit that exposed too much skin. "You did this, didn't you?"

The woman's spit flew in Zoey's face. "We all know you're the cause of this mess—"

"I'm not." Zoey wiped her face and strained to control her temper. "I'm not responsible for this—"

"Yes you are!" bellowed the large woman, her double chin wiggled like a water balloon. "Where did you put the UECs? Where are they?"

Zoey clenched her jaw.

"I. Don't. Know," she growled. "Take your finger out of my face, before I *bite* it off."

"AH!" the woman threw up her hands.

"Did you hear what she said?" she raised her voice so that everyone in the hall could hear her. "She wants to attack me! She wants to *kill* me!"

A mob of agents crowded around Zoey and her friends. Slowly, she reached for her golden bracelet and waited. She saw Tristan and Simon reach for their weapons, too.

"Where are they?" repeated the woman as sweat trickled down her forehead. "You better tell us . . . or we'll *make* you tell us—"

"ENOUGH!"

Director Hicks pushed his way through the crowd.

"What is the meaning of this?" He could see that Zoey had her hand on her weapon and he frowned. "Why are you attacking these young Sevenths? Have you lost your mind woman?"

The large woman put her hands on her hips. Zoey could see great sweat stains under her arms.

"Director Hicks, we know this girl took the UECs—"

"No, she did *not.*" Director Hicks seemed to grow taller and towered over the woman.

She cowered and said nothing. He glared at the gathered agents.

The large woman crossed her arms over her bugling chest. "If *she* didn't do it, then *who* did?"

Director Hicks didn't answer right away. "We still don't know."

He glared at the woman. "Now, I suggest you forget this ridiculous notion and think of a solution instead of *creating* more problems."

He looked at Zoey.

"But Director Hicks," said a middle-aged agent who looked like he was about to coach a little league team, "the UECs were our only hope. How can we shut them down the portals without them?"

Director Hicks pulled on the sleeves of his plaid jacket nervously, like he was hiding something. "Our scientists are working hard at creating new ones, but I'm afraid they won't be ready for another few days . . . maybe a week."

Zoey, Tristan, and Simon shared a look. Simon mouthed the words "*a week!*"

Agent Frank had given them twelve hours.

"So, while we wait for the new UECs to arrive, I want everyone to settle down and regroup with their teams and come up with new strategies. We have mountains of work to do. Go on now."

Director Hicks's fingers twitched at his sides nervously, and when Zoey looked into his eyes, she could see that he knew a week was too long,

"Any ideas as to what we do now?" asked Tristan as the mob of agents dispersed.

Zoey glanced over her shoulder to make sure no one was listening. "We stick to the plan."

"We do?" questioned Simon, and then he lowered his voice. "But how? We don't have our secret weapon anymore."

He raised his brows. "You look like you've already got something in mind? What's the plan, oh mighty one?"

Zoey tossed the useless strap onto a nearby table.

She took Tristan and Simon by the arms and said, "I don't know yet. But we can't give up now. We'll figure something out. But right now, we need to *go*. Come on!"

With Tristan and Simon behind her, Zoey tore down the hall and raced across the grounds to the Wander Inn. They pleased Aria by inhaling a late supper and asked her to pack them each a midnight snack.

Zoey shut her bedroom door. "All right. Who's got a watch?"

"Nobody wears watches anymore, girl," laughed Simon. He pulled out his cell phone. "We use these babies."

"Anyway," said Zoey a little annoyed that she could never afford one of her own. "You'll keep track of time, got it?"

"Got it." Simon slipped his phone back into this jacket pocket.

"And the food." Zoey tossed Simon the three meals. She watched him stuff his backpack and then filled her own bag with water bottles. She zipped it up and hoisted it over her shoulders. "You guys ready?"

"Ready," chorused Tristan and Simon.

"You can still back out, you know." Even though she meant it, Zoey hoped her friends would accompany her. She needed them.

"You're not going anywhere without me," said Tristan, and Zoey felt her cheeks burn.

"Don't forget me," said Simon. "You need at least one guy with a cell phone."

"Let's do this."

Zoey withdrew her double-sided mirror from inside her jacket and flipped it open. "Grab hold of my arms and squeeze in. I need to have all your reflections in the mirror."

Simon grabbed her left arm. "You know *where* we're going, right?"

"Not really. Don't look so freaked out. It'll be fine—"

"Says the girl who has *no* idea where we're going," said Simon.

"Shut up, Simon, and let her concentrate," said Tristan. "Or do you want our legs to end up somewhere in Africa?" Simon glared at Tristan but kept his mouth shut.

Zoey filled her mind with images of Muttab. She pictured the eight-foot black-cloaked figure with a white face mask under its black hood. Her skin tingled. Her reflection wavered. Her friends looked like flickering ghosts in the mirror.

"Ready!" she called. Her friends' grips tightened.

"One . . . two . . . THREE!"

With a *pop*, they vanished.

Even before Zoey felt the full effects of the mirror-port, her feet met solid ground. The air moved beside her, and she felt the presence of her friends. She blinked and looked around.

They stood on a rocky island with brilliant white beaches surrounded by a turquoise sea, but she had no idea which sea. Her jacket flapped in winds that smelled of salt and tropical flowers. Great waves smashed against the rocks and showered Zoey in salt water. Overhead, deep maroon clouds raced against a sky the color of blood. The effects of the Great Junction had reached this little island, too.

A few hundred yards away, a white castle with many turrets and towers overlooked the sea below. Its graceful ivory walls gleamed in the sun like a giant jewel. It was like an elegant and magical fairytale castle from a painting. Zoey had never seen anything so majestic and beautiful in all her life, and she had to restrain herself from running over to it.

The earth vibrated under Zoey's sneakers as though the castle's magic was alive in the ground and in the rocks.

"You found it," yelled Tristan over the wind. "It's beautiful."

He turned towards her. "You knew you'd find it, didn't you? The castle that never stays put in the same place for long . . . and *you* found it."

Zoey smiled in spite of herself. "I did."

Perhaps she was the only Seventh or human being for that matter who *could* find the secret castle. Agent Franken had known she could find it, and his belief in her had given her the extra courage she needed at first to set out on this crazy quest.

"We better hurry. Who knows how long it will stay here."

"Man, it's like *ninety* degrees here!"

Simon tossed his jacket on the ground. "My sweat glands are on overdrive."

After about ten minutes of clambering up the sandy road, Zoey brushed the dust out of her hair and looked around.

Magic sparkled on every surface of the castle like a thin layer of chalk, and the glass spires of the turrets gleamed as if they had been enchanted.

They strolled through a gateway below an ornate arch and up a flight of stone steps where they stopped in front of two colossal glass doors.

"Now what?" Simon spit some sand from his mouth.

"Do you think someone's expecting us? I mean—they are *sorceresses*. Maybe they saw us coming in their crystal balls or something."

Although she couldn't explain it, Zoey agreed with Simon. She felt like they were being watched somehow, as though the castle walls had eyes.

Tristan turned to Zoey as if he expected her to decide what to do first.

She raised her fist and knocked four times on the castle doors.

They all stepped back.

Simon looked around nervously. "Who do you think will answer the door—?"

Suddenly the doors screeched loudly and swung open.

Tristan peered inside.

"No one," he said and he turned around. "There's no one there."

Simon whistled. "Oooh . . . spooky. This is so cool!"

Tristan reached inside his jacket pocket for his dagger, but Zoey grabbed his arm.

"No, don't," she said, shaking her head. "They might take that as a threat. We're here to ask for their help. We can't anger or frighten them. This is our only shot. Let's not jeopardize it."

Tristan slipped his weapon back into the folds of his jacket, but he didn't look too pleased about it.

"Fine, but I don't have a good feeling about this place. I feel like the walls have eyes, and they're glaring down at us in a *bad* way."

Zoey nodded. "I know. I feel the same way. But we don't have a choice. We need their help. Come on, let's go find Muttab."

The truth was Zoey didn't know how Muttab would greet them. When she had met her the first time, she hadn't been exactly friendly or engaging. Maybe she would be angry that Zoey had come to her house uninvited.

Zoey swallowed her fears and walked through the doors. She didn't know what to expect. Even though Muttab was her mother's friend, she had been told that the Minitians weren't forthcoming with humans. She kept thinking about what Agent Franken had said, *the key is to* persuade *them, which will prove to be a difficult task, nearly impossible . . . it'll be a lot harder than you think . . . .*

Somehow, she knew he was right. They were about to find out.

They walked on cold marble floors and stepped into a grand foyer. The echo of their footsteps shattered the omnipresent silence. A series of white marble columns supported arched ceilings nearly two hundred feet above them. Zoey felt a thick electric energy, and the smell of incense stained the air like a heavy perfume. Was that magic she felt? It had to be.

After getting over the initial shock of walking in such a grand and elegant castle, Zoey noticed the first strange signs of wear.

Upon closer inspection, the polished floors were cracked, like something heavy had landed on them repeatedly. Deep fissures crisscrossed the outer walls like jagged veins, and chips of marble and dust carpeted the floors. Even one of the tall columns was cracked and fractured. Everywhere she looked, she saw signs of destruction, like a bomb had gone off.

"Something happened here," she said. "The castle's been damaged somehow. Maybe an earthquake? Looks like it."

Tristan inspected a large fissure in the limestone wall. "Maybe. But maybe it's a side effect from moving around so much. The castle moves, remember?"

Zoey nodded. Tristan was right. This had to be an effect from constantly moving. The bones of the poor old castle were suffering from age and movement.

The foyer opened up into a room the size of a school gymnasium. The walls were lined with alcoves that were filled with magnificent tapestries and crystal sculptures of creatures Zoey had never seen before. Even in here, the floors were cracked, and there were fractures in the columns and walls.

As they traveled deeper, all of Zoey's instincts told her to get out of there, to run and never come back. If things went wrong, they'd need a fast way out, and the castle's front doors were getting further and further away. She repressed a shiver.

The coldness of the room chilled her bones and dulled her spirit, as if she would never laugh or smile ever again. The space was unnaturally empty. There was no furniture anywhere, not even a chair or a simple candlestick. Didn't witches burn candles? Were the Minitians hiding somewhere, waiting to spring a trap? She'd have to find out. They *had* to ask for help. They had no other options. They needed a spell to become invisible.

"There's no furniture in here," whispered Zoey although her voice carried a lot louder than she had first anticipated. "Castles do *have* furniture, don't they?"

Tristan frowned, "I admit it's a little weird, but we're the first Sevenths ever to set foot in this castle. Maybe this is *normal* to the Minitians."

Zoey kept walking. Tristan did have a point. Maybe they were spiritual creatures and only furnished their castle with what was truly necessary. Was there a library where they studied their magic? Or beds—if they even slept? And without mouths, did these creatures even eat?

"Hey, check these out! They're awesome," said Simon as he inspected the head of one the crystal sculptures. "Totally weird, but totally cool. I wonder what they're for?"

"They're *not* for touching," warned Tristan.

Simon made a face. "Nah. I think they're supposed to scare whoever comes in here. I mean, just look at the detail on their faces—they look real, and it's super scared, like a horde of flesh-eating zombies tried to eat it."

He poked his finger into one of the ears. "I saw an art exposé at the Mocca art museum in Toronto like this before, except the sculptures had no skin, and you could see all the muscles, tendons, guts—"

"Nice," said Zoey. "Remind me never to check that out."

She stopped and inspected a crystal sculpture of a human man dressed in nineteenth century clothes. Her blood froze when she looked at his eyes. There was something that seemed almost *real* about them. The face was the face of absolute terror, like it had been sculpted moments before the subject died in excruciating pain. There was something oddly familiar about the face, too. It was so lifelike that she could almost imagine him waking up and talking.

"Told you they were weird." Simon poked the statue in the ear with his finger. "Loads of weird."

"But they look so—"

"Real," answered Tristan. He examined a crystal statue of a little woman who reminded Zoey of the one of the leprechaun gang. She could have been one of their wives.

"This feels *wrong*, for lack of a better word," said Tristan. "I don't like it. I don't like this place. We shouldn't have come—"

"We *had* to come, remember?" urged Zoey. "We have no choice; they're the only ones that can help us."

She glanced around the room, her bravery diminishing the more she lingered in the eerie castle. "Even if this place is a little . . . strange—"

"It's more than a little strange. It's dangerous."

Tristan walked off, leaving Zoey staring at the back of his head. It was such a lovely head. She cursed herself for thinking such a thing at such a time.

Tristan was right.

Zoey frowned. All the sculptures had one thing in common—fear. It was as if whoever sculpted them made sure their subjects had been constantly terrorized. Maybe the Minitians weren't as friendly as she had hoped.

"So, where are these *sorceresses* anyway," said Simon as he unsuccessfully tried to pick the nose of the man in the statue Zoey had inspected moments before.

"I'd have thought they would have shown up by now, since we're like *trespassing*." Simon looked up, "Maybe they're . . . *gone*. It would explain the lack of furniture. I know—maybe they saw the end of the world in their crystal balls and magically transported themselves to another universe."

Zoey could tell by the anxious expression on Tristan's face that he felt the same way.

"They're here," said Zoey. "I can *feel* them watching us. It's creepy. Don't you feel it, Simon?"

"I just feel hungry."

Zoey smacked him on the arm. "You better stop touching those. They're probably like their *prized* possessions or something. Besides they're the only things in here, so stop playing around with them. Didn't your mother ever teach you to *not* touch things that didn't belong to you?"

Simon ignored her and kept poking. "Nope. She's the one that encouraged me to do it."

As they ventured further, they came to the end of the great room and walked through a corridor that opened up into another chamber.

The new space was like a circular cathedral. The ceiling was so high it was lost in the gloom. The blood-red sky peeked through a series of tall, skinny windows, and the red light made the gleaming white walls look like they were stained with blood.

Shadowy corridors led off in different directions. The silver walls were carved with scenes from another world where Minitians battled giant elephant-like creatures under planets and stars that Zoey did not recognize. In one scene a group of Minitians kneeled before a godlike creature with antlers.

But it was the floor that made her the most nervous. The white marble was inscribed with black symbols and runes. It was as though the floor was a giant curse. She did her best not to step on them. Just like the other rooms, this place had suffered damage as well.

"Don't step on the markings," Zoey warned.

"I wasn't planning on it," Simon muttered.

Tristan scanned the exits. "Which way do we go now—?"

WHO ARE YOU!

A voice blared inside Zoey's head.

HOW DARE YOU ENTER THE WHITE FORTRESS!

Zoey fell to her knees in excruciating pain. Over her own screams, she could hear Tristan and Simon wailing, too. But she couldn't even move to help them, because her own agony pinned her to the floor.

But then the pain stopped as suddenly as it had appeared.

Zoey opened her eyes.

Twelve tall black-robed figures with featureless white faces stood in front of them.

CHAPTER 10

THE HIGH SORCERESS

White-hot pain exploded behind Zoey's eyes again. Her vision blurred from the agony. Tears streaked down her face as she pressed her hands against her head. All she wanted was for the pain to stop. Please let it end. Her brain was on fire.

Once more, the pain vanished as fast as it had appeared. Zoey could see that Tristan and Simon were both hunched forward on their knees. Their faces were red and wet, and their breathing was shallow.

Who are you! Repeated the same voice inside her mind. It was a woman's voice, strong and commanding.

Speak now, or you will all die!

Just as the searing pain started again, Zoey raised her hand. "Stop! Please! I'll tell you!"

The pain vanished.

Zoey's body shook, and she didn't even bother to try to stand. She had no idea which of the Minitians spoke to her; they all looked identical except that some were a few inches shorter or taller. And the fact that they *didn't* have mouths wasn't exactly helpful.

Heart hammering in her chest, Zoey wiped the tears from her eyes.

"My name is Zoey St. John," her voice cracked, and she strained to continue. "And these are my friends, Tristan Price and Simon Brown."

How did you find the secret fortress? Are you sorcerers disguised as little children? What kind of magic is this? We sense a force of power . . . something different . . . .

Zoey glanced at her friends for support. She wasn't sure if she should reveal her talents to these obviously hostile and suspicious mystics. Her friends' faces were just as unsure as hers. Although she couldn't explain why, she had the sudden feeling that she better keep her talents to herself.

"We're Op—Agents," corrected Zoey. "We're here on official business—"

Why have you forsaken the oaths and trespassed into this sacred place? Those who dare walk into the white fortress will die a most painful death. It is known.

Again Zoey tried to figure out who had spoken, to try and seek a connection, but it was impossible. She glanced at each face and then said, "Uh, I—we didn't *know* about any oaths. The agency didn't tell us. I'm sorry—"

Suddenly, the light dimmed and darkness thickened around Zoey and her friends. On either side, an army of shadows appeared—tribes of ghouls with long spindly arms and legs, demons with red eyes and veiny bat-like wings, twisted bulbous creatures with boils and leaking yellow pus, masses of putrid worm-like beasts with hundreds of gaping maws full of teeth, and clusters of floating, transparent deformed specters.

The air turned cold, and invisible icy hands squeezed her throat. She wanted to run. She was facing a horde of horrors that would snap anyone's sanity. But she knew that she and her friends would most certainly die if she ran.

The human lies, hissed another voice that was deeper and hoarse like an older female.

They are enchanters, tricksters. Kill them all! Kill them! They're polluting our home with their presence.

The shadows rustled and shifted. Hundreds of horrible glowing red eyes focused on Zoey and her friends. As the shadows neared, Zoey could almost feel her life drifting away. The sounds of scuffling got louder. The darkness became even deeper. She could tell Tristan and Simon were on the verge of panic, too. She had to stand her ground for all of them. She had to make things right, or they were all going to die.

With every bit of strength she could muster she bellowed, "MUTTAB! I'm looking for Muttab!"

The shadows vanished. The room was bright again.

The Minitian line parted, and a single figure stepped forward. It looked exactly like the others, except it was clad in the purest flowing white robes. The tallest among her sisters, her robes billowed around her like white watery light as she crossed the room. Zoey squinted as the sorceress neared. It was like staring up at the sun. The Minitian had no eyes, nose, or mouth under her white hood. Where her face should have been, Zoey could only see a blank white façade, like a mask, just like the others.

The white sorceress stooped over Zoey. Her power radiated from her like heat from a fire. Her pointy white boots peeked from under her robes.

How do you know that name? Questioned a soft voice inside her head. Somehow Zoey could tell it was older than the other two voices, and it had more kindness in it.

At first, Zoey was afraid to answer. She didn't want to feel the scorching pain in her head or to see the horrible demons that came from the shadows again. But something inside her told her it was safe to speak up. It was as if the white Minitian was *making* her feel more at ease, like she was putting a *spell* on her . . . .

Please, you can tell me, Zoey St. John . . . .

It was weird. The voice sounded a lot like Aria's. If she closed her eyes, she could swear that Aria was standing in front of her and not the white sorceress. This was magic again. At first, it had felt like dark magic, but now she wasn't so sure anymore. The voice didn't seem to want to hurt her.

Zoey could see Tristan and Simon waiting for her to answer. She didn't want to disappointment them.

"She was—*is* my mother's friend," she said finally, glad her voice was even.

The white sorceress loomed over her but didn't say anything.

Zoey wiggled uncomfortably under the stare of the white witch. Even though she didn't have eyes, Zoey could still *feel* them on her.

She tried to gather her thoughts and suddenly realized what she needed to say.

"She . . . she delivered a message to me from my mother. My mother's name is Elizabeth Steele—do you know her? No, probably not, stupid question."

Zoey fumbled with her words. "The thing is . . . I thought I could ask Muttab or you for help—"

This beast dares *asks the High Sorceress for help!* A loud voice bellowed in Zoey's mind.

They should all die for such insolence! Never has a mortal spoken so out of terms. Only death could make this right again.

Zoey looked over to Tristan and Simon. The stress on their faces and the whites around their eyes, told her that the voices spoke to them as well.

With dread creeping inside her, she looked back at the group of Minitians. They all looked the same. How could anyone tell them apart? Was Muttab among them? Maybe she had led her friends into a trap—

The ground beneath Zoey's feet trembled. A rumble like the roar of thunder bounced inside the chamber. Dust and debris cascaded down on Zoey and her friends like heavy snow.

The Minitians ran for cover as part of their castle ceiling fell on them. They were restless, fidgeting on the spot, and looking around nervously. This wasn't an ordinary occurrence. Zoey could almost sense the fear in them. They were afraid, but of what? What was happening to their beloved castle?

A black-robed Minitian inched forward. She cocked her head in their direction.

High Sorceress, we must rid ourselves of these mortals. *Are the shades of the white fortress to be thus polluted? Their mere presence is a mockery of our sacred laws. Those who seek and find the white fortress are our enemies. This is a clever plot to undermine us, to use children. Do not be fooled. They must be killed! The humans and the Mysterian must die!*

A mixture of anger and fear welled in Zoey. She knew coming here was a risk, but she didn't realize that their lives would be in danger. She had thought that she just needed to persuade them to help. Now it seems that she needed to persuade them to spare their lives.

Yes, we must rid ourselves of the vile beasts, said another voice.

YES! Chorused many voices at once.

Kill them!

"I think if we want to make a run for it . . . the time is *now*," whispered Simon. A faint smile twitched on his lips. She knew he was only trying to make everyone feel better.

The high sorceress waved a delicate hand.

It is curious that three children have found their way into the white fortress when it is known that only those who possess magic can break through the barriers. You say you are not magicians, but then how did you find the fortress if not aided by our enemies?

"Please, we're not sorcerers; we're *Sevenths*," began Zoey. "We only came here to ask for help—"

Our enemies have tried to steal our secrets and failed. Those who are foolish enough to attempt to trespass pay with their lives. And on this day you *will die.*

Zoey stopped breathing and the blood left her face. She turned and looked at her friends. Tristan clenched his jaw and drew his blade, but Zoey knew his blade would be no match for magic.

Simon looked green and avoided Zoey's eyes.

It all seemed like a bad dream. How did her mother befriend such a hostile group? Where was Muttab?

The high sorceress inclined her head.

Children are foolish creatures. You will be given a test . . . if you fail, you will die.

Zoey frowned as she tried to make sense of what the sorceress had just said.

"What? What kind of test? What does that mean—?"

Suddenly the room darkened, and for a horrible moment, Zoey thought the demon shadows were back. She moved towards Tristan and Simon and grabbed her boomerang.

Survive this test, and I will grant you safe passage back to your lives. But you need to prove to us your worth. If you live, then perhaps we shall discuss what you need from us. We shall see . . . .

Zoey's mouth tasted like metal. "What does that mean? Survive what? What kind of test?"

"Hopefully it's not a math test. I suck at math," muttered Simon.

"I don't like this," said Tristan as he gripped his blade in his hand.

"You're not the only one." With her boomerang firmly in her hand, Zoey scanned the room.

The sorceress raised her hands. Her thin pale arms peeked from the sleeves of her white robes.

Who will survive the first test? Or will you all be lost . . . ?

Before Zoey could protest, the chamber dissolved into darkness.

CHAPTER 11

MASTERS OF ILLUSIONS

Zoey sat at a kitchen table.

She felt sleepy, like she had just woken up. She smelled coffee and pancakes. A man with dark hair and dark eyes sat across from her reading his newspaper. He seemed oddly familiar.

"Don't forget to drink your orange juice. You need more vitamin C," said a woman's voice.

When Zoey looked up, her jaw dropped.

A woman with fire-red hair and big green eyes walked into the kitchen. She wore a fitted white shirt and black pants. "And don't forget your father and I are going to dinner tonight with Kathy and James, so you'll be on your own."

She popped a piece of toast into her mouth.

"M—mom?" Zoey's mouth was dry. It felt odd to say that word, but she didn't understand why it should.

Her mother sipped the rest of her coffee and set the empty mug in the sink. "What is it, dear?"

Zoey looked across the table. "Dad?"

Her father looked up from his paper. "Hmm? What?"

Again, Zoey had a strange feeling in the pit of her stomach, but then it faded when she looked at the smile on her father's face. She could see love in his eyes. Her father *loved* her.

What's wrong with me?

"Nothing." Zoey shrugged, gulped some orange juice, and settled her glass on the table. "I just feel weird today."

Her mother put her hand on Zoey's forehead, and Zoey couldn't help but smile up at her mother. How beautiful she looked, she wanted to reach out and hug her.

"Huh, well, you're not warm, so you don't have a fever," said her mother, and then she checked her cell phone. "But don't take any chances. Make sure you wash your hands often at school . . . there could be a bug going around. I don't want you to get sick."

"I will."

Zoey couldn't stop smiling. Her parents were here with her. They were awesome. This whole scenario was awesome. And yet she still felt like something was off, like there was something missing . . . .

A ring came from the front door.

She didn't know why, but Zoey stood up and blurted out. "I'll get it."

She pushed her chair back and ran down the hallway, feeling happier than ever. She pulled open the door.

"Hey, you ready?" said Tristan. His smile sent Zoey's stomach into a series of spasms.

"Tristan?"

"Yeah? What? Did you forget we were going to go to school together?" Her stomach twisted in knots again when he smiled.

"Uh . . ." Zoey rubbed her temples. "No, it's just I'm feeling weird today. Let me get my bag—"

A lanky teen with blond hair strolled along the street across from Zoey and Tristan. She felt as though she knew him.

"Simon?"

The boy stopped and looked at Zoey strangely.

"You know him?" asked Tristan, peering at the teen who was now coming towards them.

"Of course I do, and so you do."

Tristan shook his head. "No, I don't."

Zoey frowned. Simon stood at the bottom of the steps looking confused.

"I know you, don't I?" said Simon. "At least, I think I do. This is so weird. I feel like I'm having a déjà vu on repeat."

Zoey's head pounded, like someone was hitting it with a hammer. She glanced back towards the kitchen. Her mother and father were laughing together. They seemed so happy. But then their voices sounded watery and far away. Her gut told her that something was off . . . but what was it? She couldn't put her finger on it.

"Zoey?" questioned Tristan. "You're frowning like you have a headache or something."

"Yes . . . no . . ." Zoey inspected Simon at the foot of the stairs. He was talking to himself and seemed lost.

"Something's wrong," she said. "I feel it."

Tristan leaned forward. "What's wrong?"

"All of this." Zoey raised her arms. "You, Simon, me, my parents. It's an illusion."

Tristan knocked on the wall. "Feels pretty real to me. You sure you're ok?"

The ground wavered, and Zoey felt like she couldn't stand. The more she thought that this world was an illusion, the more the illusion faded, like a curtain was being lifted and the truth was being revealed.

Tristan looked confused.

"It's not real," she insisted. "None of it. You guys—this is a trick! Remember?"

"Zoey?" Her mother stood in the hallway. "Are you going to invite Tristan in for some breakfast?"

Zoey felt as though her heart was breaking. Part of her wanted to stay in this illusion with her parents. It was all she'd ever wanted—a real family—a mother and father, but they weren't *real*. This wasn't real. Tears rolled down her cheeks.

"This isn't real!" she howled. "It's a spell."

As soon as she said it, more of reality came to her. She remembered the white fortress, the white sorceress. The Minitians. This was their doing.

The layers of illusion folded and twisted her sense of reality. Zoey felt like she was floating away from her body. She felt scared and out of control, like she would never find her real self or the real world again.

Ignoring her mother, Zoey grabbed Tristan's hand and pulled him down the steps. With her other hand, she grabbed Simon's and squeezed. "This is an illusion. We're not really here."

Simon shook his head. "I'm feeling weird. I think I'm going to puke."

"You're not going to puke." She pulled her friends in closer. "We just have to break through it—"

"Zoey," crooned her mother. "Why don't you come in? Your father wants to show you what he's thinking of getting you for your birthday. It's real special; you're going to love it!"

More tears spilled down Zoey's cheeks.

"This . . ." her voice cracked. "It's . . . not . . . real. I've never met my parents. I'm an orphan! Remember?"

Tristan hesitated. "I—I remember. Yes. You told me about it the first time we met—"

"That's right."

"Zoey, I love you," said her mother as she stood in the doorway. She reached out. "Come, my darling girl. Come give your mother a hug."

"UH!" shouted Zoey. "Get out of my head. This isn't real!"

"This isn't real," repeated Simon. "If this isn't real, then where the heck are we? What is this place?"

Zoey ignored her mother. "I don't know, but we're definitely still in the fortress. Come on guys, we need to break the spell—"

"You're too late," laughed her mother. "You have failed, Zoey St. John. Now you must pay for what you have done!"

Suddenly, her mother's face warped, and her body stretched. Her skin turned paper-white; her clothes shimmered and became white robes.

The high sorceress snapped her fingers.

Holes opened in the ground beneath Zoey's feet. She pushed Tristan and Simon aside just as tendrils of black smoke broke through.

"RUN!" she screamed.

"Where?" said Simon. "If this isn't real, where are we supposed to go?"

"This way!" Zoey pulled Tristan and Simon with her. They ran down a street, leaped over a garbage can, and came to a halt in front of a deep pit.

"Is this part of the illusion?" asked Simon, gasping for breath. "If it is . . . I want my money back."

"Why aren't we waking up?" said Tristan as he tested the pit with his foot. "I mean, now that we *know* it's an illusion, why isn't the spell breaking?"

"I don't know, maybe it takes time."

Zoey glanced behind her. The sorceress was following behind them. Tall black tendrils of smoke rippled beside her like great waves.

Somehow, Zoey knew they were in the same fortress. They were running around aimlessly, back and forth like hamsters in a cage, while all the sorceresses watched in amusement.

They tore down the street. But when Zoey thought they were reaching the end of the road, it kept going on and on, as though it were being stretched in a visual effects scene.

How could they break free of the spell? She hated the white sorceress for playing with her head. It wasn't fair. Her eyes welled with tears. She wanted to scream. How could this have happened? It wasn't supposed to happen this way.

And then she heard chanting in a language she couldn't understand. The voices were all around them in the air.

The street and buildings grew more solid, and the smell of pavement and freshly cut grass grew more intense.

But she knew it was a trick, a trick of the mind. The Minitians were trying to drive them insane. Desperately, she tried to break free. But it was like trying to fight off a god—it was pointless.

The light intensified and lit up the chamber. Then a beam of light shot out of a crystal and hit her square in the face. At first it hurt, like a slap in the face, but then she couldn't feel anything at all except for the burning in her eyes.

She tried to blink, but her eyelids wouldn't respond. Even when she tried to look away—she couldn't. It was as though the light had trapped her.

Zoey felt like she had jumped into a freezing lake. She felt colder and colder. The beam of light was sucking the energy out of her. Her soul was being pulled into the crystal.

Her body hardened and cracked as thick scales formed over her skin. But she knew it wasn't scales. She was turning into crystal.

The hardness reached inside and clamped down on her lungs. She was suffocating. She was dying. She wished she could have spent more time with Tristan. She thought she heard a voice call out her name, and then another voice screamed angrily.

Her vision blurred. The light disappeared and there was only blackness—

Zoey felt her body float. She thought that this was what it was like to be dead. Her soul was floating away . . . .

She hit the floor hard with a thump.

She blinked the white spots from her eyes and looked around. Tristan and Simon moaned on the floor next to her. They hadn't been turned into crystals. They weren't *dead*.

Zoey was happy to feel a stabbing pain in her side and legs. She wasn't dead. Maybe a bruised rib—that was good.

The crystal still hung in the air above their heads, but its light was dimmed as though someone had shut it off.

"Is this heaven?" said Simon, as he lay on his back with his eyes open. "Am I dead? Can I have a girlfriend now?"

Zoey scrambled to her knees and felt her energy slowly return as the blood rushed back into her body. She rubbed her hands to get the blood flowing again. "No, you're not dead."

"Oh," said Simon. He struggled to a sitting position. "For a minute there, I thought we were goners for sure. I felt my life being sucked out of me, like the lights were going out, and I'd never wake up."

The Minitians still stood around them in a circle. Their bodies shifted as if they were waiting for something. Maybe this was just the beginning and they were going to keep torturing them.

As the blood surged back into Zoey's legs, she wondered if she could outrun them.

Tristan rubbed his eyes and stretched his legs. He turned to Zoey. "Why do you think they stopped—?"

High sorceress!

Zoey turned towards the sound of the new voice.

A Minitian came towards her from the other end of the chamber. Her white face was expressionless. She lowered her arms and crossed the room. Her black robes spilled around her like waves of black water, and the other Minitians parted and let her through.

She stood face to face with the high sorceress and pointed to Zoey and her friends.

You cannot take the lives of these children. They are innocent.

The high sorceress didn't move. When she spoke her voice was soft but full of anger. *Why did you stop me? What is the meaning of this, Muttab?*

"Muttab!" Zoey scrambled to her feet, but Muttab raised her hand and Zoey halted.

These mortals dared to enter the white fortress! said another Minitian. *They should pay the price.*

They should die like the others. They are evil.

"Who is she calling evil?" exclaimed Simon. "They're the ones trying to kill us!"

Muttab turned and addressed the Minitians. *Sisters, these children are no threat to us.*

The high sorceress cocked her head. *But how can you be so sure, Muttab? How else did they find us if they were not aided by our enemies? Only powerful dark sorcerers can find the fortress. You know this. How do you know these are not dark sorcerers disguised as children to trick us? Do not be fooled, sister.*

Muttab motioned towards Zoey. *The red-haired child is called Zoey. Her mother is my friend—*

How can that be? Said the high sorceress. *A friend you say? Minitians do not make friends with mortals. How can this child's mother be* your *friend?*

Muttab turned and faced Zoey and for a moment Zoey thought she could see her face change, as though the white mask softened, but it was difficult to tell what her mother's friend felt.

Her mother sought our help years ago, began Muttab. *She searched for the fortress, but could not find it. Her powers weren't strong enough, unlike her daughter's. And one day, beyond the boundaries of our magic and fortresses, I sensed a deep and profound sadness. As I began my search for this sorrow, I found the mortal, Elizabeth.*

Elizabeth begged for my help, continued Muttab. *She had a child with her, this child.*

She pointed at Zoey, and Zoey tensed.

She told me of her own abilities and of the dangers that followed her and her little girl. She asked for a concealment charm, to hide and protect her child from evil—the same evil that threatens this world today.

The Minitians shifted nervously.

And just like her mother, the blood of the Originals flows in the girl's veins. She has the power to manipulate portals and create her own. That is how she found us.

Zoey is not *the enemy. Her mother is my friend, and I'm sure Zoey came here for a good reason.*

All the Minitians' invisible eyes were on Zoey. It was a really creepy feeling, but she found the courage to speak up.

"High Sorceress," said Zoey. Her voice was braver than she felt, but she stayed on her knees. She knew she had spoken out of turn again, but she didn't care.

"I apologize if coming here was wrong and in violation of your sacred castle laws, but we meant no disrespect. Honest. We wouldn't have come if we had a choice, if the sake of the world didn't depend on it."

The Minitians fidgeted. Their voices cried out in Zoey's mind.

What does this child know of the fate of this world?

147

As if in answer, the ground heaved, buckled, and rolled like water. Zoey stared transfixed as a large fissure opened up and cracks snaked around the marble floor. A giant piece of the castle's ceiling fell and crashed with a thundering boom inches from Zoey.

The red sky was black with ominous clouds and lit up by a phenomenal lightning display. The thunder clap that followed shook the earth, and the sound waves, as strong as any earthquake, smashed into the walls of the castle.

"Zoey! Watch out!"

Tristan pushed Zoey out of the way just as a chunk of stone from one of the columns crashed to the floor and shattered into millions of tiny pieces.

The Minitians cried out as they scrambled for cover as more of their castle walls crumbled around them. Everyone panicked, except for Muttab and the high sorceress, who didn't move.

The earthquake finally ended, and the thick gray dust settled.

Zoey coughed the dust from her lungs and turned to Muttab. "What's happening to your fortress?"

It was the high sorceress that answered.

It is dying . . . .

"But how can it die?" asked Zoey. "It's a building made of stones. It's not alive?"

It is *alive,* said the high sorceress. Her voice was consumed with pain, and Zoey could feel the faceless tears in her voice.

She continued. *This fortress is alive with our magic. Our magic is tied to this world, as is the fortress. The white fortress is the core of our power. Our magic flows in and out of it like blood in your mortal heart. The world is dying and thus our magic and fortress will die, too.*

The white Minitian hung her head. Zoey couldn't help but feel sorry for her, even though she had just tried to drive them insane.

Zoey, said Muttab with a hint of urgency in her voice. *What help do you require from us?*

"We need a potion or a spell to make us invisible," said Zoey. "I'm not even sure you can do that, but it's the only way that we can get through to the portals and shut them for good—"

"But we still need something to destroy them," noted Simon.

He turned to the Minitian. "Um, Muttab . . . do you guys have like explosives or something that can blow up the portals? We kinda lost ours."

No, said Muttab. *Our magic doesn't work in that way. But I can help you with an invisibility potion. The rest I'm afraid is up to you.*

"We'll find a way to shut them down," said Tristan, his voice full of courage and determination. "The hardest part is to get past the Alphas undetected. Once we're on the other side, we'll have enough time to look for something to use to blow up the portals. All we need is to find something equivalent to the UEC bombs."

Zoey smiled at him. "We'll find something. I know we will."

The ground trembled, and this time the windows above exploded. Shards of glass shattered on the ground like heavy rain.

"If we don't get out of here soon," said Simon as he plucked glass out of his hair. "There'll be nothing left of us."

Muttab grabbed the high sorceress's hand. *Do not fret, sister, there is still hope. Hope in these children.*

I am sorry I ever doubted them.

With that the white sorceress turned on her heels and disappeared down a dark tunnel.

Quickly, said Muttab. *Follow me.*

Zoey dashed after Muttab as she led them through one of the tunnels. They arrived inside a chamber the size of an office. The room was filled with jars churning with green slime, scrolls of old parchment, pots with strange spidery-looking yellow plants, countless empty pots, and mountain of decrepit books. The only source of light came from two large candles mounted on the walls.

Muttab crossed the room. She picked up a small glass container that looked like a saltshaker. But instead of salt, tiny green sand-like crystals filled half the bottom. She gave the vial to Zoey.

Just a small amount will do. Don't use too much.

"Why?" said Simon as he peered curiously at the container in Zoey's hand, "What will happen if we use too much—?"

Suddenly, the shelves rattled and collapsed. The jars and pots, parchment scrolls, and books all crashed to the ground. The castle roared and howled, like it was in pain. Zoey jumped out of the way as a strange slimy ooze neared her foot.

Come on, urged Muttab. *You must hurry. It's not safe for you here.*

The Minitian's legs were long, and Zoey struggled to keep up. They dashed into the larger chamber with the shattered Seeing Crystal, but the other Minitians were gone. Without stopping,

Muttab crossed the chamber in giant leaps. Zoey followed the sorceress through the foyer and out the front doors.

Keep running, she urged. *Don't stop and don't look back until you reach the shoreline. Go!*

"But what about you?" said Zoey, "I have so many questions! I want to know about my mom—"

Muttab pushed her away. *There's no time! Get your mother back, Zoey. And shut the portals before it's too late. Go on!*

"Let's go, Zoey," pressed Tristan. He grabbed her arm and pulled her along.

"But—"

Zoey forced back the tears in her eyes. With a final look back at the Minitian, she ran down the white sand path with Tristan and Simon.

The ground shook beneath their feet again. A large crevice split open in front of them, and they leaped over it as a large section of the path crumbled away into the sea. But they didn't stop. They didn't look back until they reached the beach.

Zoey turned with her heart in her throat.

A giant cloud of dust erupted where the white fortress had once stood gleaming like a jewel in the sun. Now there was nothing but a pile of rubble.

CHAPTER 12

A TEASPOON OF

MAGIC

Zoey, Tristan, and Simon hid behind a large pine tree and watched as an army of agents battled with masses of moving red uniforms and vile, ominous beasts. Tall spider-like creatures with raw, leaking sores hacked at an unsuspecting female agent. Her scream died in her throat as the creature broke her neck and then wrapped her in a cocoon. An Alpha hybrid creature with furry moth-like wings and two giant bug eyes grabbed two agents at once and tossed them like basketballs into the mouth of a dinosaur.

Agent Barnes and Agent Lee stood back to back and fought with a red lizard the size of an elephant with three heads and long purple tongues like whips. But they were still far from the portal.

Their science officer, a young woman, shot small lightning bolts at the blue portal. But the bolts bounced back, and the portal didn't even shimmer.

Desperation marked the faces of every agent and science officer still standing. They were throwing anything and everything they had at the Alphas and the giant portal. But Zoey could see it wasn't enough. Even if they did succeed at breaching the Alpha army and attacking the portal, she knew that to destroy the Great Junction once and for all, they had to shut the portal on the Nexus side as well.

"Simon, how much time left?" Zoey was worried that they had spent too much time in the white fortress.

Simon pulled out his cell phone. "Just a little less than seven hours left."

"It didn't feel like we spent five hours with the Minitians," remarked Tristan. "We could have been trapped there forever."

"I'm just glad we didn't end up at the bottom of the ocean with the rest of their castle," said Zoey.

She pulled out the small glass vial with the green crystalized sand. She shook it and examined it closer. "There's something written on it."

Tristan leaned forward. "What does it say?"

"*Sprinkle one teaspoon . . .*" she read, "*over subject . . . do not . . . do not . . .* the rest is completely worn off. I can't make it out—"

"Let me see that." Simon grabbed the container out of Zoey's hand. "*Do not . . .* I think that's an *A* and then *L L*—*do not all?*"

Zoey grabbed it back. "That makes no sense at all. Well, I'll go first."

She unscrewed the lid and tipped a small amount of the green crystals into her palm. They sparkled in the dim light like emeralds.

"I guess that's about a teaspoon. Okay, here goes nothing."

She raised her hand to the top of her head and sprinkled the green sand all over herself.

A cool sensation rippled over her body like ice cubes rolling over her skin. She waited for about ten seconds and then looked down at herself and sulked. "I can still see me. Can you guys still see me?"

"Yes." Tristan took the vial. "Maybe it takes a few minutes to work. Let me try."

He sprinkled some of the contents on himself waited, and then gave the container to Simon.

"Maybe you didn't sprinkle enough." Simon dumped the green sand over his body.

"Simon! What are you doing?" hissed Zoey. "It says a teaspoon not a large bucketful."

Simon shrugged and pocketed the nearly empty container. "We'll see."

The three of them waited in silence, and Zoey started to get impatient.

"Anyone noticing any changes?"

Tristan shook his head. "Nope."

"I'm hungry," said Simon. "Does that count?"

Just when Zoey thought that maybe Muttab's potion had been defective, a rumbling sound came from her belly like a hungry growl. And then . . . nothing.

"Hey, isn't that Director Martin," Simon pointed towards the portal. "I'd recognize that ugly face tied to a pole, upside down, and blindfolded."

Even from the distance and covered in shadows, Zoey recognized that hateful scowl, that condescending smile, and those accusing eyes. It was indeed Director Martin. He strolled among the Alphas and mystics like it was a regular walk in the park. No one paid any attention to him, like he wasn't even there. He was walking straight for the portal.

Zoey's eyes widened. "He's got my bag! That's Agent Franken's bag with the UECs. But why does *he* have it?"

"And why aren't the Alphas stopping him?" said Tristan.

Zoey watched as the director passed a mass of Alphas and werewolf-babies and stepped right through the giant blue portal.

"What the—?" Simon stepped away from the tree and pointed.

"Did you see that? He just walked right by them and into the portal like nobody's business. Guys, what the heck's going on?"

Tristan pulled Simon back. "I don't know. I'd never thought *he* would be a traitor—"

"I would." Zoey checked that her weapon was secured on her wrist.

"Zoey, why are you smiling?" inquired Simon. "Did I miss the memo? Is this *'We all love Director Martin Day'?* Let's bake him a freaking cake! I thought you hated the guy."

"I do hate the guy," said Zoey. "But now we have a chance to get my bag back—and the UECs. We find Director Martin—"

"We shut the portals," finished Tristan. His smile matched Zoey's.

"Uh . . . dudes . . . I think the spell thing is working," said Simon.

Zoey looked at the spot where she had last seen Simon. At first she thought he was completely invisible, but as she looked she could see traces of him, like an optical illusion. But it was more than that. Grass and tree bark and branches reflected on him. It was as though he was reflecting off what was around him, like he was painted with mirror paint. He wasn't invisible, but rather he was giving off the illusion of invisibility. And when she looked where Tristan had stood moments ago, his body was just like Simon's, reflecting off his surroundings. If she focused, she could see her friends through the illusion, almost like trick-photography. If she knew where they were, and what to look for, she *could* see them. It was ingenious. She hoped this disguise was clever enough to fool the Alphas. They only needed a few minutes to get through to the portal.

"This is so awesome," exclaimed Simon's voice. "Think of all the things we could do! If we live though this, I could totally use the green stuff again and check out the girls' washrooms. I've always suspected theirs was nicer than ours. Plus it doesn't smell like pee."

"I'm going to pretend like I didn't hear that." Zoey laughed, took a few steps forward, and stood in the clearing. It was a little suicidal. She *was* in the perfect spot to get noticed. But that's what she wanted. A few Alphas rushed by, and then two werewolf-babies and a worm-like creature with a bearded face, but they never even glanced her way. Muttab's potion worked. They couldn't see her.

"Guys," whispered Zoey, "get over here."

The mirror effect was so good that even Zoey had to concentrate really hard to see her friends.

"Ouch!" she cried as something hard hit her in the nose.

"SHH!"

"Hey! That's my foot!"

"Lower your voices!" hissed Zoey.

"That's my *other* foot!"

"Okay, okay," said Simon's voice. "But Tristan pushed me."

"Sorry," laughed Tristan. "Didn't see you there."

"Ha, ha."

Zoey scowled. "Do I have to tie you two together or can you manage to make it across by yourselves?"

There was still two hundred feet to cross before they made it to the portal, and they had to get Agent Franken's bag back.

"Remember," she whispered as they huddled together. "We're not exactly invisible so try not to draw any attention our way. We might just be able to make it across without them noticing us. Be careful and try not to bump into anyone."

"Why do I get the feeling that was directed at me?" whined Simon.

"Because it probably was," mocked Tristan.

Zoey wanted to slap them both. "Come on."

With her boomerang in her hand, Zoey lead the way. She was ready if anything was to happen, but she hoped to make it across safely. She suspected that the real dangers were on the other side of that portal.

They slipped and zigzagged through the battle. The smell of blood and sulfur hung heavily in the air like horrid burning incense. Desperately trying not to cough or breathe loudly, Zoey dodged a large female Alpha with spiked hair and two large machetes in her man-like hands.

"Now that's a handsome man," whispered Simon once the woman was out of earshot.

Just as Zoey was about to turn around and slap Simon for real this time, another Alpha charged in her direction. Tristan pulled them both out of the way, and the Alpha ran passed them and kicked an agent in the gut.

"Don't stop," said Tristan in a low voice. "We're almost there."

It was difficult to see through the dim light, and Zoey wondered how Tristan could see so well when she could barely make out his face. Maybe it was because of his Mysterian blood.

Another group of Alphas rushed by, but they crept further along without being discovered.

Zoey looked up. The giant blue portal was only twelve feet away. They had made it.

"Hey, what's that?"

Zoey froze. Tristan and Simon both crashed into her, and the three of them toppled to the ground.

An Alpha man rushed their way. He had extra badges on the front of his uniform, and Zoey was sure he was of higher rank. A large sword hung in his right hand.

"What is it, Captain?" another Alpha joined him.

The Captain lifted his sword inches from Zoey's face, and she backed away.

"There. You see that? I thought I saw a young girl's face right here."

The other Alpha shook his head. "Don't see anything. You sure?"

Zoey's skin started to tingle. She looked down at herself. Her hand was visible. It looked like a severed hand floating in the air. She hid it behind her back and held her breath.

The Captain eyed the spot where they lay. His eyes rolled over them.

Zoey felt Tristan's hand on hers and then he squeezed. Slowly, and as silently as they could, the three of them rose to their feet—

"There! Look! I see them!"

Zoey cursed. She could see half of Tristan's face and Simon's jeans. Things were not good.

"Time to go!" said Simon.

"KILL THEM!"

The captain swung his sword dangerously close to Zoey's abdomen. She jumped out of the way just as the blade sliced through her shirt.

Zoey grabbed her friends by the arms. "Get to the portal!"

They were still half invisible, and it worked in their favor. They charged through the crowd of unsuspecting Alphas without being seen. The portal was just a few feet away. Zoey's nerves tingled. She was almost there.

"Don't let them get to the portal!" cried the captain.

The giant blue portal was so close now that Zoey felt a cool breeze brush her face. It was as though the portal was sucking her in. For a split second she felt fear. What was waiting for them on the other side?

Tristan and Simon's images wavered beside her. With a last effort, she held her breath and leaped through—

CHAPTER 13

THE NEXUS

Darkness. Silence.

Zoey's limbs felt heavy and restrained, like she had fallen into thick pea soup. She didn't dare to breathe. What if she suffocated? The effects of stepping through the portal weren't at all the same as using the mirror ports. Her body hadn't rematerialized, and she hadn't broken apart into miniscule particles. She just felt like she was floating and slowing down. It was as though time stood still and she had stopped moving.

She couldn't see or sense Tristan or Simon although she was sure they had entered the portal at the same time. But she felt alone. Stuck. Maybe they couldn't pass through to the other side, and they were all going to die . . . .

And just when she thought she'd be stuck there forever, her shoes touched solid ground. Dizzy and disoriented, Zoey moved on instinct with her boomerang ready. Simon and Tristan landed beside her, completely visible. Their eyes were out of focus, like they were just waking from a dream. She felt exactly the same.

Seconds passed. The effects of the portal wore off. The portal stirred, but nothing came through.

They weren't being pursued.

The portal on this side was not at all like the portal on her side. Instead of the watery light-blue surface, this side was red and churning like hot magma. She took a careful step back.

When she realized she was still holding her breath, she let it go, took a deep breath, and coughed. Her throat stung like she had swallowed liquid bleach. The air was thick, hot, and reeked of sulfur. It was almost like a poisonous gas. How long could they breathe this toxic air before it killed them?

"This place smells like my Grandpa Gordon's bathroom," said Simon as he pinched his nose.

"I never realized how different the portals would be," she coughed, trying not to think too much about the quality of the air. "On our side it's blue, and on this side it's red, thick, and angry looking."

"That's not all that's different," she heard Tristan say. "Look."

Zoey turned around.

Vast red deserts of smoke and ash spread out before her. High winds blew sand into her eyes and thunder roared from above. The sky was a ruby color with dark maroon clouds moving fast against two suns. In the distance, black mountains with jagged peaks rose like spears. Rivers of black waters snaked in and around the land like dark worms. From what she could see, there was no plant life, no greenery—nothing, just miles and miles of red deserts and black mountains. The land was harsh and unforgiving. The Nexus was unlike anything she'd ever seen.

Thunder boomed. But this time it sounded as though it was coming from underground. The ground trembled below Zoey's feet. A few hundred yards to her left the ground opened up. An area as large as a lake collapsed and disappeared down into the crevice.

"Looks like the Nexus is struggling with the Great Junction, too," said Tristan, his face worried.

Zoey nodded. "Means we don't have much time to find the missing bag *and* my mother."

"It looks like a giant bowl of tomato soup," noted Simon as he turned away from the portal. He rubbed his belly. "I'm so hungry! Where's the food?"

"Simon?" said Zoey, her voice rising. "You're the one who was carrying the food. Where's *your* bag?"

"Ooops."

Tristan loomed over him. "What do you mean *oops*? Where's the food? Don't tell me you forgot to bring it?"

"I, I . . ." began Simon. "I just put it down for a second when we were sprinkling ourselves with the magic salt."

He shrugged. "I guess I must have left it by the tree."

Zoey glared at Simon, but then her expression softened. "I don't want to fight. If forgetting the food was the worst that could happen to us, then we still have a real chance."

She reached inside her backpack and pulled out a water bottle. "At least we'll be hydrated. Here, have some water." She tossed Simon her bottle and did her best not to look angry or disappointed. She doubted they were going to starve to death anyway. They only had a few hours left. It wouldn't matter if they starved if the end of the world was on its way.

Something nagged her. "Guys, pull out your DSMs. Hurry."

She waited until they all had them opened in their hands. "Flip them open. You see anything different?"

"Yeah," noted Tristan. "My reflection's off. I look like a ghost. I'm not *solid*."

Simon stared at his DSM, "What do you think that means?"

"I think I know." Zoey stared at her own phantom-like reflection and waited. When their specter-like reflections didn't shimmer, she looked up at her friends.

"It means they don't work here, we can't use them to get back. It means the only way home is back through *that* portal."

Tristan pocketed his DSM. "What about you? What about your abilities? Maybe it's different?"

Zoey concentrated on the Hive. She had been able to create her own anchor points before, but after a minute had passed, her image still didn't shimmer.

"Nothing, sorry," she said a little deflated. "I can't make it work." She was just like any other Seventh.

Simon tossed the bottle of water to Tristan. "So, now what? This world is probably just as big as or bigger than our world. How are we supposed to find Traitor-Martin?"

"There." Tristan kneeled. "Fresh tracks. It has to be him. They head out north towards those black mountains over there. If we hurry, we might catch him."

Zoey stared at the ground and dug into the red sand with her boomerang. "And if we don't hurry the wind will blow away the tracks. Come on, we *need* that bag."

With Tristan in the lead, the three of them followed the tracks in a jog. As they ran, Zoey glanced a few times behind her. She was still expecting some Alphas to come through the portal, but they never did. It was odd that they hadn't chased them.

They passed a curved stream of black water that bubbled like hot oil. As she examined it more closely, a pair of eyes broke the surface and blinked at her. Zoey lost her footing and tripped.

Tristan whirled around. "Zoey? Are you okay?" He pulled her up.

Zoey stared at the water. "I saw something."

"What?" Simon leaned over the stream. "I don't see anything."

"That doesn't mean there's nothing there," warned Zoey. "I wouldn't get too close to that water . . . there could be Grohemoths, or something more evil."

Simon jumped back. "Right. Let's not disturb the water."

"Come on," urged Tristan, "I'm losing the tracks."

After about a half hour of running, Zoey thought her lungs would burst.

"Water," she heard Simon grumble behind her. "I need water."

Tristan stopped and turned. "How much water do we have left?"

"Just two bottles," said Zoey. "We need the water for the way back."

Simon pinched the cramp at his side. "What?" his face was as red as the sand. "Listen, I need just a sip, just a sip. Please."

"We can't. Maybe if we walk the rest of the way? This air is really hard to breathe. I don't think I can run anymore, either." Zoey's legs started to shake.

Simon hung his head. "I'm going to die. We're all going to die."

Tristan wiped the sweat from his brow. "Okay, I think we're getting close anyway. I can sort of see a city near the bottom of the mountains there."

Zoey squinted into the wind. Tristan was right. She could barely make out the silhouette of a city below the black mountains. She hoped her mother would be there somewhere.

"I'm so hungry I could eat my own foot," whined Simon, dragging his feet.

"The tracks lead to that city," pointed Tristan. "We get to the city, and we'll find Director Martin—"

"And punch him in the face," said Simon brightly.

"I have a feeling it won't be that easy," said Zoey. The black mountains loomed in the distance like an upside-down clawed hand. She fought down an eerie feeling in the pit of her stomach.

"Sure it will," she heard Simon say behind her. "You hold him, and I'll use his face as a punching bag."

Zoey turned around—

"Simon! No!"

Green crystals dribbled from the corners of his mouth. His eyes widened at the realization of what he had just done. He spit on the ground, but it was too late. He'd already swallowed most of crystals the Minitians had given them.

Zoey smacked the empty bottle from his hand.

"You idiot! You're not supposed to eat that stuff! You're supposed to sprinkle it over you!"

"I'm sorry. I don't know what I was thinking," said Simon backing away. "I was so thirsty and hungry, I—I wasn't thinking clearly. I found it in my pocket. I don't know why I ate it. I don't know why I do most of what I do. But it's weird, I feel better now."

He smiled at his friends. "Hey, this stuff's not that bad, tastes like sugar—"

"Your mother must have dropped you on your head too many times."

Tristan picked up the empty bottle. He started laughing. "I can't believe you swallowed this stuff. It could be toxic."

Simon lost his smile. "You think so?"

"Yes!" Zoey yelled angrily. "I thought you were supposed to be the smart one."

Simon looked frightened, but then he shrugged. "It was dumb, I see that now. But nothing's happening to me. Maybe it doesn't work if you swallow it?"

Tristan snorted.

Zoey glared at him. "This isn't funny."

"Yes it is."

"I give up." Zoey examined Simon one last time. "I guess you were lucky this time."

She turned around and gazed at the mountains and the surrounding grounds. "We've been lucky so far. Hopefully our luck will still stand."

"I have a good feeling about our trip," said Simon. "I love road trips."

Zoey whirled around. "This isn't a—" the rest of her sentence caught in her throat.

Simon wasn't *Simon* anymore. An old man was wearing Simon's clothes. His hair had turned white, and his face was creased with wrinkles. He was four inches shorter, skinnier, and he hunched over like he needed a walker. He blinked at them with tired wet eyes.

"Oh, man, this is *bad*," said Tristan staring at Simon. "Dude, you're like . . . *old*."

Simon swallowed hard. "What? What are you talking about?"

He wrapped a hand around his throat, "What's wrong with my voice? It sounds like I've got a serious case of tonsillitis. You guys are freaking me out. I can see my legs and my shoes so I'm not invisible—urgh . . . I *hate* my voice. Why are you staring at me like you've seen a ghost?"

"Because you *are* a ghost." Zoey pulled out her DSM. "Seriously, look."

Simon held the mirror and stared at himself. His face paled and then turned a greenish color like he was about to be sick.

"Oh, this *is* bad, I'm—I'm *ancient*. I'm a senior citizen without the benefits," his voice cracked.

Then a small smile appeared on his chapped lips. "I kinda look like a sexy version of Einstein—like his *hot* brother." He paused. "Do you guys think this is a permanent thing? Like I've wasted all my life, and I'm going to die soon of old age? Oh man, what's my mother going to say when she sees me? She probably won't even recognize me!"

Zoey shrugged. "I don't think you're going to die. What you swallowed was magic, so hopefully it'll wear off."

"You better hope it'll wear off," commented Tristan. "It's not like we can ask the Minitians for a remedy potion."

"It'll pass, Simon. I'm sure it will."

He looked frail and weak. "So . . . how do you *feel?*" asked Zoey. "Do you feel old?"

Old man Simon jogged on the spot and then did a set of straight punches.

"I feel the same," his face crinkled into a large smile. "I feel some restrictions. My bones crack a lot, but basically I feel the same."

Zoey sighed. "Well, that's a relief."

Tristan laughed again, and she shoved him hard. He wasn't making things easier.

Simon gave them a weak smile. "I guess this is payback for my stupidity."

He gave Zoey back her DSM. His hands looked bony and were peppered with age spots.

"At least it's not going to get any worse. I mean, I'm already close to my death bed—"

A gurgling roar thundered from behind them.

Zoey whirled around, forgetting Simon's transformation temporarily, and looked up into the face of an enormous gray beast.

CHAPTER 14

BLACK WATERS

Zoey's blood turned to ice.

The creature was hairless, with thick, gray reptilian-like skin. Its elongated maw snapped with rows of pointy, black teeth. It stood upright on its hind legs. The creature looked like a cross between a crocodile and a grizzly bear, a deadly combination. Black oily water dripped from it like it had just crawled out of the black stream. Its powerful tail slashed eagerly behind it, waiting. Small, evil white eyes measured them, contemplating whom to eat first.

Zoey could smell the stench of rotten meat and spoiled eggs.

"What kind of mystic is that?" Zoey backed away slowly and raised her boomerang over her head.

"Don't know," answered Tristan as he angled his dagger and planted his feet. "Never seen one like this before."

Simon planted his feet and aimed his slingshot. "Who wants to go first?"

"This isn't a *game*, Simon," said Zoey. She marveled at Simon's sudden bravery. It was almost as though his transformation into a modern grandfather had given him more courage. Maybe his alteration *was* a good thing.

"Of course it's a game," said Simon as he aimed his weapon. Zoey heard his bones crack like popcorn. "It's a game of life and death, and I don't plan on losing."

The beast growled a wet growl like it was gargling its own mucus.

"Tasty," mumbled Simon.

With a splashing sound two more of the creatures emerged from the black stream. Their white eyes gleamed with hunger.

"Wonderful," muttered Simon. "Now we each get a pet lizard."

With ferocious speed like a tiger, one of the creatures came at them thrashing its sharp talons. Its snapping teeth sounded like a machine gun.

Tristan moved forward and met it head on. He dodged around the beast as he slashed repeatedly with his weapon.

In a blur of red sand, the second creature leaped in the air. Its massive tail hit Simon across the chest. He flew twenty feet and crash-landed on a heap of sand. His frail body lay crumbled. He wasn't moving.

Zoey moved in Simon's direction, but the beast turned and charged like a crazed rhinoceros.

She dodged sideways and rolled on the ground. A massive talon just missed her head, and she stood up on the other side of the creature with her boomerang ready. She hurled her weapon and hit its head with a loud *crunch*. The creature was stunned for a moment. But as she caught her returning boomerang, something heavy crashed into her back.

Her face hit the ground, and she tasted blood in her mouth. A beast landed on her legs and sunk its talons into her flesh, biting at her thigh. She raised her head. Another creature appeared and dived for her face. Its clawed feet and toothy mouth snapped at her eyes and nose.

She reeled backwards, ducking and slashing her weapon as hard as she could. But every hit only seemed to anger the creatures. Their teeth sank into her neck, and their claws dug into her scalp. She screamed and roared and twirled, stabbing and slashing wildly.

Tristan latched on to one of the mystics' tails. He heaved and managed to pull it off Zoey. She felt lighter. She rolled over and kicked the other creature in the face with the heel of her shoe. The beast stumbled backwards, and she took the time to struggle to her feet.

The crumpled gray carcass of the beast that Tristan had managed to kill lay at her feet. White liquid oozed from the deep gashes in its lifeless body, and steam rose from it like the vapors from onions. Through her watering eyes, Zoey could see that there were still two more. And who knew how many others could emerge from the black waters.

The air seemed to get thinner and thinner with every passing minute, like it was being slowly squeezed out through the portal. She was hot, thirsty, and tired. If the air got any worse, she didn't see how they could even walk to the city. It was like breathing poison. It was slowly killing them.

Tristan cursed, and shielding his head and face he hit the second beast with a powerful blow and sent it sprawling on the ground. But in one easy flip, it regained its feet and launched another attack. He managed to grab it by the neck and twisted it in a headlock.

Simon . . .

The lack of oxygen had affected her brain, and she had momentarily forgotten about him.

Zoey charged towards the spot where he lay. But before she could get to him, the third creature sunk its talons into her flesh, and she cried out as she felt warm blood trickling down her back. She hung in its grasp with her arms and legs dangling like a doll's.

The more she struggled, the deeper the talons tore into her flesh. In her terror, she had a moment of clarity.

Arching her right arm, she jabbed the left edge of her boomerang into the beast's right eye.

The creature wailed.

Zoey fell to the ground with her boomerang still clutched firmly in her hand. She slowly got to her feet, her eyes never leaving her opponent.

White liquid oozed out of its punctured eye like yolk from a shattered egg, and Zoey felt sick to her stomach. Shaking its head, the lizard creature thrashed at the ground, wailing. It raised its head and focused its unspoiled eye on Zoey, hissing and growling, making the hairs on the back of her neck rise. Now it was hurt and *really* mad.

Over the hissing of the creature, she could hear Tristan's battle cries. He was still fighting.

The creature circled her, snapping its jaws.

Zoey could see Simon's body lying on the ground behind it. He still hadn't moved from the spot. If he wasn't dead, he was seriously injured.

Her hatred for the creatures intensified. She wanted them to pay for what they had done to Simon. She planted her feet, glared at the beast, and waited.

It lowered its head, kicked up sand behind it, and then charged.

But Zoey was ready for it.

She whipped her boomerang at the creature as hard as she could and opened a large gash on its forehead. But the creature grabbed her returning boomerang and then turned its remaining eye back on Zoey.

"You better give that back," said Zoey. "It doesn't belong to you."

The beast laughed a wet laugh. And then it sliced a deep cut along its left forearm. Zoey could see white blood seeping from the wound. It placed the boomerang below its wound and let the blood trickle over it.

Zoey frowned. What was it doing?

The creature's blood bubbled. It was acid, and it was eating through her boomerang. The molten gold from her melting boomerang pooled at the creature's feet and then disappeared into the sand.

Her beloved weapon was destroyed.

The creature angled its head. Its lips rolled over its teeth and it seemed pleased at the panic on Zoey's face.

Zoey stared at her hands. She had never imagined in a million years that she'd lose her precious boomerang. It was like losing a limb.

She searched the ground and grabbed a rock. It wasn't much of a weapon, but it was better than nothing.

The creature snarled in delight.

Zoey stood her ground. Whatever happened, she was going to die fighting.

The black water beast crouched down low, and then with rows of black teeth flashing it came at Zoey again.

"Zoey! Get back!"

Tristan pushed Zoey out of the way just as the beast's giant mouth neared her head. His blue skin glowed. He side-kicked the creature and sent it staggering back. It came at him, again and again, but Tristan blocked, dodged, and parried every strike. Crying out in frustration, the creature charged Tristan's neck. It was going in for the kill.

Tristan faked to the right, spun, came up behind the creature's left side, and slashed it across the neck. He jumped back as the acidic white blood spilled out of the beast. It hissed one last time, and then dropped into the sand and didn't move again.

"That was close. I thought it was going to kill me. Thanks." Zoey got to her feet.

"That's what boyfriends are for." Tristan smiled at her and for a moment she forgot where she was.

The winds blew at Zoey's back, and she wiped the sand from her eyes. She glanced back the way they had come. She couldn't even see the portal anymore. Everything was covered in dust. It looked like a huge sandstorm was brewing. She could hardly see fifty feet away from her. They needed to get to Simon before he was lost in the sand blizzard.

His body was already half covered in red sand.

"Simon!" she dashed across the red field and fell to her knees next to Simon. She had forgotten about his transformation into an old man and was shocked at his pale wrinkled face. He looked like a real corpse.

"Is he alive?" Tristan kneeled beside her.

"I don't know," Zoey said as she found her voice. She wiped the sand from his face as softly as she could. Gently, she reached out and put a hand over Simon's mouth.

"I . . . I can't feel anything. I can't feel his breath. It's too windy. It's no use!" Her heart raced as searched for signs of life and cursed the high winds. What if Simon *was* dead? She'd never forgive herself. *He can't be dead. Not like this.*

She rested her ear on his chest. A soft *thump, thump, thump* sounded in her ears.

"He's alive," she said as the tears fell freely down her face.

Tristan sat back in the sand. "Thank God."

Zoey shook Simon's shoulders gently. "Simon? Simon can you hear me? Wake up!"

She looked over at Tristan. "He's not waking up."

Tristan sat up in the sand. "I don't know. Maybe he suffered a concussion or something, but at least he's alive."

"Yes," sighed Zoey. "He's alive, but *you're* going to have to carry him. I'm not strong enough. You think you can carry him all the way to that city?"

Tristan sheathed his dagger inside his jacket. "Yeah, his old bones probably don't weigh much anyway."

He looked up at the sky. "But we better hurry; this storm is getting worse. We won't be able to see a foot in front of us soon. It'll be a miracle if we can still find the tracks."

Zoey got to her feet. It wasn't just the storm that worried her. She kept checking her wrist, hoping her boomerang would magically reappear. It didn't. She tried hard not to freak out, but she felt like somebody had stolen one of her hands.

"What's wrong?" Tristan saw her hand around her golden bracelet and frowned. "Zoey, where's your boomerang?"

"Gone. Destroyed. One of the creatures melted it with its acid-like blood."

It was strange to feel so attached to something that wasn't alive, but without her weapon Zoey felt naked, exposed, weak. She stared at the ground.

Tristan reached into the folds of his jacket and drew a small dagger. "Here, take this one. It's a spare. I know it's not the same, but at least you have something to protect yourself with."

Zoey flipped the dagger in her hand. It was much lighter than her old weapon, and the rough handle felt awkward against her skin, but she needed to get used to it quickly.

"Let's go," she said, trying not to sound too disappointed. "Maybe we can help Simon in that city—"

"You come with us now, or you die," said a voice behind Zoey.

CHAPTER 15

NEXUS CITY

A group of the strangest creatures she'd ever encountered stood behind Zoey and Tristan.

Although tan-colored robes were draped over their Hobbit-sized bodies, and their faces were hidden beneath their hoods, Zoey could see their small pointy features. They formed a ring around Zoey and Tristan and watched them with large, glowing green eyes. Some of them brandished deadly looking spears while others held automatic weapons or wore belts of grenades over their shoulders. With the strong winds, Zoey hadn't heard them until it was too late. They looked like miniature ninjas. Even without their numbers and weapons, they still had the upper hand because they were stealthy and knew the lay of the land.

One of the hooded mystics pointed a long, sharp spear at Zoey's face and spoke in a chipmunk-like voice with a heavy accent.

"Leave weapons or you die."

At first Zoey almost started laughing. She had to remind herself that she had a razor-sharp weapon pointed at her eyes. She glanced over at Tristan, and they tossed their weapons to the ground. She wished she had her boomerang with her. She raised her hands in surrender and backed up next to Tristan. She leaned towards him and whispered. "Please tell me you know what these mystics are."

"Chacras," answered Tristan. Zoey couldn't tell by his tone if they were dangerous or not. They looked pretty dangerous.

"Are they *friendly*?"

"Not sure." Tristan eyed them curiously for a moment. "They're mostly traders, and merchants. They trade weapons."

"Well, they're pretty *loaded* with them," said Zoey.

She raised her voice. "These are the only weapons we have. Take them, and leave us alone."

Simon was still unconscious. They needed to get him some help fast.

The Chacras that was pointing the spear at Zoey backed away and began conversing with the other Chacras. They spoke quickly in a high-pitched language that sounded like an audio clip on fast-forward. The Chacras' voices rose as disagreements erupted among them. She couldn't tell who their leader was. She sensed that they didn't have a leader and acted as a collective.

"What's going on?" Zoey whispered. Tristan shrugged.

Finally, the voices calmed. One of the Chacras raised his spear and pointed it towards the city.

"You come with us. Leave the dead one. Cannot make trade with dead one—"

"What?" Zoey stepped forward. "He's *not* dead, you overgrown chipmunk. He's hurt."

She stood protectively in front of Simon. "I'm not going anywhere without my friend."

The Chacras raised their spears at Zoey. "He old. He dead. You do what we say."

Zoey knocked the spear out of her face.

"I don't think so. You'll have to kill me," she growled. "He's just hurt . . . he's unconscious."

If they tried to hurt Simon she swore would tear them apart with her bare hands. Well, at least she hoped she could.

The Chacras raised their weapons at her and yelled angrily.

One of them yelled something that seemed to calm the others down a little, although they still shifted nervously and held their tiny fingers on the triggers of their big guns.

Tristan stepped carefully over to Zoey.

"Zoey, we can't shut the portals if we're dead. You're upsetting them, and in case you haven't noticed, there's a lot more of *them* than *us*."

Zoey knew Tristan was right, but she felt overly protective of Simon because he was injured and because he was an old man.

"You worth more living. No dead, no dead," said the Chacras. It shook its head and lifted up three fingers. Zoey noticed that its skin was a light yellowish color.

"We make *three* trade. You take friend with you. Three trade. We make trade in city. You come now." He shoved his spear at Zoey.

"I swear I'm going to break that spear over his head—"

"*Zoey*," warned Tristan. "Let's do what they say. We need to get to the city anyway. Think of them as our guides."

"Fine. Okay. We'll go with you." She waited for Tristan to lift Simon up on his shoulders and then followed the Chacras.

The Chacras moved fast across the red dunes. They looked more like they were gliding than walking. And when Zoey glanced down, she noticed that the only footprints in the sand were hers and Tristan's.

Every now and then a Chacras would hit Zoey or Tristan with the blunt edge of a weapon. "Faster. You move faster."

"Okay, okay," hissed Zoey.

The lack of oxygen and food was taking its toll. Zoey was beginning to struggle just to walk. Sweat poured down into her eyes, and she concentrated on putting one foot in front of the other and not falling over. Tristan's face was strained and dirty. She could see that his skin was back to its natural olive color, which meant he was relying on his non-Mysterian strength to carry Simon. She could tell he was tiring, too.

After what seemed to be two hours of walking, all she could see was a wall of red sand. They were in the eye of the blizzard. How did the Chacras know where they were going? She realized that even in their misfortune they had been *lucky* the mystics had found them. They would never have made it to the city without them.

Then the winds died. Zoey looked up and quickly understood why.

The city was cupped protectively at the bottom of the black mountains, as though two giant hands were holding it up. She had been so preoccupied with trying to breathe and not trip she hadn't even noticed that they had arrived at the city. The winds didn't reach them here, and the air seemed easier on her lungs.

The city was huge—the size of a major metropolitan city in her world. But instead of tall glass and metal skyscrapers, the Nexus city was a jumble of mismatched subterranean and above ground dwellings made of clay and the black stones from the mountainside. Thousands, perhaps millions, of mystics scurried around in the labyrinth of streets and passageways.

Two colossal stone statues carved with the body of a lion, the upper torso and head of a woman, and eagle wings guarded the entrance of the city. They looked like Sphinxes. They had ruby eyes, and they frowned to ward off intruders. Zoey was both impressed and frightened by the looks on the women's faces. Both statues held signs. One was written in a language she couldn't understand. Although the other was damaged, she could read it. *NEXUS CITY*.

Zoey had absolutely no idea how many cities there were in the Nexus, but she hoped this was the capital and prayed that Director Martin and her mother were here somewhere.

Zoey heard a whining sound and turned to see a large cow-like creature with long brown hair pulling a wagon. Another Chacras sat in the driver's chair, and some of Zoey's abductors went to speak to him.

"You get in," said the Chacras who spoke English.

He hit the end of his spear against the back of the wagon. "Get in. We go to city. We make trade."

He ushered Zoey and Tristan into the wagon. She was so grateful for a break from walking that she didn't need to be told twice.

Tristan laid Simon gently on the floor. Zoey quickly slipped her backpack off and placed it carefully under his head. He was pale, really pale. She tried to wake him up with a little bit of water on his mouth and face, but it didn't work. She took a small sip to rinse the sand from her mouth and gave the bottle to Tristan.

The English-speaking Chacras and two others jumped into the back of the wagon with their weapons drawn. The rest of the group spread out and disappeared back into desert. Zoey watched until they were swallowed up by the red storm. Apparently they felt that Zoey and Tristan were no longer a threat. Why? Whatever the reason, it made her more nervous.

"Uttik, tuk, tuk," the driver called as he lashed the reins. The beast whined, and then the wagon shifted and bounced. Zoey sat with her back against one of the side panels, and Tristan sat across from her. The touch of each other's feet was their only source of comfort. The Chacras still pointed their weapons at them, and Zoey tried to ignore them as she took a closer look at the city.

Like any major metropolitan city, the streets of Nexus were packed with creatures big and small. A dog-like creature with a large human face and tall rabbit ears walked beside a creature with a large green body, long tentacles, wings, and talons. Blue-skinned females with backwards feet shopped in a store tended by a small bear-like, hairless beast with spikes. Behind them coiled a large serpent with horns, and beside it was a hideous monster made of deceased human body parts. It reminded Zoey of Frankenstein. She recognized clay golems from her studies. An enormous black dog with blue flames around its head talked with moth and human hybrids with yellow glowing eyes. Everywhere she looked she saw more mystics she'd never seen or heard of before. The mystics paid no attention to her and Tristan, like they weren't very interesting. She wondered why that was. Were humans a regular thing in the Nexus?

The deeper they ventured into the city, the deeper her sense of dread.

Was her mother here? This city was enormous. How would she ever find her? It would take years to go through every building. She could see that Tristan was thinking the same thing. The city was just *too* big, and they were running out of time . . . .

The wagon came to a halt before the tallest building in the city. It stood around ten stories high and was made of a black stucco-like material. Red painted animal bones formed the moldings around the rows of windows. The front door was also made of large red bones, as though they were still fresh and wet with blood. It looked like a black cathedral, a bone church.

"Those doors are seriously disturbing."

"SIMON!" She threw her arms around him and squeezed.

"Zoey—can't—breathe," said Simon into Zoey's shoulder. "Seriously, you're *killing* me."

Zoey released him. "Sorry, it's just . . ." she hesitated, her heart thumping, "I thought you'd never wake up. I'm *so* happy to see you're okay."

Tristan shared a smiled with Zoey and then patted Simon on the back. "Really glad you're back with us, man. You had us really worried."

"What? And miss out on all the fun?" said Simon. "Not a chance."

He pulled himself up and rubbed his head. "I have a nasty bump on my head."

He hesitated and then asked, "Am I still . . . old? Or do I look like me again?"

Zoey saw the glint of hope in his wet blue eyes. She didn't want to disappoint him, but she couldn't lie either. "Sorry, Simon, but you still look like someone's grandfather."

Simon was silent for a moment. "Where are we? And what's up with the hooded munchkins?"

Tristan quickly explained what had happened after Simon had blacked out.

"So this is Nexus City, eh?" said Simon as he examined his surroundings. "What do you think the Chacras are going to do to us—"?

The front doors made of bones swung open.

A tall, hunched creature with long spindly legs and arms and a round torso that looked as though it was filled with air walked down the stone steps and made for the wagon. It had no visible neck, a small, flat bald head, and lopsided shoulders. It wore a white lab coat and looked at them with bulbous pink eyes. The coat was stained with burgundy and green spots, and Zoey thought she could see chunks of flesh splattered over the front and sleeves.

"That dude looks like a cross between Dr. Frankenstein and Mr. Hyde," laughed Simon.

Zoey glanced at Simon. She still felt weird that her friend's voice and face looked and sounded so old. She hoped the effect wasn't permanent.

"It's worse than that," said Tristan. He leaned back and lowered his voice. "He's an Anerak."

Zoey's throat tightened. "Those are the mystics Mrs. Dupont sold my mother to . . . the doctors."

Tristan nodded. "I wouldn't call them doctors. They're rumored to be responsible for *unethical* experiments. They call themselves doctors, but they're the worst kind of doctor *monsters.*"

When Zoey had first discovered that Mrs. Dupont had sold her mother to these experimental doctors, she did her best *not* to imagine the worse, but she couldn't help it. It was impossible *not* to visualize the atrocities in her mind, and now she could finally put a face to this evil.

As the Anerak spoke to the Chacras, its thin lips spread into an evil smile. Zoey wondered if the creature had smiled like that right before it had poked and prodded her mother. She glared at the creature in the white coat.

"What do you think they're talking about?" asked Zoey.

One of the Anerak's bulbous eyes watched her, while the other focused on the Chacras it spoke to.

Tristan leaned forward, frowning. "Probably making a trade."

"You mean *us*." Although Zoey wasn't thrilled at the idea, she still really wanted to know why the lab-coated creature looked so familiar.

And then it hit her.

The Anerak was the creature from her nightmares—the ones torturing her, performing experiments on her while she was chained to a bed. It was all coming back to her. The doctors in her nightmares weren't *human* doctors. They never were. They were Aneraks. Zoey had the horrible feeling that the girl in her dreams wasn't her at all—it was her *mother*. As the realization hit her, she knew it was the truth. Somehow, she had seen her own mother being tortured. Her stomach was in knots. She had to be alive . . . .

After a brief conversation, the Anerak dismissed the Chacras with a wave of its skeletal hand, and the Chacras waddled back towards the wagon.

"Out!" it barked and shoved Zoey. Its eyes widened at the sight of Simon sitting up, but it didn't say anything. It looked pleased.

"Okay, okay, I get it." Zoey jumped down from the wagon. She felt slightly revived after the short trip and helped Simon down.

The Chacras shoved Zoey, Simon, and Tristan up the steps. When they stood at the top of the stone steps and faced the Anerak, the creature drummed its gangly fingers together in excitement. Up close it was taller than Tristan and much, much uglier. Its pale greenish skin was covered in pimples, scabs, and oozing blisters.

"Humans!" said the Anerak in a voice that sounded like it had swallowed an accordion. "Good, good, yes, yes."

It paused for a moment, measuring Zoey. A small, triumphant smile twitched on its lips, and she had the eerie feeling it had seen her before. It was almost too pleased to see her. While one of its pink swollen eyes still focused on Zoey, the other rolled over Tristan like he was the next best thing to candy. But when it examined Simon, both of its eyes focused on him. Its thin mouth was slightly open in astonishment.

"You are *old*," it said in more of a question than a statement. It poked him repeatedly with its pencil-thin finger.

"Hey, stop that!" growled Simon and he took a step back. "I'm not a wax figure. I'm real you know. I'm *alive*."

The Anerak leaned over him, its long nose inches from his face, and sniffed. "You smell young, but you look old? Why is that?"

"It's called *aging*," grumbled Simon, as he tried to wiggle away from the creature.

"Very curious." The Anerak stood back. "Old . . . and very ugly."

"Look who's talking, stick-man," muttered Simon. He leaned away from the Anerak's curious eyes, like he was afraid they were going to jump out at him.

"No matter. We can still perform the Dream Purge."

Simon paled. "What's the Dream Purge?"

The creature ignored him, and its eerie smile widened. "I am Doctor One. You may address me as *Doctor One*."

"Is this freak for real?" chortled Simon. "I feel like I'm stuck in a really bad rerun of the Outer Limits—" He was struck in the back of the head with a spear, and he fell to his knees.

Tristan moved to defend Simon, but a gun and two spears were aimed at his head. He froze. The muscles in his face twitched, and Zoey could see his skin tingle with a little blue hue. She met his eyes and pleaded with him. She didn't want him to get hurt, and somehow she knew she needed to get inside that building, even though every inch of her was screaming *not* to.

Doctor One scratched a scab on his arm and then flicked a flaky piece away.

"Humans are very hard to come by in these parts. You are very *rare* commodities in our world and *very* expensive," said the doctor happily. "But as you stand here before me, I can see that you were

191

all worth the trouble . . . and more. My little friends have done very well today, very well indeed."

The doctor drew a small bag from the folds of its coat and tossed it to the Chacras. Their kidnapper examined the contents of the bag and seemed satisfied.

There was something odd about the way the good doctor was eyeing them, more like a mortician than a doctor.

Zoey shared a worried look with her friends. If they were going to make a run for it, now was the time.

Just as she thought about running, something cold and heavy was latched around her neck. She jumped back in surprise, but the collar tightened around her neck like a metal scarf.

"Hey! What's going on?"

She tried to pull it off, but she couldn't. Before she could react further, the Anerak seized her arms and chained her wrists together.

Zoey was stunned. What had just happened? Tristan and Simon were shackled with large metal collars around their necks just like hers, like they were dogs.

Tristan fought against his restraints. His skin shone blue, and he tried to break free desperately.

"It's pointless, Mysterian," said the doctor. "Even with your strength, you cannot break free. A word to the wise: keep your energy for later. You will need it."

The creature grinned, its pointy teeth blackened and rotten.

Zoey glared at the doctor and raised her wrists. "Why are you doing this? We haven't done anything."

Doctor One's smile sent a chill through Zoey.

"What did you expect? That we'd throw a party in your honor? You can't just waltz into our world without suffering the consequences. You agents imprison our kind when we venture into *your* world. It's the same here. There are rules. Trespassers are dealt with harshly. But it's lucky my friends found you first—"

"I don't feel very lucky," grumbled Simon. "I guess it's these chains. They're weighing down my otherwise *high* spirits."

One of the doctor's pink eyes rolled in Simon's direction. He still seemed puzzled by Simon's age.

He waved a thin, bony arm in the air. "Now, you will follow me inside in *silence*. Your *kind* is not permitted to speak. I'm anxious to begin."

Zoey frowned. "Listen, you need to know something. Both our worlds are in danger—"

The metal collar tightened around her neck immediately. She was suffocating. Black spots danced before her eyes as she tried desperately to remove the collar, but she could hardly think. She staggered and then fell to the ground. She tried to focus, but she went spinning into darkness.

CHAPTER 16

THE DOCTORS ARE IN

When Zoey regained consciousness, she was lying on the floor. She blinked at a pair of white boots with pointy toes. She looked up at Doctor One. He held a remote control.

"No more talking from now on," he said darkly. "If you don't want me to use the collar again, you will do as I say. If you speak, I will use it again and again until you start bleeding from the ears, and then I'll fry your brain like eggs in a pan. Nothing gives me more pleasure than to torture *agents*, but I would prefer to present you to my colleagues unspoiled. Do you understand, agent?"

Zoey moved her lips but no words came out. She wheezed as she tried to breathe normally again. Her throat burned like she had swallowed a gallon of bleach. Her head still throbbed and she felt a pressure in her ears like when she used to dive at the local pool.

"Just a nod will suffice. You are not permitted to speak."

She glared at the doctor and nodded.

"Good," said the doctor. "You show a degree of compliance. You'll do very well."

Tristan helped Zoey to her feet. He looked like a tiger ready to lunge for the kill. It felt amazing to be held by Tristan. If he hadn't been there with her, she didn't think she could go on. Her head felt like it had split in two.

Tristan smiled weakly and whispered. "I got you—"

"No more talking," hissed the doctor, his scabby face twisted in fury. He pointed his contraption at Tristan menacingly as though it were a gun. "I'm warning you. One more word, *Mysterian,* and I will fry your brain like fritters!"

Tristan glared at the doctor like a chained animal. If the chains were off, Zoey knew he'd tear the good doctor apart like a piñata.

Doctor One waved his contraption. "Now, I can either make this very painful for you or pain free. It's up to you. If you speak, I will use the collar on you. If you try to run, I will use the collar on you. Try anything at all—"

I will use the collar on you, mouthed Simon so only Zoey and Tristan could see.

"I will use the collar on you," finished the doctor. "Now, if you'll follow me." Doctor One walked up the steps and through the front door.

Zoey wiped her dripping nose, and when she looked at her hand, her fingers were stained with blood.

Reluctantly, Zoey, Tristan, and Simon followed Doctor One.

If the bones on the exterior were gloomy and foreboding, the interior of the building was much, much worse. Her instincts warned her not to enter.

They stepped into a vast chamber with dirt floors and bone walls. The bone cathedral building was just that—made of bones.

Centipede-like creatures as big as puppies scuttled across the ground and large cockroaches the size of rats scurried at their feet. An enormous chandelier made from bones and tiny skulls hung from the center of the chamber and cast shadows of screaming faces. Garlands of skulls and bones draped the vaulted ceiling like Halloween decorations in a haunted house. Whoever had built this place had to have been mad. It was as though they had dug up an entire cemetery and had used the bones as decoration.

Zoey could see that her friends felt the exact same way— completely flabbergasted and just a little grossed out.

"Keep up, or I'll press the button!" warned Doctor One. He led them through the main area and then into one of the many corridors.

Zoey ground her teeth but said nothing. She didn't want to feel that pain ever again.

They passed a display case of skulls and bones that looked as though someone had taken an axe or a sledgehammer to them. Doctor One mumbled to himself as they walked. Where was he leading them? She had no idea how much time had gone by but she knew time was running out. Somehow, they needed to get rid of the collars and chains. They needed a plan, and they needed it fast.

The corridor opened to another chamber with a spiral bone staircase that moved like an escalator. The doctor moved towards a door behind the staircase. Zoey was sickened to see that the door was made of flesh. It was quilted together with thick black leather thread and looked like it was made of *human* skin. To add to the horror, the handle was a human skull painted black.

"Well that's reassuring," grumbled Simon.

The doctor grabbed the skull and pushed.

Zoey knew she needed to get their collars off before they could do anything. And she knew the only way to get them off was with that remote control. She didn't want to let it out of her sight. They followed the doctor.

The room had the same dirt floor and bone walls. It was about the size of a small shop with a staircase leading up to a second level. There were no windows, and a series of single light bulbs poked out from the jaws of skulls hanging from the ceiling. Shelves stocked with dusty books and jars lined the far wall. Bottles whose contents looked disturbingly like organs in green churning liquid covered the jumble of tables in the room. If it weren't for the strong sulfur smell and the dissected bodies on the tables, it could have passed for a normal laboratory. A device like a vintage gramophone played dark music in the background.

Zoey passed a table where a human had been cut up and sewn back together badly. She looked away.

They made their way deeper into the room where two creatures in blood-stained lab coats stepped away from one of the tables.

Doctor One greeted them and said, "My colleagues, Doctor Two and Doctor Three."

They were both Aneraks like Doctor One. Doctor Two looked like he had never eaten. He had crazy spiked hair and looked like a tree in a lab coat, with branches for arms and legs. He had a mouth the size of a button and no visible nose. He regarded Zoey suspiciously with tiny pink eyes.

Doctor Three was short and had no eyes, just two small holes for a nose, and a mouth that stretched all the way back to his ears. And when he smiled, his teeth were tiny little skulls. Zoey suspected they were *not* his regular teeth.

"I have found us more humans!" Doctor One clapped his hands excitedly like he had just won the lottery.

"We'll have more live tissue samples—" He held his breath, "We can finally perform the Dream Purge!"

Zoey shared a nervous look with Tristan and Simon.

Doctor Three smiled even more widely and spoke with a lisp.

"We should do it while they're still alive!" His green tongue rolled over his skull-like teeth. "I want to see the life go out in their eyes. It's so . . . invigorating!"

Doctor Two nodded, opened his tiny mouth, and said, "Miut, mit, miut, mit."

Doctor Three smacked him on the back. "What? Speak up? We can't hear you."

The tree-like doctor frowned.

Doctor Three shrugged and then smiled happily. "Doctor Two agrees. Strap them into the Dream Purge chair, and we can begin immediately."

"Yes, of course, Doctor Three," said Doctor One.

He turned towards Zoey and smiled. "Ladies first."

He pointed to a dentist-like chair with leather restraints for the feet and arms. A metal ring with tubes and wires like a helmet was mounted just above the headrest. The chair had once been white, but now red marks stained its dirty gray upholstery.

Zoey felt sick.

"Move!" bellowed Doctor One as he threated Zoey with the remote control.

But Zoey couldn't move. She just stared at the bloody chair.

Doctor One moved to press the remote control, but Tristan charged forward and knocked him down.

"Leave her alone!" yelled Tristan through gritted teeth. "I swear, once this collar is off, I'm going to kill you—"

The rest of his threat died in his throat, and he fell to his knees. He rolled on the ground, twisting and crying out in agonizing pain.

"You shouldn't have done that."

Doctor One got to his feet and pointed his remote at Tristan. His expression changed from anger to delight at the sight of blood pouring from Tristan's nose and ears as he convulsed in pain on the ground.

"STOP!" cried Zoey. She made her way to the chair.

"I'm going—see? Please *stop*." She knew she wasn't allowed to speak, but it worked.

Doctor One released his finger on the trigger and stepped over Tristan's body.

"Get on the chair," repeated the doctor as he made his way towards her.

Tristan staggered to his feet and moved next to Simon. His face was swollen, and his nose and ears were still bleeding, but at least he was alive and standing on his own. Their eyes met, and she knew he'd give anything to trade places with her.

Simon's wet eyes said it all. He was scared. They were all scared.

Zoey stood next to the long chair. Doctor Three was waiting for her. He patted the chair invitingly. His pale, wet, and scabby skin looked like melted cheese up close. Doctor Two sat at a table behind the chair and typed on a keyboard.

Zoey managed to haul herself up onto the chair. Her heart pounded like a machine gun.

"Lie down all the way please," said Doctor Three.

He moved towards the head of the chair.

Zoey did as he asked and rested her head on the headrest. The chair reminded her of her visits to the dreaded dentist, but now she wished it *were* a dentist appointment.

The doctors didn't bother tying the restraints around her arms and legs, probably because she already wore the collar and handcuffs. And she could use that to her advantage . . . .

Click!

The heavy cold metal hat dropped around her temples, and a piercing pain that felt like a ring of needles had just punctured her skull blinded her momentarily. She reached up to touch her head, but Doctor Three slapped her hands away.

"Don't move," he barked. He moved around the chair so that Zoey could see him clearly.

"Just try to relax. It never works well when the subject is stressed—the dreams turn out to be nightmares. We *don't* want nightmares."

Zoey frowned. What was he talking about?

Doctor One shoved Tristan and Simon forward until they all stood near the edge of her chair. He waved his remote control like it was a gun. He was close now. She could almost reach the remote with the tip of her shoe—

Doctor One moved over and stood next to Doctor Three.

Zoey took a chance and spoke up, enunciating her words very quickly, "What are you going to do to me?"

Doctor Three leaned over Zoey. His face was so close that she could smell his rancid breath and could count the sores and zits on his face. Where his eyes should have been, she could only see blistered and flaky skin.

"We're going to take your dreams, of course," said the eyeless doctor eagerly.

Tristan and Simon both shrugged.

"What do you mean take my dreams? You can't *take* my dreams. It's impossible. Dreams happen when you sleep. It's a state of mind, a consciousness. It's not tangible."

She knew she was pushing it by speaking again, but the doctors didn't seem to mind now that she was already positioned for their experiment.

Doctor Three adjusted wires around Zoey's head. When he was done he licked his lips and said, "The Dream Purge is a device that *extracts* dreams." He knocked the top of Zoey's head twice, "through these mind wires."

He moved his hands along the black wires that went from Zoey's metal helmet to a rectangular basin filled with a blue fluid. "We transfer the dreams to this reservoir tank until they are ready to be extracted."

Zoey stared at the thick blue fluid. It looked more like mucus than water.

"But why do you want to do that?"

Doctor Three lost his smile. "Because the one thing we *desire* above all else in the world we Aneraks cannot have."

"And what's that?" asked Zoey.

"We cannot *dream*." Doctor Three hesitated for a moment.

"When we sleep, we experience only emptiness, a vacuum, nothing. Imagine our surprise when we experimented on our very first human—"

"We discovered dreams," interjected Doctor One. His bulbous eyes rolled around in their sockets like little whirlwinds. "Thousands of wonderful dreams."

Doctor Three picked at one of his front skull teeth, yanked it out, and tossed it on the ground.

"Why should you humans dream and not us? What makes you so special that your mind produces wonderful projections while you sleep?"

Zoey wasn't sure if she should answer, so she didn't.

"We purged our first human dreams centuries ago," continued the eyeless doctor. "It was the most glorious feeling, finally to dream! A door of endless possibilities opened to us. Once we'd glimpsed what it was to dream, we needed to have it. We needed to dream again."

He shuffled over to Zoey's dream-helmet and began adjusting latches and wires.

"And now we're going to take your dreams, agent girl. We're going to take *all* your dreams. Yours *and* your friends."

These doctors were completely and utterly *mad*. Whatever this thing was, this dream purge, Zoey knew she wouldn't survive. These mad scientists were going to lobotomize her if they started rummaging around in her brain.

"With *three* new brains, we'll have enough dreams to last us for years," said Doctor One, leering at Tristan and Simon.

"The dreams of children are much more potent, innocent, and filled with ingenuity, imagination, and creativity. They are the source of dreams. This is a *dream* come true."

He laughed at his own joke. Even Doctor Two joined in with a mousy kind of laugh that made Zoey want to punch him in the face.

"What happens after you take our dreams?" Zoey tried to pull her head away as Doctor Three's stained lab coat brushed her face.

"You die, of course," answered Doctor One. "But don't worry, we don't waste *any* parts. You'll be glad to know that your skin and bones will be added to our wall collection. Your organs, and especially your brain, will be used to test our new meta-creation theory."

Zoey didn't want to know about their new psychotic theories, she just wanted out of the chair. If only Doctor One could move a little closer, she could reach the remote with her foot and maybe kick it over to Tristan. But he was too far away. She couldn't reach him . . . .

"Power it up!" Doctor Three backed away. Even though he didn't have eyes, Zoey could tell he was thoroughly excited. He licked his lips eagerly like a snake smelling the air.

Doctor Two reached over to a large metal box and flicked a switch.

"Ut, wut, vit!" he called.

The lights flickered and a loud humming resonated through the chamber like the droning of a giant refrigerator.

"NO!" screamed Zoey. "STOP! Please, don't do this!"

She bucked like a wild horse, but Doctor Three pressed her legs down hard. His smile made her want to scream even louder. She tried to move her legs but she couldn't. The doctor had the strength of five men.

"Our worlds are collapsing," she cried desperately. "Haven't you noticed? They can't survive a permanent portal. We have to shut the portals down, or we'll all die!"

Doctor Three laughed. "Shut the portals down? Now why would we want to do that, silly agent girl? We are *grateful* to Mrs. Dupont for being clever enough to generate the Great Junction. Because of her, we now have an *endless* supply of humans. An endless supply of dreams!"

Zoey blinked the sweat from her eyes. "You can't dream if you're *dead*. I'll telling you the *truth*. It's why we're here. We need to shut the portals! Both our worlds will be destroyed if we don't."

"Fiddles and sticks." Doctor One dismissed her with a wave of his hand.

"It's not like we haven't heard *that* one before—the end of the world, blah, blah, blah . . . ."

He laughed a sick wet laugh.

"The True Eye cult have been preaching the end of the world for years. But they just try to scare us so that we will obey them," continued Doctor One.

He looked at Tristan and Simon with a sinister smile on his scabby face. "Fear can make us do anything."

Zoey caught Tristan's eye. He looked green. Simon was more of a purple shade. He looked like he was about to have a heart attack. She was not persuasive enough. The doctors didn't believe her.

Doctor One and Doctor Three exchanged a dark look, and then Doctor One yelled, "Activate the Dream Purge sequence!"

Zoey stopped breathing.

"Tat, sot, ich!" called Doctor Two. He leaned over his keyboard, and with a long, spindly finger he pressed down on a single key.

The lights flicked. The skulls in the lighting fixture seemed to move. The humming got louder and louder. From the corner of her eye Zoey saw small blue and red flashes of electricity move slowly from the tank to her head.

She tried to move her head, but the metal helmet dug into her skull. What would happen when the energy reached her?

Flashes of Tristan appeared in her mind's eye.

She thought of her mother.

She had failed everyone . . . .

The terror of what was about to happen overwhelmed her. She watched helplessly as a surge of electricity danced around her head like a ring of blue and red light.

It was over.

Just as she was about to close her eyes, Tristan charged forward.

Doctor One raised the remote—

CRACK!

The power went off.

CHAPTER 17

LOCKED UP

Darkness.

Zoey let out a shaky breath. Had she only just imagined it, or did their precious machine malfunction?

She blinked repeatedly, trying to adjust her eyes to the new darkness. She could hear sizzling and smell burnt rubber. It was just like the smell when one of the computers back at the Hive had overheated and then fried. Then she heard the click, click, click of boney fingers hitting a keyboard.

She smiled.

"You idiot! What did you do?" bellowed Doctor Three.

He let go of Zoey's legs. She could hear his feet shuffle across the ground, and then the sound of a fist hitting something hard.

"Did you connect the wires properly? Did you check the trans-cranial direct current stimulation before plugging it into the tank? Why is this always happening? Do I have to do everything myself!"

"Miet, nut, tah tah," the voice of Doctor Two growled in the dark. Even though Zoey couldn't understand him, she knew just by his tone that he was angry, too. He clearly didn't appreciate being blamed for whatever had happened.

Someone snorted, and she recognized Simon.

There was some more banging, and then something fell to the floor.

"There was a surcharge of energy from the fuse box," said Doctor One. "It's fixable, but it'll take some time, a few hours at least."

As her eyes finally adjusted, Zoey could make out the moving silhouettes of three white lab coats fidgeting with the tank to her right. She could see Simon's white teeth smiling, as though he had used a glow-in-the-dark toothpaste. Although Tristan's face was lost in shadow, the whites of his eyes were on her, and they were smiling, too.

"*Losers,*" whispered Simon. Zoey stifled a laugh.

Click.

The lights came back, and Zoey blinked away the white spots from her eyes.

The three Anerak doctors where huddled together by the tank with confused expressions on their flaky and diseased faces.

Doctor Three looked up and then shuffled towards Zoey. He flicked a lever on the wired helmet, and she immediately felt a sting as the pins that had pierced her skull retracted. The doctor removed the helmet and placed it gently on a table nearby.

Zoey stretched her head and neck.

"It's unfortunate we lost power," said Doctor Three. "And it pains me that we are left without your dreams. But it's just a temporary glitch. We'll have the Dream Purge up and functioning again in no time at all."

"Great," mumbled Simon.

Doctor One charged towards Simon, and pointed the remote at his face like a blade. "Did I hear you say something, old man?"

One of his eyes was on Simon, while the other twitched and focused on Tristan.

Simon pressed his lips into a thin line and shook his head.

The mad-eyed doctor made a face. Yellow liquid trickled down from his nose and onto his lab coat. "I'll take these three to the holding cells with the others."

Others? Zoey cringed at the thought of brainless, starved, and mutilated souls, kept alive only to aid in the mad scientists' experiments.

"Fine," muttered Doctor Three. "Give them some Seeder milk. We need them *relaxed* if we want good dreams. The last human gave us horrible nightmares. I don't want to experience that again. Yes, it's better that they rest."

Doctor One grabbed Zoey roughly by the arm, yanked her off the bed, and then shoved her into Simon and Tristan.

"Follow me this way," he said and pointed towards the door with the remote. "And no talking if you still want the use of your brains."

Zoey glanced back. Doctor Two and Doctor Three stood beside a large cauldron she hadn't noticed before. They were examining what looked like a boiled tibia bone.

They followed Doctor One down the corridor in silence. He stopped before an old oak door with a small opening at the top. He pulled a key from his front coat pocket, and the door screeched loudly as he pulled it open.

"In!" ordered the doctor.

Zoey stepped in first.

She was in a small jailhouse with individual cells separated only by metal bars. The hot stale air smelled of decay and waste, and other things Zoey didn't want to think about. A single light bulb hung from the ceiling on a stringy wire and cast long shadows. It was nearly impossible to see clearly.

They followed the doctor down the small path between the two walls of cells. A bundle lay at the back of the first cell. When Zoey got close enough, she saw that it was a man. He was lying on his back and staring blankly up at the ceiling. Even in the dim light she could see nasty lacerations where his mouth had been sewn shut with thick black thread. His head had been shaved, and a ring of red, angry blisters from the Dream Purge helmet peppered his scalp.

Uncontrollable hatred rose in the pit of Zoey's stomach. She hated the doctors even more than Mrs. Dupont.

The cell next to the unconscious man was empty, but the cell opposite was occupied. A woman whose eyes and mouth had been sewn shut lay in a fetal position in a wet puddle on the floor. Her shaved head was bruised and bleeding from puncture wounds, too.

Zoey's tears cooled her hot cheeks. Were these people from her own world? Had they accidently stepped through a portal? Her knees wobbled, and she struggled to keep from falling.

Another form lay against the far wall in the next cell, but Zoey couldn't see the face or tell if it was alive or dead. When she looked at her friends' faces they were grim and angry.

Doctor One led them to the only cell without a decaying body in it.

"This is your new home," he said as he unlocked the door and pulled it open. "I trust you'll find it comfortable enough. Get in."

Zoey, Tristan, and Simon stepped inside without uttering a word. The doctor locked the door.

"I'll be back later with some Seeder milk," he said.

His face twisted into a smile. "But don't get too comfortable. You won't be alive long enough to enjoy your new home."

His throaty wet laughter made Zoey want to throw up. He turned on his heels, clicked the lock closed, and left the chamber.

"Is it safe to talk now?" whispered Simon.

Zoey sighed and did her best to ignore the smell. "I think so—"

"Good," said Simon, and he let out a string of curse words.

"Feel better?" Tristan inspected the small cell closely.

"Yes," answered Simon. "But I'd feel a lot better with a Big Mac in my belly. If that dream machine doesn't kill me, I'm seriously going to starve to death."

"Trust me," said Zoey as she tried to pull open their cell's door, "dying of starvation would be a heck of a lot better than what's waiting for us if we don't break out of here soon. I don't even want to know what that milk is—sounds disgusting."

Her eyes moved to the decomposed and mutilated bodies in the other cells, and she imagined their screams and cries.

"Did the spell wear off yet?" asked Simon hopefully, and then his face fell. "My voice still sounds old, so I guess I'm still a senior citizen. Great."

Zoey raised her hands awkwardly, careful not to hit Simon's face with her chains. She rested them on his shoulder.

"Sorry, Simon. I wish I had better news. But look on the bright side, we're all still alive."

"Yeah, but for how long?" Tristan walked over to her and raised his wrists.

"If only we could get these collars and shackles off, we'd have a chance. I can't fight with this thing around my neck. We're like chained animals."

"I know. We need to get them off, but how and with what?"

Zoey wrinkled her nose. "It's hard to concentrate with the dead bodies and the smell—"

"Actually that was me," said Simon with a sheepish smile. "What? I'm a senior citizen remember? I can't control my bodily functions."

Tristan shoved Simon playfully, and Zoey was glad he was feeling better.

"Simon, can you reach your phone?"

Simon wiggled his shoulders until he was able to reach his front pocket and retrieve his phone.

"How much time do we have left?" asked Tristan.

Simon glanced at the phone. "We've got about two hours left. It's not much, but if we can get out of this sewage prison, we still have enough time to find the UECs and blow the portals."

"Simon, is there a light on your phone?" Zoey had an idea.

"Yeah . . . ."

"Is it really, *really* bright? Like *blinding* bright?"

"Of course it's bright. It's an LCD light. It's *uber*-bright."

Tristan smiled. "Zoey? What are you planning?"

Zoey looked at her friends.

"Well, I was thinking—the remote that controls the collars, the one that Doctor One has with him all the time, since it powers the collars *on and off*, it would make sense that there'd be a button on that thing that would *remove* the collars and *these*," she said and raised her shackles.

Simon tried to whistle, but it came out sounding like a cat's meow.

"Good plan. Just one problem, how do we get our hands on the remote? I mean, I don't want to be the bearer of bad news, but you said it. He has it *on* him all the time. How can we even reach it if we can't even move our hands?"

213

"He's right," said Tristan. "The moment we *move* and try something, he'll activate the collars again."

He wiped the sweat from his brow with his arm. "I thought I was going to die earlier. I've never felt pain like that before."

"We're going to blind him with Simon's phone," said Zoey.

"We'll have to be fast. We have to surprise him, and in that nanosecond we can grab the remote. We know he's coming back soon, so we better get ready. We've only got *one* shot at this, so we need to make it count."

"So . . . I'll blind him while—"

"I'll get the remote," said Tristan.

Zoey had a feeling that the remote was not the only thing he wanted to *get*.

"Right," said Zoey. "And *I'll* distract him."

Simon jumped on the spot. "Good plan, Zoey St. John."

He rubbed his hands together. "Man, it might actually *work*."

Zoey knew her plan was farfetched. So many things could go wrong. And if by a miracle they did escape, how would they ever find Director Martin? What could they accomplish without the UEC?

Zoey exhaled deeply and made fists with her hands. "It's *going* to work, it has to—"

"Zoey?" A low voice came from behind her.

Zoey's blood froze.

She searched her friends' faces, but *they* hadn't uttered her name. Very slowly, Zoey turned towards the sound of the voice.

The bundle that Zoey had thought was dead was standing and facing them. It was impossible to see it clearly in the shadows. The figure stood still and did not move.

Zoey inched towards the figure. She couldn't explain why, but she wasn't afraid. Something inside told her that it wouldn't harm her. The slight build and soft voice was female. But who was she?

"Who are you? And how do you know my name?" demanded Zoey.

The woman took a careful step forward, and a shard of light spilled onto her face—

It was like staring in a mirror. Zoey was looking into her *own* face.

CHAPTER 18

REUNITED

Zoey gasped and staggered back. Her knees weakened, and she couldn't breathe.

Tristan grabbed her and steadied her.

"Zoey? What is it? Do you know this person?"

The woman stepped closer. Now her face was fully visible between the metal bars. Her head was completely shaved except for a few bright red strands that fell below the ring of bloody, red puncture marks. Her thin, frail, and hollow face still held traces of beauty, and her large green eyes were alert and mesmerizing like precious jewels. Her filthy clothes hung loosely over her thin body like she hadn't eaten in months. She was clearly weeping at the sight of Zoey. She didn't look at anyone else, just her.

Zoey couldn't look away from the woman in the next cell either. It was the face in her dreams, the face on the photograph.

"Zoey? Who *is* that?" asked Tristan again.

"I know who she is," said Simon finally. "It's her. It's Zoey's mom."

Elizabeth glanced briefly at Simon and Tristan, and then her eyes settled on her daughter again.

"My beautiful girl. I never thought I'd ever see you again. The last time I saw you, you were just a little girl staying with the Turner foster family. Now look at you. You've grown so tall. You're a young woman now."

Simon and Tristan both looked at Zoey, waiting for her to respond. Her lips moved, but no words would come. When she had played out this scene in her head—when she had imagined meeting her mother—she had hugged her mother and kissed her. She had told her all about her abilities and her friends. She hadn't been a scared little kitten like she was now. It was almost as though she would break the spell or lift the veil from the dream if she moved.

Sensing the awkwardness, Simon stuck out his hand through the bars.

"Simon Brown at your service, Zoey's mother," he said proudly.

Elizabeth shook Simon's hand and smiled. "Please, call me Elizabeth."

Her voice was soft and kind, as if she hadn't spent months being abused like a lab rat by the mad doctors.

But still Zoey couldn't move.

Tristan let go of Zoey gently.

"I'm Tristan Price, Zoey's—" he hesitated, "—friend."

He stared at his feet.

And still Zoey didn't utter a word or move.

Her mother watched her daughter lovingly. Warily, she reached a shaking hand through the bars. "Zoey? Come here."

It was like someone had cut down her bonds. Finally, Zoey could move. With her heart thundering against her ribcage, she leaped forward and grabbed her mother's ice-cold hands.

The effect was instantaneous. Tears spilled down her cheeks as she took in a shaky breath. She slipped her hands through her mother's fingers and squeezed. She desperately wanted to reach out and hug her, but the shackles around her wrists prevented her.

Simon and Tristan backed away, giving them their private moment together.

After a few moments, Elizabeth let go of her daughter and frowned.

"Zoey, what are you *doing* here? Didn't you get my message from my friend Muttab?"

Zoey looked into her mother's eyes. "Yes I did."

Her mother's face fell. "So the Agency found you, and you decided to stay, even though you knew your life was in danger."

Zoey stared quietly into her mother's face. The same dreaded collar was wrapped around her mother's neck, just like hers. And when she spoke next she avoided her mother's eyes.

"I had to. I wasn't willing to give it up." She looked up and met her mother's eyes again. "You don't understand. You don't know what it's like to grow up feeling that you're a freak. I didn't have any friends. I had no one to talk to. When the Agency found me, it was like . . . it was like I was finally home."

Tears trickled down her mother's face. "I understand, Zoey. I know it was a lot to ask, and I know how angry and confused you must feel right now, but please know I did it only to *protect* you. I had to hide you from the Agency, from the double agents and those working for Mrs. Dupont. If they had found out who you were and discovered your abilities, they would have used you and then killed you. It was the only way to keep you safe."

"I know," said Zoey. "But they still used me—"

"What?" Elizabeth's eyes grew fierce. "What do you mean?"

"The lovely Mrs. Dupont used me. She used me to set in motion the Great Junction. I tried to stop her, but I couldn't. And now we face the end of the world because of me."

Her mother pressed a hand on Zoey's shoulder.

"Not because of you, but because of her." She hesitated. "I knew something must have happened when she sold me off to the Aneraks. So she took you instead. She knew you were much more powerful than I ever was. She's been obsessing about the Great Junction for years. I was a disappointment. She could never open it with me."

Zoey glanced back at her friends. "And now we're here to try to destroy the portals."

"How?" asked her mother.

"With bombs," answered Tristan. "UECs given to us by our science officer. He got hurt, so he had to stay back at the Hive."

"So it's just us," added Simon happily.

Elizabeth studied Simon for a moment. "Aren't you a little old to still be in service, Mr. Brown? I'm sure they agency could have found someone else to assist Zoey and her friend Tristan."

Simon's jaw dropped. "Oh my God, she thinks I'm an old geezer! But I'm not old! I'll be fifteen in two months!"

He lowered his voice when he realized he was yelling. "This royally sucks!" he whispered.

Zoey quickly explained how Simon had ingested the potion Muttab had given them. Her mother stared at Simon but didn't say anything. Zoey wasn't sure if that was a good thing or a bad one.

Tristan pulled at his collar. His frustration increased with every new try.

"Urgh! If I don't get this collar off soon, I think . . . I don't know what I'm going to do. I think I'm going to go *crazy!*"

"We're going to get them off," said Zoey with more determination than she felt. "And then we're going after Director Martin."

"There's an agency director to help us?" questioned Elizabeth. "Is he somewhere near?"

The smile on her mother's face pained Zoey. She shared a look with her friends.

"Not exactly. He's a traitor. He stole our bag with the UECs in it. We need to find him and get the bag back."

Elizabeth measured her daughter and her friends. "Are you sure about that? Are you *positive* it was him?"

"We're sure," said the three teens in unison.

"Well, I'm very sorry you all got involved in this mess."

She wrapped her hands around the metal bars, and Zoey noticed the dried blood and scars on her mother's hands.

Zoey wrapped her fingers over them. "We're going to get you out. I promise."

Elizabeth gave her a weak smile. "The Aneraks are dangerous and mad. I've seen horrible things, things that should only exist in nightmares."

Tears spilled down her mother's cheeks. "I've been a part of their experiments for months. No one has ever escaped. They're all dead. They're not about to let us go—"

"That's right, *human*," said a voice behind them.

Before Zoey could even turn around, her collar slammed her against the wall and pinned her there. It was like the collar had been magnetized. She howled in pain and kicked her legs desperately, but the invisible force wouldn't let go. Her feet dangled in the air like she was a puppet on a string. The cold metal around her neck burned hot as it squeezed tighter. She tried to scream, but her mouth wouldn't move. She couldn't even swallow.

She could see that Simon and Tristan were pinned on the wall next to her, struggling with the collars, their mouths open in silent screams, and their eyes wide in absolute terror.

Zoey tried to focus. A shadow moved in front of her eyes.

"Don't waste your time thinking up of a plan to escape, agents." Doctor One laughed as he pointed his metal remote at them.

"There is no escaping. What you have is too precious. We want your dreams. And we will *have* them."

He unlocked the door to the cell and stepped through. He carried a bottle of white liquid, and Zoey knew it wasn't milk.

"Leave them alone!"

Zoey she could see that her mother was pinned against the wall in her cell, too.

"Use me! Take my dreams and let them go," Elizabeth pleaded between great gasps of breath.

Doctor One wrinkled his diseased face into a smile. "Of course we will still use your dreams, silly human."

He crossed the cell and examined the three teens. "But we will have theirs as well."

He stood next to Zoey and raised the bottle to her lips. "Drink this, and the pain will stop. I promise."

Zoey blinked the tears from her eyes and gagged at his vinegar-like breath.

"Don't drink it!" screeched Elizabeth.

Her face turned a deep shade of burgundy. "It's a sedative. It'll drug you."

She gasped for breath. "Don't do it."

"Don't listen to that vile human," purred the doctor.

He tipped the bottle into her mouth. "Drink, and you and your friends will live. I promise."

The doctor's wet, pink eyes whirled in their sockets making Zoey dizzy.

"No, Zoey, don't drink it," pleaded her mother with her last breath. "He's lying."

But Zoey opened her mouth.

The doctor smiled as he poured some of the white substance down her throat.

Zoey swished it around in her mouth, on her tongue, and around her teeth. It tasted like strong cough syrup and burned the inside of her cheeks and gums.

Doctor One inched closer to make sure she had swallowed it. His ugly, twisted smile widened as he got nearer—and then she spit her mouthful into his face.

The doctor cursed and staggered back in surprise. The bottle slipped from his hand and crashed to the ground, spilling the contents.

"Simon! Now!" screamed Zoey. She spit again and again, trying to get the taste out of her mouth.

Simon reached into his pocket with trembling sweaty hands, pulled out his cell phone, and dropped it.

CHAPTER 19

TRAPPED

Zoey gasped at the phone on the ground. Their last hope was fading away like a dream.

Simon let out a tiny cry. "It's not my fault! It's these old hands! I've got arthritis. It slipped."

Doctor One's face twisted in a frightening smile, like the smile a serial killer gives before he kills. He bent over and grabbed the phone. Twisting it in his hand, he examined it.

"Now, what kind of contraption is this? Is this one of the image players?" He looked at Simon. "One of the other humans had one with him. It was a delight to watch, but it won't play anymore."

He shook the phone and frowned. "Tell me, old man, how does this device work?"

Simon's face was a nasty shade of purple, and his eyes bugged out of his head like they were about to pop.

"I'll show you," he gasped. "But you'll have to release the collar," he struggled to inhale. "Can't—breathe."

Doctor One studied him for a moment, and then he pressed a button on his remote.

Simon fell to the ground.

"Okay. Now show me, old man," ordered the doctor.

Simon staggered to his feet. He glanced quickly at Zoey and Tristan, and then he faced the doctor. "You have to hold it really close to your face. That's it. Now hold it there. Good, now—"

"I still don't see anything," grumbled the doctor. "You better not try to fool me, human. I will kill your friends if this is a trick."

Simon raised his hands and did the peace sign. "I'm not. I *swear*, Agent's honor."

Doctor One glanced at him distastefully but kept the phone near his face, admiring it like a new toy.

Zoey glanced over to Tristan, and he gave her an *I don't know what he's doing* look.

She looked at her mother. Her face had gone a gray color, and she could hardly keep her eyes open. Whatever Simon was planning on doing, he needed to do it fast.

"So, what now?" pressed the doctor, his lips curled. "How do I make it work?"

Simon swallowed hard. "Yes, that's it. Hold it *really* close to your face, yeah, near your eyes—exactly. Perfect, that's how it works. Now, see that tiny button on the left side? Yes, that one. You just need to press it—"

A piercing white light blasted out of the cell phone directly into the doctor's eyes.

"AHH!" he bellowed. "I'm blind! I can't see! You've blinded me!"

He staggered around, rubbing his eyes, ranting and raving, howling like a wounded animal. "I'm going to kill you all!"

Simon didn't waste any time.

He kicked the doctor hard in the chest. The Anerak reeled backwards and landed spread eagle on the ground. The remote fell from his grip.

Simon leaped over and picked up the remote. He fumbled with it in his hands.

"Simon—hurry," hissed Zoey. She didn't think she'd be conscious for much longer. She could hardly keep her eyes open.

"I'm trying. I'm trying." Simon hurriedly flipped the remote in his hand and ran his fingers over the metal.

"Simon!" yelled Tristan, "What are you waiting for? Do it! Do it now, or we're all going to die."

"If it were written in *English*, I'd know what to press," answered Simon in a panic.

As Zoey began to slip into the darkness, she heard Simon call out, "I think I got it!"

Her collar released, and she fell to the ground next to Tristan. She could see her mother lying on the floor in the next cell. She wasn't moving.

"Mom!" Zoey shook the bars on her cell. "Mom, can you hear me?"

She knew her mother was already weak from the experiments she had endured. Maybe this had been too much for her frail body.

As Zoey's bottom lip trembled, her mother turned towards her.

"I'm fine," said Elizabeth.

She tried to look brave, but she looked grim and sick. Zoey knew another violent blow would finish her. She had to get her mother out of here, out of the Nexus.

Zoey stiffened and blinked back the tears. She staggered to her feet.

Tristan leaned over Doctor One, his face was as angry as Zoey had ever seen it.

"How do we take the collars and the shackles off?" he demanded.

The doctor squirmed on the ground. "You will die for this, humans! I will kill you—"

Tristan's boot crashed into the doctor's abdomen. "If you don't tell me soon, you're the one who's going to die!"

The doctor spit the blood from his mouth and smiled. "I'm going to enjoy seeing you die, *Mysterian*."

Just as Tristan was about to stomp on the doctor, Zoey pulled him away. "You better tell us, Doctor One, or Tristan *will* kill you. I'm sure about that."

The doctor scowled at them. "Even if you do leave here, you will not survive in the Nexus. Our kind do not take three young humans roaming around in our city lightly. We will kill you."

"We'll take our chances," said Zoey. She loomed over the doctor. "Tell us! Or I swear *this* face is the last one you'll ever see!"

Tristan raised his boot—

The doctor shrieked. "Enough! I will tell you." He cowered as Tristan lowered his boot.

"Go on then." Zoey turned around. Her mother sat with her back against the wall, watching them.

Doctor One's bulbous eyes fixed on Simon. "The release lever is the green triangular button on the controls."

Simon looked up at his friends with a *do we trust this dude* look on his face. But he pressed the green button anyway—

CLICK!

His collar and shackles broke apart and fell at his feet.

"Sweet." He rushed over to Tristan, pointed the remote and pressed the green button again. Tristan's collar and restraints fell to the ground. Smiling, Simon did the same for Zoey and then leaped over to Elizabeth's cell and released her from her collar.

"Thank you," she said weakly.

Zoey glared at the doctor on the ground. Kneeling beside him, she searched his pockets and drew a set of keys. She grabbed her collar from off the ground and moved towards him.

"What are you doing?" squealed the doctor. He tried to back away, but Tristan pressed down on his chest with his boot.

"Giving you a taste of your own *medicine*, doctor."

With a click, Zoey secured the collar around the doctor's neck. Then she bound his wrists together with the metal shackles.

"There, all done. See? You didn't even feel a thing."

Doctor One grimaced as he tried to pull off his metal collar. "You're going to *pay* for this! I'll see to it personally that you all die a slow and painful death—"

"Not if you die first, scumbag," said Simon. He pocketed his cell phone and the remote. He looked at his friends. "What? Might come in handy later."

Just as the doctor tried to yell for help, Zoey hit him in the neck, and he gagged. She didn't feel any remorse for the Anerak. He had tortured her *mother*.

"Stay down and be quiet," she growled. "Good doctor."

Zoey waited for Tristan and Simon to exit the cell and then she locked the door behind them.

Doctor One squirmed and cursed. Blood and spit flew from his mouth, and his rolling eyes made him look like a massive and ugly iguana.

Then she hurried over to her mother's cell. After trying three different keys and kicking the door, she finally heard a satisfying *click* and pulled it open. She ran over to her mother and hugged her for real this time.

She pulled away and helped her mother to her feet.

"Can you walk?" As Zoey said the words, her own legs felt liquid, and she wondered if they'd support her weight.

"Yes," answered Elizabeth. Zoey could see more purple bruises near her temples, and an angry red and purple bruise around her neck.

"I'll run if it means getting out of here," her mother smiled.

Zoey slipped off her backpack and pulled out the second to last water bottle. "Here, drink this. You need it."

Her mother drank half the bottle and then gave it back. "Keep the rest for later. I have a feeling we'll all need it."

Zoey swung her backpack back onto her shoulders and turned to her friends. "Let's get out of here before the other doctors start wondering what happened."

As they made their way out the chamber door, Simon turned around and smiled at Doctor One. "Can you smell that?"

The doctor looked perplexed. "What? What smell?"

"That's the sweet smell of revenge, my friend." Simon smiled, "Later loser."

Zoey shut the chamber door behind them, and together they made their way down the corridor and past the spiraling bone staircase.

They met no one. The dirt floor muffled their steps like a thick carpet.

As they passed the flesh-door of the doctors' experiment chamber, she heard Doctor Three's voice. "Why do you suppose it's taking so long for Doctor One to bring us one of the humans?"

Silence, and then, "Tut, zag, heim," answered Doctor Two.

There was a pause, as though the doctors were pondering their options.

"You stay here and I'll go fetch him," said Doctor Three.

Zoey froze. They all halted in the middle of the chamber like deer caught in headlights. If the doctors came out now, they'd be found. She heard the shuffling of feet coming from behind the door.

"Behind the staircase!" whispered Zoey and pulled her mother with her.

The door swung open.

They crouched behind the staircase, and Zoey knocked her head on one of the bones. The sound resonated, and she prayed the doctor hadn't heard it or *seen* them. Holding her breath, she raised her head carefully and peered through a gap in the bone railing.

Doctor Three stood at the threshold of the door. His eyeless face angled slightly, as though he was trying to hear something. His large elongated mouth twitched. His green tongue flicked like a snake tasting the air. Finally, with a swing of his long coat, he scurried out the door and disappeared down the dark corridor.

Zoey let out her breath and whispered. "Hurry, before he comes back."

In silence, the group left the staircase and made their way down the last corridor to the front door.

Just as Zoey reached out towards the skull handle, Tristan stepped forward and grabbed her arm. "Wait," he said as he let her go. "Where are we going?"

She turned to her mother. "Do you know your way around the city?"

Elizabeth shook her head. "No, I was blindfolded when they brought me. I've been in this place ever since."

"Zoey, we're not going to find the Director," said Tristan. "We don't have any weapons. Our only hope is to sneak out of the city and make our way back to the portal. Our scientists have probably made more UECs by now. For all we know, there are agents already putting them in place."

"But what if they aren't?" said Zoey. "What if you're wrong, and our only hope is in that bag?"

Zoey knew her mother was weak and wouldn't be able to search around the city for a man they might never find. She might die. Zoey knew she had to decide.

"We can't stay here," said Tristan gently. "Your mom needs help."

"I'm fine," dismissed Elizabeth. "Don't worry about me. If you need to search the city, then we search the city."

Zoey knew what she needed to do.

"No, he's right, mom." The word *mom* felt strange on her lips, but it made her mother smile. "We'll never find the director. The city's too big, but we still have enough time to make it back to the portal."

"And hopefully we won't meet any of the Chacras again," noted Simon.

"Or anything worse," added Tristan.

Zoey glanced back towards the corridor. "Okay, so how do we sneak out of the city? Any great ideas?"

"I have one," said Tristan. His skin started to shine as though it were painted with glowing sapphires.

Elizabeth's eyes widened. "You three are full of surprises," she laughed.

Tristan smiled at Zoey. "I'm the only mystic here—"

"*Half* mystic," corrected Simon.

Tristan ignored Simon and withdrew the chained shackles from his jacket.

"Wrap these around your wrists without locking them. You'll be my prisoners. Stay behind me in a single file and keep your heads down. With a little luck, we'll be out of the city in less than forty minutes."

"Handsome and smart, the dude's got it all. Life's not fair."

Simon whispered, "Seriously, good plan man."

Zoey wanted to kiss him. He was the most beautiful creature she'd ever seen.

"It's genius," she said.

They wrapped the chains around their wrists, stepped behind Tristan in single file, and walked through the door.

The street was crowded with every mystic from *The Mystic Manual*. Beasts, half-man beasts, and giant insects turned and watched as they followed Tristan. For a horrible moment, Zoey feared their great plan had failed, but the mystics ignored them. They were nothing more than prisoners on a regular transport.

Tristan did his best to retrace their route, venturing deeper and deeper into the city. The air was hot, and smelled of sulfur, burning wood, and oil. Zoey peered around without raising her eyes. The mystics didn't give them a second look. One look at Tristan, and the rest was history. His stride was confident, and he had a mean look in his eye. It was working.

After a half hour of wandering through the city, Zoey started to feel more at ease. She raised her head slightly and looked straight ahead. In the distance she could see that the imposing Sphinx-like statues that towered over the entrance to the city lay about a hundred yards away. She smiled. They were going to make it—

"HUMANS!" cried a voice from the crowd. "Imposters! Don't let them get away!"

Simon slowed down, hesitated, and nearly stopped.

"Keep moving," hissed Tristan from the side of his mouth. "If we stop now—we die!"

He marched on without turning back. The others followed quickly behind him. Blood pounded in Zoey's ears, and sweat trickled down her face and back. Her mother was struggling to keep up. If they had to stop and fight, the outcome would be grim. They had no weapons and her mother was too weak to help. She forced the panic from her mind and ignored the voice that kept whispering that they were doomed.

"There! Stop them! Stop the humans!"

Tristan stopped abruptly. Simon crashed into him. Elizabeth gave Zoey a worried look.

"Thought you could get away, eh? Well, well, well, you were *wrong*, humans!"

Even before she saw him, Zoey recognized that eerie, harmonica-like voice. She looked up.

Doctor One stood in front of a crowd of mystics and pointed a long scab-covered finger at them.

"You're going to pay dearly for this."

Everyone on the street backed away from them, as though Zoey and her friends were contagious, no doubt from something the good doctor had given them.

"This is bad, isn't it?" whispered Simon.

Zoey stood protectively in front of her mother.

A group of black helmeted mystics with long sharp swords stood beside Doctor One. Even with their faces hidden in shadow, Zoey could see their tusks and long angry snouts. They looked like a cross between a man and a wild boar.

Doctor One beat the air with his gangly limbs. "Keepers! Arrest them!" Arrest those humans, and take them back to my lab!"

The keepers moved swiftly and surrounded Zoey and her friends. They drew their swords and then advanced—

"STOP!"

A tall woman dressed in a skin-tight baby-blue leather pant outfit pushed her way through the ring of Keepers.

Even in this land of strange and unsettling creatures, the woman's face was still the most disturbing Zoey had ever seen. She would never forget it. It was a face of horrors, of too many plastic surgeries gone wrong—the face of a cat. Her slick white hair only magnified her disproportionately large cheekbones and tiny nose.

The woman's smile was contorted by her bulbous red lips.

Mrs. Dupont held out her arms and said, "And so we meet again, Zoey St. John."

CHAPTER 20

LORD GIGOR

Mrs. Dupont's smile widened as she approached. Her small black eyes sparkled meanly like she was about to play a cruel joke.

A flash of red caught Zoey's eyes. A dozen Alphas in red uniforms pushed their way through the crowd and formed a protective barrier around their mistress, like soldiers making way for their queen. A tall, strong-looking man stayed close at her side, like a personal bodyguard. He surveyed the crowd intensely, almost fearful. His single white eye twitched nervously, as though he wasn't excited to be here, like he *didn't* want to be here. His hand rested on the gun holstered at his waist.

"What's wrong? Nothing to say?" teased Mrs. Dupont as she stopped in front of Zoey.

"You usually have lots to say, my dearest Zoey. Are you feeling all right? Are you sick? Are you ill? You don't look ill, but I can't say the same for your mother. Oh, dear, she has seen better days. How are you, Elizabeth dear? Enjoying your new home with the Aneraks?"

"Leave her alone," said Zoey angrily. The woman's repulsive face made it even harder *not* to hate her. It was inevitable. Zoey's hatred for her had grown like an infection, consuming her soul. She wanted Mrs. Dupont dead. Not just because of what she had done to her and to her mother, but because of what she had done to the relationship between them. She'd grown up alone and disconnected from her mother because of this vile woman.

Mrs. Dupont's smile grew wider at the distress on Zoey's face.

"What's the matter? Did I say something wrong? Did I say something to *upset* you? Oh, dear, I do apologize."

She laughed a hair-raising, sick laugh.

Zoey leaned forward slightly. She wanted to reach out and strangle her with her bare hands. She knew it was a barbaric reaction and she would probably get killed for it, but she couldn't control herself. But just as she raised her hands, she saw something that made her stop.

Nazar was staring at Elizabeth with the strangest look on his face, like he had just suffered a great loss. A shadow in his face revealed that he was troubled by the state of her. But why? Why would Mrs. Dupont's rightwing man feel anything at all for her mother? Didn't he put her here as well?

Elizabeth only glared at Mrs. Dupont, her hands in trembling fists. Zoey squeezed her mother's hand and flinched at the ice-cold feel of her skin.

"What do you want from us?" said Zoey angrily. "You already have your *precious* Great Junction. Why don't you just leave us alone? Haven't you done enough?"

"Me?" Mrs. Dupont waved a manicured hand like a pageant queen. "*I* want nothing to do with you, but our gracious host would like a word."

Her sausage-like lips sneered, and she snapped her fingers. "Bring them!" she ordered.

The Keepers moved in, pointing their gleaming black swords at their necks. Instinctively, Zoey backed away until she, Tristan, Simon, and her mother all stood back to back.

"Wait just a minute!" Doctor One waddled forward and pointed a finger at Mrs. Dupont. "I've already paid handsomely for these humans! They belong to me!"

He scratched his arms nervously, and yellow liquid oozed from his deep gashes. "We still need to perform the Dream Purge! You cannot take them. They belong to me!"

Mrs. Dupont looked slightly annoyed. "They belong to your ruler, Gigor. He's asked for them. You don't want to disappoint him, do you?"

Doctor One's mouth quivered.

"You know what happens when he's disappointed," said Mrs. Dupont. "Is that what you want? To disappoint him?"

"No-no," stammered the doctor and then frowned. "But I've already paid for them."

"What's it to me? Take it up with him. I couldn't care less." Mrs. Dupont turned on her heel and marched away through the crowd.

Nazar hesitated for a second. His face looked drawn, and he still appeared to be preoccupied with Elizabeth. But then he disappeared after his mistress.

The Keepers motioned with their swords.

Zoey could see the entrance to the city. They were so close. Another fifteen minutes, and they would have been long gone. She looked at Tristan who appeared to be blaming himself for their predicament. But none of this was his fault.

There were a hundred things she needed to say to him, needed to tell him, needed him to know. There were a thousand words she needed to speak, needed to whisper, needed him to hear. She wanted to reach out and tell him that it wasn't his fault, and that his plan had been a brilliant one, but the Keepers growled menacingly and prodded Zoey's chest with the tips of their swords.

"Uh, guys," said Simon, looking grimly at the razor-sharp sword pointed at his neck. "If you don't want to become living shish kebabs, I think we better move. Like *now*."

Reluctantly, Zoey, Tristan, Simon, and Elizabeth followed the Keepers down the road. Zoey's legs were like lead and her heart was heavy. She had failed in her quest. She had failed her friends, and worst of all, she had failed her mother.

The more they walked, the more a plan of escape seemed ridiculous. They weren't going anywhere, except to meet Gigor. Who was this Gigor anyway? The fact that he made deals with Mrs. Dupont didn't paint him in a very good light. For all she knew, Gigor was as evil and horrid as the psychotic woman, or maybe even worse.

Mrs. Dupont walked ahead of them, deep in conversation with Nazar. Were they discussing how they were going to kill everyone? The way Nazar had looked at her mother still bothered her, but she wondered if she hadn't actually imagined the whole thing.

They had arrived at a colossal building without a roof, like a baseball stadium. Built of black stone, it stood out among the other buildings like a giant spaceship. She could hear mumbled voices inside.

They followed Mrs. Dupont and Nazar through an archway and into an open area the size of a baseball field. Like a sports stadium, rows of seats circled the field, and doorways led to upper levels. Keepers guarded every exit.

Thousands of mystics sat in the seats. They were drinking, chanting, and some were even dancing. It was like a big party before the show. And Zoey had a horrible suspicion that she was it.

They made their way along the right side of the stadium, towards a raised platform on the upper first level.

An enormous creature with two massive black horns sat on a large throne made of bones in the middle of the platform. Its skin was the color of fresh blood, and it had a series of black symbols tattooed all over its body and face. It looked humanoid from the chest up, but hooves peeked from the bottom of its leather black pants, and talons gleamed at the ends of the thing's fingers. It looked like a cross between a man and a bull.

Two large troll-like bodyguards in metal breastplates and armor sat at his sides. Zoey suspected the creature didn't need them and that they were more for show than for protection.

But then Zoey saw something that was more upsetting than the giant bull-man. A young woman wearing a metal collar stood in the shadows with a tray with food and bronze cups. Although her face was bruised and blood seeped from a cut on her lips, Zoey recognized her. Her name was Sonya, and she was an Agent. But how had she gotten here?

Mrs. Dupont stopped and raised her arms in the air. "Gigor, my lord. I bring gifts, as promised."

The great red beast smiled. His eyes looked like black bottomless pits and his black forked tongue flicked out of his mouth as he spoke.

"So, these are the agent trouble makers? They are just children with an old man and a sick woman!" Gigor's laugh resonated like an earthquake.

He flicked his hand, and Sonya shuffled forward, her feet shackled with chains. He took a goblet from her tray and drank from it. For a moment he sat silently.

When he stood up suddenly, his long black cape spilled behind him.

"Why are they such a threat to you, Mrs. Dupont? I see nothing extraordinary about them apart from the Mysterian. Is he why you wanted to bring them to me? Mysterians are of no value to me. But still, he will play his part in the games."

Zoey frowned and mouthed to Tristan, *what games*? He shook his head and shrugged.

Mrs. Dupont pushed Zoey and her mother forward roughly. "I'm not talking about the Mysterian. These two have the blood of the *Originals*."

Gigor regarded Zoey and her mother lazily. He still didn't seem interested.

"I never cared for the Originals. I never saw anything special about them. Humans with gifts, that is all. Mortals are weak. What good are they if they do not provide me with some entertainment? They will all join in the games. That is what I promised my people."

Mrs. Dupont smiled. "Of course, my lord. It will be an enormous pleasure to watch them die."

She turned to Elizabeth. Her face twitched in a failed attempt to look apologetic.

"This is what you get for lying to me about your daughter," she spat. "If you had told the truth years ago, we could have avoided all this unpleasantness now."

"Unpleasantness?" hissed Elizabeth. "You're crazy. You've always been crazy."

The cat-faced woman laughed softly. "I will rejoice watching you die, Elizabeth. And your troublesome daughter will die alongside you. You've been meddling in my affairs for too long. But I won. You lost. Goodbye."

Mrs. Dupont walked away. Her Alphas moved with her, but Nazar stood still. His face was drawn, and his eyes were fixed on Elizabeth.

"Nazar," Elizabeth pleaded. "Don't let her do this, please. Stop her—"

But Nazar had turned away. He made his way to the first level and joined Mrs. Dupont on the platform to the left of Gigor.

Behind Mrs. Dupont, Zoey could see a man with dark hair, pale skin, and a hollow face. It was Director Martin.

The beige carry-on bag rested on his lap—the UECs.

"Zoey, do you see what I see?" whispered Tristan.

"Director Martin," she answered. She felt a flicker of hope deep inside her belly. There was still a chance to close the portals. All she needed was a miracle.

The Keepers made their way across the grounds and stood in line formation against the inner walls.

"And now, the moment we've all been waiting for," bellowed Gigor.

The crowd in the stands cheered wildly. It sounded like the crackling of thunder. He waited for the crowd to settle down and raised his glass.

"As promised, I give you four new warriors for the Blood Games!" The crowd cheered loudly, as though they were at a baseball game.

"Is it me or does that sound really bad?" said Simon. His face fell.

"I'm awesome at video games. I can even play a wicked game of Monopoly when we lose power . . . but *blood* games? Not so much. What's going to happen to us?"

"I don't know," said Zoey. "But we stick together. And we stay alive. Have faith Simon, we still might have a chance to get out of here."

She glanced at Director Martin. He had to be here for some reason. She didn't believe in faith, but this was pretty close. She had to do something before it was too late.

The crowd quieted down, and Gigor raised his voice. "Let the Blood Games begin!"

Zoey leaped forward and cried. "WAIT! STOP!"

Gigor frowned and lowered his eyes until they met Zoey. Clearly he wasn't used to being interrupted, and for a second Zoey thought he was going to lunge off the platform and step on her. But he didn't. He waited.

She cleared her throat nervously. "Mr. Gigor—uh—*Lord* Gigor," she said clumsily. "We only came here for one reason—to *shut* the portals down. Both our worlds are collapsing," she said as fast as she could. "Neither of us can survive a permanent doorway. They need to be shut down, or we'll all die."

Gigor measured Zoey and then said. "Close the portals? The worlds are collapsing?"

He laughed deeply. "This child amuses me. Child, why would I want to shut them down when *I* wanted to *open* them in the first place? Mrs. Dupont has promised me more slaves." He turned and gestured over to Sonya who was cowering at the edge of the stage.

"We have an agreement. I helped her open the portal, and in return her world will become enslaved to me!" His voice reverberated throughout the stadium like an earthquake.

Zoey looked quickly at Mrs. Dupont. She doubted that the woman would have agreed to such a thing. Mrs. Dupont wanted to rule both worlds *herself*. Zoey was sure that Mrs. Dupont had tricked Gigor somehow. She must have had something else up her sleeve, Zoey was sure of it.

But right now, she didn't have time to think about that. She needed to stay alive long enough to get her hands on the bag . . . .

Tristan moved in beside Zoey and raised his voice. "What are the rules?" he called. "There must be some rules. All games have rules."

Gigor smiled, and for the first time Zoey noticed that his teeth were as red as his skin. "Yes, Mysterian, you are correct. The rules are the same for beasts and humans. If you *survive* the games, then you may leave in peace."

Simon gave a little gasp.

Tristan looked at Zoey, his eyes filled with new vigor. "If we live, then we can go," he called out again to the mystic lord. "Do we have your word?"

Gigor raised his glass at Tristan and said. "You have my word as lord of this world. In fact, if you survive, I will personally escort you back to your portal."

He shook his head. "But no mystic or human has ever survived the Blood Games, so I wouldn't get too excited. Your death is inevitable. Still, you will be given as many weapons as you want. Good luck."

"As a senior citizen, don't I get a free pass, or a discount, or something?" bellowed Simon, but the mystic lord ignored him.

Zoey turned to Tristan and lowered her voice. "What's your plan?"

"Stay alive," he answered. "Whatever we'll be fighting, at least we'll be able to fight back with weapons."

"I can fight, too," said Elizabeth with determination. "I know I don't look it right now, but I can."

"I'm sure you can," said Zoey. "But if you get tired, stay behind us."

Just when Zoey started to wonder when they were going to get their weapons, objects flew from the crowd and landed on the ground. Daggers, swords, rocks, and even a variety of fruits were tossed at them from the onlookers. Even some of the Keepers pitched them their swords.

"Nothing like getting the crowd to *contribute*," said Simon grimly as he struggled with both hands to pick up a heavy sword. "I'm too old for this."

Tristan grabbed two black Keeper swords. He twisted them skillfully, as though he were a Keeper himself. His determination reassured Zoey that they might survive.

Elizabeth picked up what looked like a silver sword, and Zoey found a short bronze one. It felt light and balanced in her hand. The edges were sharp. She could do some real damage with it. For a second she thought about grabbing two weapons like Tristan, but she was not as ambidextrous as he was. She wished she had her boomerang, but it was gone forever. Her short sword would have to do.

"Open the gates!" bellowed Gigor. He tossed his goblet into the arena to signal the start of the games.

The sound of metal chains rattled over the cheers of the anxious crowds. Zoey turned towards the noise. Four iron gates lifted at the western end of the stadium. With her heart in her throat, she waited to get a look at whatever would come out from behind them. She felt like a gladiator.

"Stay together," said Tristan. They all stood back to back. "Don't break the formation. We're stronger together."

At first she could see only shadows behind the gates. But then they came out.

A hoard of the most horrid, vile, and dangerous creatures from her worst nightmares came hurtling towards them with one purpose—

To kill them all.

CHAPTER 21

BLOOD GAMES

For a moment, Zoey forgot to breathe.

The ground shook. It was like watching a scene from the movie *Gladiator*, but instead of great half-naked warriors lunging across the grounds, beasts from the gates of Hell had been unleashed upon them.

She could see two giant wolf creatures with glowing red eyes and fur that looked more like spikes than hair, enormous spiders the size of lions, winged beasts with the heads of women and the bodies of bats, and a legion of humanoid skeletons.

It was a savage, brutal army. Zoey understood why Gigor had said that no one had ever survived the games. How could two kids, an old man, and a sick and fragile woman defeat such foes?

"This reminds me of a dream I had once," noted Simon. His sword shook in his hand as he shifted his weight from side to side as though he was about to hit a tennis ball with it.

Zoey kept her eyes on the advancing threat. "What happened in the dream?"

"I died."

Zoey glared at Simon. "Nice."

Simon shrugged. "What? I'm just saying . . . forget it. It was a stupid thing to say, sorry."

"Just—"

Zoey suddenly was really worried about Simon. The spell still *hadn't* worn off. His face seemed to have more wrinkles than before, and he was losing more hair. Was he still aging? He caught her staring at him, and she looked away. "Just try to stay alive, okay?"

"What? More *alive* than in *this* body," Simon pointed to himself. "I'm already running on used fuel. But don't worry, I might be an old fogey, but I still have a few good moves left in me—hopefully."

"Get ready and stay together!" Tristan's voice sounded over the savage cries and shrieks from the avalanche of beasts tumbling towards them.

They had nowhere to go. There was no escaping. Their DSMs didn't work. They would *have* to fight. How could they defeat such a brutal force? They were going to die . . . .

"Zoey," said Elizabeth suddenly, and Zoey turned towards her mother. "I—" she paused as though she wasn't sure whether or not to say what was on her mind. "Be careful."

Zoey reached out and squeezed her mother's hand. "I will. We're getting out of here, mom, I promise."

Her mother's eyes filled with tears, and her own eyes burned. She turned quickly away, not wanting her mother to see her cry. She glanced over at the platform. Mrs. Dupont was smiling so much that Zoey thought she might swallow her own head. She was leaning forward in her chair like she was watching her favorite live theatre performance. She was thrilled they were about to die.

Zoey breathed in all her anger and let it fill her with energy. If she was going to die, then she'd go down fighting. If Mrs. Dupont wanted to see a *show*, then a show Zoey was going to *give* her.

The army of skeletons moved to the right side of the stadium and waited like they were the reinforcements, should things go in Zoey's favor.

The wolves reached them first. The two great beasts snarled and shrieked, and their red eyes gleamed with hatred and hunger.

"If anyone here believes in some God, it's time to pray," said Simon behind her.

Elizabeth planted herself. "Let them come."

She brandished her sword, looking braver and stronger than Zoey had first anticipated, and it filled her with more confidence.

The wolves were so close that Zoey could smell their putrid fur. She raised her sword.

"Here! Come over here!" Tristan leaped forward and away from the group. His skin shone blue as he waved his daggers like baseball bats.

"Tristan, what are you doing?" shouted Zoey. But she knew he was taking on the biggest beasts so that the rest of them wouldn't have to. She loved him for it.

The wolves howled angrily and went straight for Tristan.

A rust-colored wolf leaped towards his neck. But Tristan was ready.

The wolf dove for him, but he moved, got behind it, and wrapped an arm around its neck. He held it struggling against him while he struck with his blade, but the other wolf leaped onto his back. Tristan cried out in pain but didn't let go. He twisted his body and managed to kick the second beast off. With spit flying from its maw, it spun and reared. Three spikes rose on its back and shot straight at him. He swung his left arm and blocked two, but the third pierced his shoulder. His knees buckled. Miraculously, he remained standing.

Zoey moved towards him.

"NO! STAY BACK!" howled Tristan, and Zoey froze mid-step.

Still hanging on to the first wolf, Tristan whirled around.

The black wolf lunged again.

Tristan swung his blade in an upward arc, and the creature spun through the air and hit the ground with a nasty thud. Its severed head fell away from its body and landed in a puddle of blackened blood.

He let go of the red wolf, and it crumbled to the ground.

Zoey thought she could hear the crowd booing, but she didn't have time to dwell on that.

"SCORE!" shouted Simon defiantly to the crowd.

"Two to zero for us! Better reorganize those bets. We're winning this!"

For a second she thought Simon was about to do a *happy dance*, but he taunted the crowd with his sword instead.

Tristan staggered and pulled out the black spike still lodged in his shoulder. Blood seeped out from the deep wound, but he didn't even flinch.

He hurried back to the group, and just as Zoey started to ask him if he was okay, the crowd cheered loudly.

She felt a sudden gust of wind and looked up.

Winged creatures with fangs for teeth and stingers in their scorpion tails hovered above them. Their deeply sunken yellow eyes and heavy brows made them look as if they were grimacing with a cunning intelligence.

"Watch out for their poison tails!" cried Zoey.

She stood shoulder to shoulder with her mother and Simon.

The creatures shrieked and dove.

Zoey realized that they were going for Simon and her mother because they looked old and weak. As one of the creature's talons neared her mother's throat, Zoey swung her sword and cut the beast's hands. The creature shrieked, and with a great beat of its wings it flew back out of reach.

Tristan knew that Simon and Elizabeth were the targets, too, and he rushed to Simon's side. He struck one of the creatures with great whacks, while Simon kept his own and stabbed the third creature as it tried to get in closer.

"Take that, stinker!" said Simon as he poked it again, feeling more confident with every blow. "Don't suppose you've ever heard of soap? You smell like cat pee."

The creature sneered and lashed out its tail. Simon's feet were torn from under him. He went sprawling and lost his sword.

The creature's eyes widened in delight.

"You're mine now, human!" It flapped its wings and lashed its stinger towards Simon's chest like a venomous snake.

Zoey sprung into the air and kicked the stinger out of the way, just as it nicked Simon's jacket.

"Simon get back!" she cried and pulled him to his feet behind her. He picked up his sword and backed away.

Tristan fought the other winged beast with great strokes of his sword, and the creature shrieked angrily as it couldn't get near him.

Zoey heard a great flap of wings and felt searing pain in her shoulders as she was thrown into the air. She hit the ground hard and had the wind knocked of her. She wiped the blood from her mouth and nose as she struggled to regain her breath. Her eyes watered from the burning vinegar stench of the beast that still lingered around her. By a miracle she still held on to her sword. She struggled to her feet and turned again to face the hovering beast.

"We are going to kill you, *agent!*" hissed the bat-like female creature with a high-pitched voice that sounded like screeching tires.

"You cannot win. *No one* wins. Why don't you give up? I will give you a quick death." It sneered.

"I promise," it said in mock sincerity.

"Who said anything about giving up?" spat Zoey. She turned her blade in her hand. "I'm not afraid of you. Maybe *you're* afraid of me?"

The creature grinned. Its tail slashed eagerly behind it and then its vein-ridden face darkened. "You humans are so stupid, you don't even know when you're beaten."

"We're not beaten, not yet," said Zoey through gritted teeth as she tried to anticipate the creature's next move.

Tristan had the other creature pinned to the ground. He was winning.

"Well, that suits me fine," laughed the creature. "I'm *starving*. Human blood is the sweetest."

The creature shrieked again and dived tail first towards Zoey.

Zoey ducked, spun around, and blocked the stinger with the edge of her blade. She cried out as the force of the hit sent stinging pain up her arm, but she kept moving. If she stopped now she was dead. She turned around, panting, trying to catch her breath.

The creature's grin was gone. It came at her again with greater determination, swinging its tail like a whip. Zoey dived and rolled, and the stinger missing her completely. She kicked out at the creature's chest, but before she knew it, its giant claws had ripped into her back. She was thrown into the air again, and lights exploded behind her eyes when she hit the ground.

She rolled over, ready this time, as the beast wrapped its hands around her neck and squeezed. She raised her sword and plunged it into the back of the creature's skull.

The effect was instantaneous. The beast fell dead on top of her.

Zoey gagged at the stench, heaved the creature off her, and staggered to her feet.

She heard a gag from behind. The creature whose hands she had severed had its feet wrapped around her mother's throat.

Zoey gave a roar and charged. The creature's thin, deadly stinger flashed out. Instinctively, she went down and rolled. The beast's tail slashed above her head and missed her by inches. Not knowing what possessed her, she stomped on the tail and pinned it down. Then she brought her sword down with all her strength and severed the stinger.

The creature wailed and sent Elizabeth sprawling unconscious to the dirt. It thrashed in the air, waving its bloody stumps where its hand used to be and swinging its stinger-less tail ineffectually.

But still it stretched its black lips into an evil smile.

"You might have taken my hands and stinger, but I'm still going to kill you," it threatened. "You can't escape. You're all going to die."

It moved its talons towards Zoey's neck with lightning speed. It clawed its way through Zoey's shield and sent her scuttling back as it howled and hissed angrily.

The beast soared at Zoey again, but she waited until the last minute and then jumped up and slashed with her sword. The creature gasped and faltered.

Zoey grabbed it, flipped it on its back, and stepped on its neck. The beast squirmed like a fish, but Zoey pushed down harder. Without hesitating, she thrust the tip of her blade into the creature's skull. Its head drooped to the side.

When Zoey looked up, the last of the bat creatures lay dead at Tristan's feet. And to her immense relief, her mother stood next to Simon. She still looked frail and in need of a doctor, but she smiled at her.

"SPIDERS!" roared Simon suddenly, pointing behind her.

"Zoey, watch out!" Tristan leaped towards her, but it was too late.

A giant spider with eight glowing red eyes and mandibles the size of machetes leaped at her and pinned her down. Her sword fell from her hand.

It reared its hairy head, and shot its mandibles forward. But Zoey turned her head to the side just in time, and the creature's mandibles brushed against her ear. She was aware of Tristan's voice, but she couldn't hear what he was saying.

The spider bit down at her again, and she caught the mandibles with her bare hands. It was like trying to keep giant scissors from cutting off her neck. She was yanked and pulled as the spider tried to break free from her hold. Zoey knew the thing would chomp off her head if she let go, and she really *needed* her head.

Just as her hands slipped and the spider's mandibles reached her neck, the spider's head fell onto Zoey's chest. A hot yellow liquid flowed over her, and Tristan appeared above her. With a great heave, he rolled the spider's dead body off her and pulled her to her feet.

"You owe me for that," he said as he pulled his dagger from the beast's body. He was covered in yellow slime, too.

"I'm thinking when we get out of here we can go to dinner and a movie or something?"

Zoey grabbed her sword and smiled in spite of herself.

Another spider leaped at her. She ducked and impaled it with her sword. It collapsed to the ground on its back.

"You mean like a *real* date?"

Tristan slashed the legs off the fallen spider. "Yeah, a real date."

Zoey felt invincible, like she could do anything.

Elizabeth screamed. "Zoey, get back! Get back!"

Zoey *hated* normal-sized spiders, and she hated these giant ones even more. It was time to get rid of the spiders once and for all. She planted her feet and readied herself.

The spider screeched and leaped.

Zoey jerked away sideways and stabbed her weapon into one of its eight eyes, pushing it until she heard a satisfying crunch. The spider went limp and then it crumbled at her feet.

Zoey wiped the yellow, sticky ooze from her face and looked around. All the spiders were dead.

She looked to the platform, and to her surprise Gigor took a great gulp from his goblet and smiled at her. But Mrs. Dupont was not smiling.

Tristan moved beside her. His shirt was red with blood from the wound on his shoulder.

He caught her looking and said, "It's nothing. Don't worry about it."

"It's a lot of blood, Tristan." Although Zoey didn't know how much blood a normal person could lose without suffering the effects, she knew the amount on his shirt was bad.

Tristan shrugged. "It's nothing, really, just a scratch."

"It doesn't look like nothing," insisted Zoey.

"We did it," said Simon happily and high-fived Elizabeth. "We actually did it! We're going home! We're going home!"

Simon's good cheer and the smiles on everyone's faces caused Zoey to relax for a moment. She could almost smell the fresh baked bread in Aria's kitchen.

But just when they thought that their victory was near, the army of skeletons marched towards them.

CHAPTER 22

AN ARMY OF

SKELETONS

Simon looked like he was about to collapse.

"I totally forgot the *bones brigade*. They look pretty intense. You think we can beat those guys?"

"What other choice do we have?" Tristan's face darkened.

The armor-clad skeletons reminded Zoey of Charlie, the skeleton mascot from her biology class in high school, but Charlie didn't *move*, and he wasn't on his way to attack them. They marched in a straight line, with gleaming swords, battle-axes, and spears in their white-boned hands.

The stadium was still. The only sounds were the clicking and clacking of bones rubbing against metal. They had no eyes, and

Zoey couldn't tell where or at whom they were looking. They had no flesh. If they didn't bleed, maybe they *couldn't* be killed.

Zoey glanced up at the podium. Mrs. Dupont's smile had returned.

"They have to have a weak spot," said Zoey. "Everyone has a weak spot, right? Then so do they."

"Yeah, but they're *skeletons*!" said Simon. "How do we kill something that's already *dead*?"

"I don't know, but we have to try."

With a swish, the skeleton army raised their weapons.

"Zoey's right," said Tristan. "We need a plan. The army is a scare tactic. I'm sure everyone who's ever stood in this arena were scared out of their minds when they first saw them."

"So what's the plan then?" asked Simon.

Tristan didn't answer.

"Aim at the joints, knees, elbows, and feet," said Elizabeth. "I don't know. Maybe they'll come apart if there really is nothing holding them together. If we can't kill them, then we need to immobilize them."

"And then what?" asked Simon.

"We're about to find out," Zoey braced herself. "Get ready, here they come."

The twelve skeletons charged. There were no battle cries, no sounds of heavy breathing, just the sounds of clanking metal and the clicking of old bones. It was the most frightening thing Zoey had ever faced.

Tristan charged forward and met them head on. Zoey just glimpsed him tackle three skeletons when the other nine attacked.

A tall, chalk-white skeleton with a green and red-jeweled sword lunged at her. Her mother swung her sword at a second skeleton, and Simon jabbed and kicked a third in the tibia.

She kicked the one who had attacked her, and it staggered back. Another came at her from the side, but she slipped to the side and tried to sweep her own blade along the back of its leg. The skeleton pivoted away. It lunged, and she parried. She lunged at his shoulder, but it raised its blade, and her cut went wide. The skeleton held its left hand high like a classical fencer.

The skeleton barged forward, using its shoulder to knock her sideways. Zoey sidestepped and rolled on the ground. She came up behind it and slashed her blade across the back of the skeleton's neck.

The skeleton stood still for a moment, then its skull rolled off. It crumpled to the ground in a pile of jagged bones.

For a moment Zoey just stood there, staring at the jumble of femurs, tibias, and ribs. And then it hit her.

"The heads!" cried Zoey triumphantly. "Cut off their heads! They go down if you cut off their skulls!"

With her gleaming silver sword, Elizabeth parried, twisted around, and knocked her opponent to its knees before she sliced off its head. It crumbled at her feet.

Meanwhile, Simon jabbed and slashed and derided them, "When I look into your eyes, I see straight through to the back of your head."

He thrust his sword above a skeleton's clavicle, and its skull popped off with a *snap*.

"Thank you, come again."

Tristan swung his blades like nunchakus, slashing at their collarbones. They dropped their swords and crumbled like a pile of matches.

The entire skeleton army had been reduced to twelve piles of bones.

Thunderous applause erupted in the stadium as the thousands of mystics cheered and clapped.

"And the crowd *loves* us," said Simon.

He took a bow and then straightened up proudly and blew them kisses.

"My mother always told me I was a star." He beamed and blew more kisses. "We're awesome. We should totally go out on tour. Our stage name could be, *The Incredible Four*—"

"You're delusional, and possibly disturbed because of what you drank," Tristan nudged him playfully on the shoulder. "But, yeah, we're still awesome."

A few loud *boos* pierced through the cheers.

"Oh, no you don't." Simon's face fell. He turned around and mooned them.

"Simon!" Zoey covered her eyes. "Are you mad? No, I *know* you're mad, but are you suicidal? Why did you do that?"

She peeked through her fingers.

Simon shrugged, "I'm an old fart. Everyone knows old people get away with murder. So I'm just milking it a little bit."

"A little bit is an understatement," Tristan high-fived Simon.

Zoey felt a hand squeeze hers.

"I'm really proud of you. You're a great agent, Zoey," said Elizabeth. "This is where you belong, with your friends, and with the Agency."

Zoey squeezed her mother's hand gently. "You're not so bad yourself, mom."

Elizabeth dusted off her shirt. "Well, I used to be a really good agent until . . ." she paused for a moment. ". . . Until things got *complicated*."

Zoey frowned. She noticed a strange look in her mother's eyes on the word *complicated*, almost as though the word complicated had meant *her*.

"What do you mean by *complicated?*"

"I hate to break up this Hallmark moment," interjected Simon. He pointed his sword at the platform. "But I think the Red Bull wants a word."

Gigor stood at the edge of the platform with devilish smile on his face. Zoey couldn't decide if it was a *real* smile or a *fake* one. His giant and muscular frame made him look more like a God rather than a mere lord of the Nexus, and his black cape billowed around him like a cloud.

He looked at Zoey and her friends and raised his goblet. "Well done! Well done!"

He paused and waited for the crowd's cheers to quiet.

"I must admit, I hadn't given you more than five minutes in the ring before my *dead* pets killed you all. I'm surprised that you are still standing. Quite spectacular, really. You humans never cease to amaze me."

He looked over and showed his red teeth to Mrs. Dupont. "You've provided me and my guests with a very *entertaining* match, the best we've had in five hundred years! And I thank you for that."

The crowd burst into applause again, but dread began to grow in the pit of Zoey's stomach. What if the great Gigor had lied and wouldn't keep his promise? Maybe a promise meant something completely different in the Nexus.

As if reading her mind, Tristan spoke up. "What about our deal? Your rules? We won, so we can leave right, or was that just a lie?"

Gigor's tattooed face was expressionless.

"Tristan, what are you doing!" hissed Zoey. "If you make him mad, we're not going anywhere."

But then Gigor laughed a deep, throaty laugh. "Come, come, young Mysterian. I am a Lord of my word. You won the games in a fair fight. You are free to go—"

"WHAT? NO!" Mrs. Dupont jumped to her feet. "You *can't* let them go. It wasn't part of *our* deal. You told me they were going to die. They must die!"

Zoey narrowed her eyes. "I really, *really* hate her. Why does she always have to ruin everything?"

"What did you expect?" answered Simon dryly.

Gigor lowered his goblet and angled his great head in Mrs. Dupont's direction. His black cape billowed behind him, and his glistening sharp horns and hooved feet caught in the light and made him look even more dangerous and impressive. Even Nazar cowered.

But Mrs. Dupont stood defiantly before the great creature. She was definitely mad.

"No creature or human has ever survived the Blood Games," replied Gigor in a commanding and final tone. "I assumed that they would perish. But it seems these humans are skilled and worthy combatants. It was a *fair* fight, and I will not have them harmed—"

"You stupid, useless fool!" spat Mrs. Dupont. Her face was red and blotchy, and she scolded him like he was one of her Alpha pets.

"Ouch," said Simon.

"She's dead," beamed Zoey.

"She's stupid dead," smiled Tristan.

Gigor's crushed his goblet in his hand like it was made of dough.

"You *dare* insult me . . . *human*?" The clank of his hooves echoed around the stadium as he rose in front of her like a great brick wall.

Mrs. Dupont trembled in rage.

She pointed a red manicured finger down at Zoey and the others. "You promised me that they would die. If I had known that you wouldn't keep your word, I would never have brought them to you. I would have killed them myself!"

A group of heavily armed Alphas made their way towards the platform and stood behind their mistress like a protective wall, ready to strike at her command.

Gigor sneered at her army like they were nothing but little red ants about to be squished.

"Be careful where you tread, *human*. I can destroy you and your puny army with a flick of my wrist."

Two troll-like beasts with daggers, warhammers, and maces hanging from their leather belts rose from their seats and flexed their muscles like wrestlers before a match. Their hands were the size of hubcaps. Then a platoon of Keepers stepped from the shadows, drew their swords, and stood guard behind their master.

"This is going to be *goooood*," said Simon gleefully. "I wish I had some popcorn. My money's on the Keepers . . . you?"

Mrs. Dupont's pinched features contorted into a hideous grimace.

"Is that a threat? Are you threatening me? Me? The one who gave you a doorway to my world? The one who promised you thousands of humans?"

She started to laugh. "You're nothing but a thoughtless beast!"

The two trolls charged at Mrs. Dupont. She pulled out a gun and shot the first one in the head, but the second troll grabbed the gun and twisted it out of her grip. Then it wrapped its enormous hands around her neck.

Nazar shot pointblank into the beast's skull, and it slumped to the ground.

The Keepers moved like a black wave towards Mrs. Dupont and Nazar, but her Alpha army stepped to her defense. Shouts and battle cries erupted like a thunderstorm as the two armies slashed, stabbed, and ripped away at each other. It was madness.

The crowd cheered as Mrs. Dupont and Nazar disappeared into the chaos of the battle.

"Hope she dies," said Tristan. "She deserves what she gets."

Zoey didn't think the vile woman had a chance. The Keepers were better fighters, and her precious Alphas wouldn't last much longer.

Gigor stood back and watched the ongoing battle lazily, as though he knew his Keepers would finish off the Alphas soon enough. He had a new goblet in his hand and drank while he watched the show.

At the other end of the platform, Director Martin cowered in the shadows. He had been a fool to trust Mrs. Dupont, and now he was probably going to die.

The UECs were still in his bag. If she could get to it, they'd still have a chance to blow up the portals. This was their only chance. She *had* to take it.

"Stay here!"

She ran across the field towards the stairs.

"Zoey! Where are you going?" shouted Tristan. "ZOEY!"

But Zoey's mind was set on one thing only—to get the bag.

She sneaked up to the first level and flattened herself against the wall. The Keepers and the Alphas were preoccupied attacking each other. No one noticed her.

Director Martin cowered against the far wall. His eyes were on the battle, and his back was to Zoey.

She sneaked up behind Director Martin and tapped his shoulder. "Excuse me?" she said in her most innocent voice.

Director Martin whirled around, and Zoey punched him in the nose.

He stumbled back, blood trickling down his face. "My nose! You stupid girl! I'm going to kill you for this!"

He lunged for her, but Zoey jabbed him in the throat with her fist. He fell back, choking and gasping for breath.

"Thanks for keeping it safe for me. I'll take that now."

Zoey grabbed the bag and kicked him in the chin. He fell to his knees.

"How could you do this to your own—"

The rest of her words died in her throat. She stepped back.

Director Martin's skin bubbled and blistered. His fingers transformed into gleaming black talons, and the rest of his skin peeled away and fell to the ground in a pool of black liquid. Blunt spikes jutted out from his back, and Zoey could smell the stench of sulfur and rotten meat. He turned and glared at Zoey with four large red eyes.

It was the same creature that had killed her foster mother.

"You're a skin demon," said Zoey.

She pointed the tip of her blade menacingly at it. "What happened to the *real* Director Martin?"

The demon smiled evilly and revealed rows of jagged glass-sharp teeth.

"I killed him," it laughed. "I killed him, and I took his place. Like I'm going to kill—"

Zoey kicked the skin demon in the head, and it fell over backwards.

"Looks like you were wrong, demon."

She stole a look inside the bag—two UEC bombs rested at the bottom. She cradled the bag close to her chest and turned to leave.

"And *where* do you think you're going with that?"

Mrs. Dupont grabbed Zoey and held a knife to her throat.

"I should have *killed* you when I had the chance. But I won't make the same mistake again.

Zoey felt the cool blade press harder against her jugular.

"*Die* you miserable, weak, little agent—"

"Let her go." Elizabeth held the point of her sword against the back of Mrs. Dupont's head.

Mrs. Dupont sneered. "Elizabeth? How good of you to join us. Aren't you glad I've brought your daughter back to you? It's like an overdue family reunion."

"I said, let her go, *witch*," said Elizabeth with venom in her voice. "Or I will shove this blade from the nape of your neck to your forehead."

With a strength Zoey didn't know Mrs. Dupont possessed, the woman grabbed her by the throat and tossed her in the air.

Zoey dropped her sword so that she could protect the bag with her body and crashed into a row of chairs. She turned over and groaned. She waited a second, but she didn't explode into a million pieces. The UECs were still intact.

"Have you seen what you look like, Elizabeth?" teased Mrs. Dupont. "You're in no shape to fight me."

She twirled her blade in her hand.

"You're injured. You already look *dead*. You probably only have one or two good moves left in that frail, sick body of yours. You're no match for me. You never were. I will kill you first—" she paused and turned towards Zoey. "And then I will kill your miserable, meddling precious daughter."

Elizabeth waved her sword from side to side. She looked like she had been waiting for this moment a long time.

"You won't lay a hand on her. I'll kill you first."

Quietly and carefully, Zoey stepped over the chairs.

Mrs. Dupont picked up Zoey's sword. "So be it. But don't say I didn't warn you," she laughed with an ugly sneer.

"Let's finish this," said Elizabeth. "Once and for all."

"Let's."

Mrs. Dupont lunged.

Elizabeth feinted low, and then brought her sword high. Mrs. Dupont blocked Elizabeth's first blow and replied with three strikes in quick succession. The monstrous woman ducked low and slashed her blade dangerously close to Elizabeth's ribs.

Zoey held her breath as her mother darted away.

Elizabeth stumbled as she parried and blocked, trying to regain her footing and give herself some space. But then Mrs. Dupont swung savagely and knocked the sword from Elizabeth's hands.

Instead of retreating, Elizabeth leaped for Mrs. Dupont's neck.

But the cat-faced woman's strength was no match for her mother's weakened body.

Mrs. Dupont struck Elizabeth on the head with the pommel of her sword and then kicked her so that her mother went stumbling into a row of chairs. Zoey heard a gut-wrenching *crack* as Elizabeth hit her head and went down.

"Mom!" Zoey rushed forward—but something hard hit her in the back and knocked her down. Her chin hit the floor, and she tasted blood in her mouth.

"You should have stayed down, girl," said Nazar. "Now I'm going to have to kill you, and you know how I *hate* killing children."

His single white eye gleamed like a gem.

Zoey grimaced and looked over to her mother. She wasn't moving.

"Get the bag," ordered Mrs. Dupont. She paused to flatten the front of her blue outfit. "And then kill her."

Nazar's dark tailored suit and black leather gloves made him look like an assassin. He held out a gloved hand. "You heard the lady. Give me the bag."

"No." Zoey shook her head stubbornly and cradled the bag protectively in her arms.

Instantly Nazar got behind her and wrapped his arm around her throat. She reared back, but he held on. Zoey cried out in pain as he squeezed the air from her lungs. Her face burned. She couldn't breathe.

"STOP!"

Elizabeth pulled herself to her knees and raised her hand.

"Don't hurt her, please," she wheezed.

"Why not? She's been a real pest, and I've been longing to take care of her once and for all," said Nazar. His cold white eye turned to Zoey

Elizabeth steadied herself, "Because she's your *daughter*."

CHAPTER 23

A RACE AGAINST

TIME

Nazar paled.

He looked at Elizabeth curiously, trying to determine if she was lying.

He turned his attention back to Zoey. With a flash of recognition, he let her go and stepped away from her, as if she frightened him.

Zoey gasped for breath, trying to make sense of what had just happened. Had she heard her mother correctly? Did she say that this man, Nazar, this murderer, was *her* father?

Nazar looked at her like he was staring at a ghost.

Mrs. Dupont laughed nervously. "She's lying, Nazar. Don't believe her. She's desperate. She'll say anything to keep her brat alive. Kill the girl. I said kill her!"

But Nazar just stood there, looking at Zoey as though he had just laid eyes on her for the very first time.

"Look at her," said Elizabeth. "You know I'm telling you the truth—"

"I said kill her!" roared Mrs. Dupont. "Kill her, you idiot! Can't you tell the truth from lies? Don't be blind, you foolish man. Kill her, or I'll do it."

Nazar didn't move.

"You fool!" Mrs. Dupont's face twisted in fury. She raised her sword and lunged at Zoey.

"NO!" cried Elizabeth.

Nazar stepped between Zoey and Mrs. Dupont. He raised his arms and gripped Mrs. Dupont by the throat.

"Na-Nazar!" coughed Mrs. Dupont, her face an ugly purple. "What—are—you—I—can't—breathe—"

Nazar raised her in the air so that her feet didn't touch the ground.

Mrs. Dupont dropped her sword and hit Nazar with her fists. "Let—me go! What's—wrong—with you! Nazar!"

Zoey watched as Nazar squeezed his mistress's throat. He looked like he had gone mad.

"Take your mother and run," said Nazar. His voice was gentle, like she had never heard it before. "Go quickly, and use the bombs. Go!"

Zoey pushed the questions and suspicions and misgivings out of her thoughts. She wanted to ask him to come with them, but somehow she knew he couldn't come. She knew that she *had* to go.

Zoey gripped the bag tightly and ran to her mother. "Can you walk?"

"Yes," said Elizabeth on shaking legs, but she moved swiftly and followed Zoey down the stairs. Once she reached the bottom, Zoey looked back. Mrs. Dupont dangled in Nazar's grip like a puppet. She no longer spoke. She was flushed, and her eyes bulged out of her deformed face.

A cry came from the shadows. Zoey stopped and discovered Sonya hiding behind a chair. Her face was streaked with dirt and tears.

"Mom, wait!"

Zoey jumped over a row of seats, "It's Sonya isn't it?"

The girl blinked at Zoey. "Yes."

"We're getting out of here. Come on!"

"We are?" said Sonya in a dream-like state.

"Yes." Zoey steered the young woman by the elbow, and together they ran across the grounds towards Tristan and Simon.

"How nice of you to join us," said Simon at the sight of Sonya. "Simon Brown at your service."

When he saw her collar and shackles, he pulled out Doctor One's remote. "I knew it was a good idea to keep this." He pressed the release button and Sonya's restraints fell to the ground.

Tristan saw the bag in Zoey's hands, but he also saw the pain and horror on her face. He moved quickly towards her. "Zoey, what happened?"

"I'll explain later—no time," she answered.

"Simon," she urged, "how much time do we have?"

Simon pulled out his cell phone, "Man, you're not going to like this. We've got thirty-three minutes left."

Zoey's heart sank. She looked towards the platform. The Keepers stood around the platform proudly, but there was no sign of the Alphas, or of Nazar and Mrs. Dupont.

"Keep Sonya hidden between you, I'll be right back."

Zoey ran back towards the platform. She stood below it and raised her voice. "Lord Gigor," she said, "You said you would escort us back to the portal, right?"

Gigor looked surprised at Zoey's sudden appearance, and a little annoyed that she had interrupted his conversation. The giant lord looked down and nodded. "Yes, that's right."

"What's your fastest ride?" She knew she was pushing it, but she *had* to try—for all their sakes, even though he had no idea she was also saving *his* life.

Gigor looked at the bag. She cursed herself for not giving it to Tristan.

"My mother needs medical help," she blurted out. "I need to get her to our doctors right away—she's dying." She lied easily, "I don't want to lose her again."

Gigor said something to the nearest Keeper, and the creature made its way swiftly off the platform. A few seconds later, a great black coach driven by two plum-colored stags hurtled in the arena, circled around them once, and then drew to a stop. The driver climbed down and opened the door. He stood back and waited.

They all climbed in, and Zoey shut the door.

It smelled of mildew and cigar smoke, but she sat back in the red leather seats and held the bag of bombs securely.

Zoey jerked back as the carriage took off. The city vanished quickly as their ride soared over the red deserts. When Zoey was about to complain that they weren't moving fast enough, the stag-creatures tripled their speed as though they had been waiting to let loose and show off how fast they really could go.

Black, jagged mountains and red hills flew past in a blur.

"Simon—time?" asked Zoey as she tried not to show the real panic she felt.

"Less than ten minutes left," said Simon.

"Ten minutes left for what?" asked Elizabeth who had been silent the entire carriage trip.

Zoey opened her bag and inspected the UECs. "Ten minutes left before the end of the world—"

"Worlds," corrected Tristan.

"What are you guys talking about?" inquired Sonya.

Zoey looked at her mother. "We've got *nine* minutes to reach the portal, detonate one of the UECs, and then cross over and detonate the other—"

"All the while trying *not* to get attacked or killed by the Alphas," added Simon.

Her mother smiled. "Sounds like fun."

The carriage was silent for a moment.

"*Eight* minutes," said Simon. His face flushed. "I feel a panic attack coming on. Oh my God, I'm having a panic attack."

Tristan rolled his eyes. "Stop it, Simon. You're not having a panic attack. We're all a little nervous."

The carriage rocked.

Zoey peered outside the little window, but she couldn't see anything except a blizzard of red sand. She couldn't see more than a few feet. The worlds were breathing their last.

"*Seven* minutes," Simon's voice was high pitched this time. "We're not going to make it."

"Shut up, Simon," said Tristan. "We're *going* to make it."

Suddenly, everyone was thrown forward. The carriage slowed to a stop, and the door swung open.

Zoey climbed out and was immediately hit by the rough winds and the hot toxic air. She squinted into the wind blown sand and could see the giant oval-shaped portal right in front of them. Its interior churned like hot magma.

"*Four* minutes!" she heard Simon yell over the roar of the winds.

Everyone's eyes were on her. It was time, but she had to wait for the carriage to leave. If the Keeper saw what she was up to, he would stop them. Unfortunately, he was waiting for them to cross . . . .

Tristan whispered. "I don't think he's leaving."

"I know," she answered.

"If you take it out now, he'll see it," said Tristan. He moved forward and sheltered her with his body.

"I know."

Zoey withdrew the first UEC with sweaty, trembling fingers.

"I'll open it, and then toss it in the portal as I step through."

"*Two*, freaking, minutes!" cried Simon.

"Be careful," said Tristan.

Zoey couldn't stop shaking. Her head started to spin. The quality of the air was so poor that she feared she might pass out if they didn't move soon. She flattened the UEC against her chest and waited.

Tristan raised his voice. "Let's go!"

He beckoned to the others, "Everyone, through the portal, and be careful once you get to the other side, we don't know what to expect. The Alphas might still be there."

"Fantastic," said Simon. "The fun just *never* ends."

He and Sonya escorted Elizabeth through the portal, but Tristan stayed back.

"You go with them. I'll do it," he said.

Zoey shook her head "No, I'm doing this. I need you to protect my mother for me."

She knew she had to do it.

"Go! Hurry," She pushed him, but her hands slipped, and she nearly dropped the UEC. Tristan shook his head to signify that the Keeper hadn't seen. He looked once more at Zoey and then stepped through the red portal.

Zoey had less than *sixty seconds* to detonate both UECs. Praying that the Keeper couldn't see what she was doing, she moved towards the portal.

She unscrewed the lid, flicked the fuse, and stepped into the red portal.

Just as the familiar feeling of being pulled forward overtook her, she rolled the bomb out of the portal behind her.

. . . forty-five seconds . . .

And then she started to doubt herself.

Did she do it properly? Would it even work or had it been damaged somehow? Had the skin demon deactivated it?

She couldn't see or sense Tristan or anyone, and she hoped that they all had made it safely across to the other side.

Her red surroundings dissolved into blue, and her skin felt cold. As her feet touched solid ground, Zoey pulled the second UEC out of the bag

. . . Ten seconds . . .

"YOU THERE, STOP! WHAT'RE YOU DOING!"

Blurry shapes came towards her. She could barely make out their red uniforms.

"STOP HER!"

She twisted the fuse, tossed the bomb into the portal, and then ran in the opposite direction.

... Five seconds ...

Three Alphas jumped inside the portal after the UEC.

... Four seconds ...

Would they reach it in time? Could they disarm it if they did?

... Three seconds ...

Zoey staggered away from the portal as fast as she could, but her legs were stiff, like she had never used them before. She feared she wouldn't make it far enough and that the bomb would kill her.

... Two seconds ...

As she ran, she searched frantically for her mother, for Tristan, for anyone she recognized—but she couldn't find them. Were they dead?

... One second ...

She heard someone calling her name. There was a blast of white light, and then she lost consciousness.

CHAPTER 24

GRADUATION

Zoey looked at herself in an old mirror up in the attic of the Wander Inn. There had hardly been any scarring. The blast from the explosion had left her with second and third degree burns on her back and parts of her legs. She would have been horribly scarred if the Seventh doctors had not rubbed a cold, sticky, green mystic medicine onto her skin. It had stopped the pain, too. And now she admired what few scars she had left. She even thought they were cool. They were a part of her. They reminded her that she was strong, and that with a little faith, she could achieve anything.

"They don't show anymore," said her mother as she wrapped tape around a cardboard box with the word, *KITCHEN*, written in black marker. Elizabeth's hair had grown a little, and she had it styled in a pixie cut that made her large green eyes stand out and made her look like a fairy.

Zoey pulled down her t-shirt. "I know, but I still love them. I think they're really cool. They make me look like a warrior princess or a pirate queen."

"Come here and give me a hand with this, *princess*," said her mother as she taped the box closed. "You were very lucky the blast from the bombs didn't do worse. You could have been killed."

"I know, but I wasn't," Zoey smiled.

She had always wondered what would have happened if she hadn't detonated the UECs. Had the scientists been right? Would the Great Junction portals have destroyed the worlds?

Simon and Tristan had paid her regular visits when she had been recovering, so she was up to date with the latest gossip at the Hive. Rumors had circulated that the infamous Mrs. Dupont had never really existed at all, which made Zoey very angry. But she also learned that an agreement had been reached between the Agency and the Alpha Nation just a week after she had destroyed the portals. More bloodshed had been averted. The Alphas were leaderless and seemed reluctant to continue their war with the Agency. Within weeks, they had faded back into whatever dark corners they had come from.

"Aria's really kind to give us some of her old stuff," said her mother.

She inspected an old brown mug that looked like it had been painted by a three-year-old child. "We're in her debt."

"Aria's awesome," smiled Zoey.

She helped her mother haul another box over to the mountain of sealed boxes, bags of clothes, lamps, and books on their old brown sofa.

"She's been really good to me, and she wouldn't want us to think that we owe her anything. I know her. She has a huge heart and just really wants to help."

Zoey felt a little awkward speaking about Aria to her mother, but Aria had been a real mother figure for her while her real mother was missing in action.

Her mother smiled and wiped some dust off her shirt.

"I know she does. So, are you looking forward to moving into our new home?" Her mother carefully wrapped a wine glass in newspaper. "It's in a really great little town, hidden from the rest of the world. It's where I grew up, you know. It's where I met your—"

Elizabeth stared at the glass in her hand.

"Where you met my father," said Zoey. She was still trying to wrap her mind around the fact that Nazar, the white-eyed sociopath, was her dad.

"Were you guys even married? Did you love him?"

Zoey hadn't brought up the subject of her real father since their escape from the Nexus.

Her mother placed another glass carefully into a new box.

"Well, I can tell you that we were very much in love at one point and foolish, very foolish. And against our parents' wishes, we eloped and moved in together. We were both working as agents with the Agency, and things were great for a while. But then . . . he changed. He started to hang around a new group of friends, friends that became Alphas. He still loved me, but he loved power *more*. And then he disappeared. A year later I learned that he had joined Mrs. Dupont. That's when I knew that I had lost him forever."

There were still a lot of unanswered questions. Zoey had only just found out who her father was. Was he dead? Was he trapped in the Nexus forever? Had he killed Mrs. Dupont? Would she ever know?

"He wasn't always like that," said her mother when she saw the grim expression on her daughter's face.

"He was good and kind man at one time. And that's how I want you to remember him, before he became lost in that mad woman's schemes. Nazar was a wonderful person. Remember that."

Zoey nodded her head.

"I can't wait to see our new place," she said quickly.

"It's only a two-bedroom apartment," said her mother as she ripped a piece of newspaper and wrapped a mug in it. "But it's a start. We can maybe get a house next year. Would you like that?"

Zoey wanted to tell her mother that she would live under a bridge if it meant being with her. But she said instead, "An apartment's fine, really. I know I'll love it."

Besides she was curious. What would it be like to live in a city filled with Sevenths and mystics?

"I've heard that our neighborhood is just for Sevenths. I think it's cool. It'll be like here at the Hive except *bigger*. And Tristan and Simon live there, too. I'll have my friends with me, so I won't feel like a total loser. It'll be great to have a real home."

Her mother smiled warmly and sighed. "Yes, yes it will."

She reached over and squeezed her daughter's hand. "Did you see where I put the pots and pans?"

"Here." Zoey picked up an open box filled with frying pans and worn pots.

"Thanks." Her mother set the box down and began securing the top with large amounts of tape.

"So, are you excited about your graduation? It's a pretty big deal."

"I am."

"But are you feeling up to it? You've only just come back from hospital. I'm sure they'll understand if you want to sit this one out—"

"Not a chance," said Zoey. "I'm sooooo going. Tristan and Simon are coming to pick me up later. Simon has my graduation robe—I have no idea what color it'll be, hopefully not *pink*. We're all going to go together."

"Well," said her mother, "if you're sure."

"Positive."

Elizabeth regarded her daughter for a moment. "You know, that Tristan is quite a handsome young man."

Zoey turned away quickly. "Ummm."

She wasn't ready to discuss boys with her mother. She wasn't even ready to discuss boys with herself.

They spent the rest of the afternoon packing the last of Aria's supplies. And as they packed Zoey told her mother about her years with the foster families before the Agency had found her. She told her about foster #28, about the skin demon, about Agents Barnes and Lee, and about her goal to become an agent.

Zoey was having so much fun with her mother that she had totally forgotten about the time until a knock came from the door.

"Zoey?" called Simon.

"In here!" Zoey brushed the dirt from her hands, but the ink from the newspapers wouldn't come off.

"Hey, it's us." Simon and Tristan peered around the corner.

Simon and Tristan were dressed in fine black robes with gold thread weaved around the collars and sleeves. They both looked very handsome in their new robes. The Minitian's potion had finally worn off, and Simon's regular goofy face and lanky body had returned. He held a black bundle under his arm. He pulled it out and gave it to Zoey.

"The ceremony starts in half an hour."

"I know. I know. I'm sorry. We were packing—"

"You better go get ready, Zoey," said her mother. "We'll finish up later. I'll see you at the ceremony, okay?"

"Okay."

Zoey admired her gleaming black robe.

"Thank God it's not pink. Give me five minutes, and I'll meet you guys downstairs."

Zoey dashed out of the attic. After a record quick shower, she brushed her wet hair into ponytail and pulled on a pair of jeans and a white t-shirt. Finally, she put on her glistening black silk robe and admired herself in the mirror one last time.

Just before she turned to leave, she grabbed the gold bracelet cuff that she had used to secure her boomerang and clasped it around her wrist. Even though she had lost her boomerang, the bracelet had become a good luck charm. It made her feel secure.

"Ready or not, here I come," she said to the mirror, and then she dashed out the door.

Taking the stairs two at a time, she leaped towards the Inn's front door, yanked it open, and ran outside.

"Made it!" she called as she bounded towards Tristan and Simon. "Told you, I only needed five minutes."

"It was more like ten," laughed Tristan, "But who's counting anyway?"

He had a package wrapped in yellow and pink gift paper under his arm. It was stiff so it was obvious it wasn't another robe, so what was it? He didn't mention it, so Zoey decided not to ask, even though she was dying to know what it was and whom it was for.

"We should get going. The ceremonies are about to start. Shall we?" said Simon, in a politician sort of voice, like he was on his way to make a speech. He raised his chin as he made his way across the grounds.

The early summer breeze was hot, and Zoey happily inhaled the fragrances from the blooming flowers. They made their way in silence towards the new wooden stage that had been built especially for the ceremony. All the seats were occupied by agents and the families of the graduates.

Zoey saw Agent Barnes and Agent Lee shifting in their seats excitedly. They beamed at her and gave her a thumbs up. Aria and her mother waved at her, too.

Tristan waved at a beautiful woman with long, wavy brown hair and the same dark eyes as his. The handsome man next to her had gray-blue skin and was covered with dark tribal tattoos. He grinned proudly as he waved at Tristan.

"Is that your dad?" whispered Zoey.

Tristan smiled awkwardly. "Yeah, that's him and my mom. I'll introduce you later if you want."

Zoey's throat tightened. "Okay." She wasn't sure how she felt about that.

All eyes were on them as they sat with the other graduates and waited patiently. Zoey took the seat next to Stuart King, who smiled at her.

"Hey, Zoey," he said quietly.

At first Zoey wasn't sure if this was his idea of a joke. She wasn't planning on punching him out, but she would if he started something. But Stuart just looked at her kindly. Was he delusional?

Zoey frowned, but then she managed to say. "Hey."

When she looked down at his hands, she could see that the ruby ring that he had once worn so proudly was gone.

Director Hicks and all the other directors were lined up on the platform beside a table that was covered with gleaming gold badges.

"Ahem." Director Hicks raised his arms.

"Good afternoon guests and family members of the graduates, members of the Agency community, and especially the graduates. I truly am honored to stand before you on this monumental day. Today's graduation ceremony recognizes your rigorous specialized training. You've completed a three-year program in less than two. Quite remarkable! Although we have experienced some hard times, you have all shown tremendous determination, courage, and a willingness to sacrifice."

His eyes rested on Zoey.

"I would like to congratulate all of you for making it to graduation and to personally thank you for the sacrifices you have made to help save our world and the agency.

"As new agents, your mandate is to protect the human world from those who don't respect our treaties. You are charged with keeping a balance between humanity and the mystics. Your role is to uphold the laws and keep our world safe. You should not take this responsibility lightly.

"I know that I speak for each of your departments and for your families when I say we are proud of your accomplishments today. As you go forward into the profession, continue to make us proud by carrying yourself with honor, dignity, and respect. Thank you for allowing me to speak today. I wish all of you in the graduating class the best in your new profession."

Director Hicks raised his arms. "Agents, please come forward."

One by one, the graduates stood up and made their way to the platform. Zoey waited anxiously and stood at the back of the line, behind Simon. Before she knew it, she was next to go.

Although her heart was galloping like an UEC bomb about to detonate, Zoey stood proudly in front of Director Hicks.

"Congratulations, Zoey."

He handed her a golden shield the size of her palm. The words, THE AGENCY, *Department of Defense*, were etched into the gold.

She was an agent.

She clasped her badge tightly, realizing that she had finally done it. She looked up at Director Hicks. "Thank you, director."

As she stepped off the platform, the crowd erupted in applause. Zoey's grin was as wide as her head.

"We did it!" boasted Simon as he jumped around in a happy dance. "I'm a *real* agent! I'm an agent!" He fell on the ground, kissing his new gold badge.

As the other graduates made their way to their families, Aria catered for the guests with everything from fried chicken to deviled eggs, smoked salmon, fried mozzarella balls, and sausage rolls.

As Zoey made her way towards the food, she heard a loud neigh over the hum of people's voices. She halted and turned towards the familiar sound.

In the golden meadow behind the Hive, a proud stallion blazed like wildfire in red and orange flames. Firefax.

But when she blinked, the horse was gone.

"Zoey? What is it?" Tristan stared at the spot where she had been looking. "Did you see something?"

Zoey shook her head. "It's nothing."

She rubbed her eyes. "I thought I saw something, but I was wrong."

She knew that Firefax didn't belong to anyone. Although he had saved her life, she didn't expect him to hang around. But she had thought the two of them shared a connection. Maybe she had imagined him.

Tristan moved closer towards Zoey. "I have something for you."

He handed her the mysterious package. "I hope it'll cheer you up."

"What?"

Zoey was way too nervous to meet his eyes as she unwrapped it. She tore off the paper.

"You got me a *boomerang*!" She said in more of a statement than a question. She was so excited she wanted to scream.

"I never thought I'd see one again. I know how rare they are."

"Well, I noticed that you were still wearing the bracelet on its own, so I thought you'd like to have another one. You like it?"

Zoey looked straight into Tristan's eyes.

"I love it. This is the best gift I've ever received, the *only* gift I've ever received. Only a *true* friend would have known how much I missed my old one. Thank you."

"I—I wanted you to know," he added softly, "that I really care about you. A lot."

He took her hand in his.

"I know," she said finally. "Me too."

She raised herself on her toes, leaned closer, and kissed him softly.

Tristan's joy spread across his face.

But before she could say anything more to him, she heard the neighing again. This time it was louder and more persistent.

Firefax blazed like a bonfire on the other side of the grounds. While the Agents and directors jumped at the sight of the wild creature, Zoey knew why he was there.

"I think there's someone who wants to say hi," said Tristan. "Go to him."

"You sure you don't mind?"

Zoey secured her new boomerang on her bracelet. A ride on Firefax would be the perfect ending to a perfect day.

Tristan smiled warmly. "Have fun. I'll see you later, Red."

Zoey lifted up her robe and ran to the firesteed.

The horse whinnied loudly at the sight of her, and she crashed head first into his strong body and wrapped her hands around his neck. She buried her face in his fiery mane, and the flames tickled her like warm fur.

"I missed you, boy." She squeezed harder.

Firefax lowered himself, and Zoey wrapped her hands around his long orange mane. She swung her right leg over the horse's back as if she had done it a thousand times before.

The horse straightened up and thrashed his long orange tail excitedly, trembling, anxious to run.

"You ready, Firefax?"

The horse whinnied loudly in reply.

Zoey tapped Firefax lightly with her heels and grabbed his orange mane.

"Let's go!"

The redheaded girl and her firesteed galloped across the grounds with orange and red flames trailing behind them. They galloped up the hill behind the Hive and then disappeared into the sunset.

Discover the world of **SOUL GUARDIANS**

CHAPTER 1
REBORN

"**W**ait for me!" Kara jogged along Saint Paul Street. She pressed her cell phone against her ear with a sweaty hand. "I'll be there in two minutes!"

Her black ballet flats tapped the cobblestones as she avoided oncoming traffic, her portfolio swung at her side. She jumped onto the sidewalk and ran through the crowd.

"I can't believe you're not here yet," said the voice on the other line. "You had to pick today of all days to be late!"

"Okay, okay! I'm already freaking out about the presentation. You're not exactly helping, Mat."

A laugh came through the speaker. "I'm just saying …that this is supposed to be the most important day of your life. And you, *Mademoiselle Nightingale*, are late."

"Yeah, I heard you the first time...MOTHER. It's not my fault. My stupid alarm didn't go off!" Kara dashed along the busy street, her long brown hair bouncing against her back. The smell of grease and beer from the pubs reached her nose and her heart hammered in her chest like a jackhammer. She knew if she missed the presentation her hopes of landing a scholarship were over. She didn't have any money for college, so this was her only shot.

Over the heads of the crowd, Kara could just make out the sign, Une Galerie. Stenciled elegantly in bold black letters, the name hovered above the art gallery's majestic glass doors. She could see shadows of people gathered inside. Her chest tightened. She was only a block away now.

"You know, the presentation won't wait for you—"

"Yes, yes, I know. I swear I'm gonna kick your butt when I get there!" Kara growled into the phone, trying to catch her breath.

For a horrible moment she thought she wasn't going to make it on time and considered getting off the sidewalk to run along the edge of the street instead. She looked back to see how bad the traffic was.

Then her heart skipped a beat.

Less than half a block behind, a man stood motionless and indifferent to the wave of humanity that flowed around him. He was staring at her. His white hair stood out against his dark grey tailored suit. Kara frowned.

His eyes are black, she realized.

A chill rolled up her spine. The man melted into the crowd and vanished, as though he were a mere trick of the light. The hair on the back of Kara's neck prickled as a sense of foreboding filled her and the urge to scream. Who was this man?

"I think I'm being followed," Kara spoke into her cell phone after a few seconds, her mouth dry.

"You always think you're being followed."

"No! I'm serious! I swear…this guy is following me—some psycho with white hair. I…I think I've seen him before. Or at least my mother has…"

"We all know your mother is a little *nutty* sometimes. No offense, I love your mom, but she's been seeing and talking to invisible people since we were five. I think it's rubbing off on you."

"Listen. I was with my mom yesterday on Saint Catherine Street, and she said we were being followed by someone. What if this is the same guy? Maybe she's not as crazy as everyone thinks." Kara wondered if there was a little truth in her mother's visions. She loved her mother very much, and she hated herself at times for thinking her mom belonged in a loony bin.

Mat laughed. "Are you serious? It's bad enough that your mom sees spirits and demons. If you start believing in all that, they'll lock you up."

"Thanks for the vote of confidence. Remind me why you're my best friend again?" Kara decided to drop the subject. After all, the strange man was gone and her fear of him was melting away with every step, replaced by nerves and restlessness for her presentation. She focused on the gallery sign as she ran. "Okay…I can see you now."

Mat was leaning against the gallery's brick exterior. His head was turned toward the glass doors. He pulled his cigarette from his lips and blew smoke into his phone's receiver. "I think it's starting. Hurry up!"

Kara felt her cheeks burn. Her heart pounded in her ears and muffled the sounds around her. She took a deep breath, hoping it would calm the fluttering in her stomach, and she sprinted onto Saint Laurence Boulevard. Her cell phone slipped out of her hand and hit the pavement.

"Crap!" Kara crouched down to grab her phone. "Stupid phone—"

A flicker of movement appeared in the corner of her eye.

"WATCH OUT!" Someone shouted. She stood up and turned around.

A city bus hurtled towards her. She stared, transfixed. The bus kept coming.

EEEEEEEEEEEEEEEEE!

An arm reached out to her. She saw a split second image of two monstrous headlights.

And then it hit.

Thirteen tons of cold metal crushed her body. She didn't feel any pain. She didn't feel anything at all.

Everything around her went black.

A moment later, Kara was standing in an elevator.

At first, streaks of white light obscured her vision. She blinked and rubbed her eyes. The elevator was elegant...three sides appeared to be made of handcrafted cherry panels decorated with golden-wing crests. The smell of moth balls lingered in the air, like her grandma's dusty old closet. When her eyesight improved, she realized that she wasn't alone.

On a wooden chair facing the elevator's control panel covered in black fur and wearing a pair of green Bermuda shorts from which protruded two hand-like callused feet, sat a *monkey*.

It spun on its seat, wrapped its feet around the backrest of the chair, opened its coconut-shaped mouth and said, "Hello, Miss."

Kara's jaw dropped, and she swallowed the urge to cry out. She stared at the beast, terror rising up inside her.

His hairless face crinkled into a grin so that he looked like an oversized walnut. His square head sat directly on powerful shoulders. He raised his chin and looked down upon Kara. His yellow eyes mesmerized her; she couldn't look away.

He looks like Old Man Nelson from the hardware store, she thought wildly.

After a minute, Kara was able to force some words out of her mouth.

"H …hey there, little talking-monkey-person," she croaked and then whispered to herself, "This is definitely the wildest dream I've ever had. I have to remember to tell Mat about this tomorrow when I wake up." Her throat was dry like she hadn't had a sip of water in weeks. She tried to swallow, but all she could do was contract her throat muscles.

The monkey frowned. Then he growled. "I'm not a *monkey*, Miss. I'm a chimpanzee! You mortals are all the same. Monkey-this, monkey-that. Might as well call me a *dog*!" A splatter of spit hit Kara's face as the words escaped his lips.

Kara retched as she wiped the spit from her face. It was yellowish green and smelled like a bad case of gingivitis.

"Ah ...sorry, monk—chimpanzee." She rubbed her hand on her blue jeans and made a face. "This is *beyond* weird. I thought you *couldn't* smell anything in dreams, at least that's what I thought. But this...it actually smells real and totally gross."

The chimp glared at Kara with a mixture of disdain and indignation. "*Chimp* Number 5M51, if you please."

He then began to scratch his behind, and only stopped once he noticed Kara's disgusted expression.

"You'll be arriving at your destination momentarily." And with that, he turned his attention back to the control panel.

Gradually, Kara began to feel more awake, as though she had woken from a long, deep sleep. Reality slowly crawled back in along with the fear that perhaps this *wasn't* a dream. She bit her lower lip as she told herself to *think*.

"Um, what destination? Where are we going?" she asked, her eyes focused on the talking chimpanzee.

Chimp 5M51 turned his head and smiled, exposing rows of crooked yellow teeth. His eyes locked onto hers. "To Orientation, of course. Level One."

"Orientation?"

"Yes. All mortals who have passed must go through Orientation. That's where you're going." Chimp 5M51 clamped his feet around the edges of the chair and extended an abnormally long arm in the direction of the elevator's control pane. He pointed to the brass buttons.

Kara leaned over for a better view. The panel read:

1. Orientation

2. Operations

3. Miracles Divisions

4. Hall of Souls

5. Department of Defense

6. Council of Ministers

7. The Chief

A feeling of dread slowly rose up inside her. She stared at the panel, dizzy, her knees weak like she was about to collapse. "This…this doesn't make sense. I…I'm dreaming. This is a dream!"

Kara shut her eyes and pressed her back against the elevator wall, trembling. "It *can't* be happening. It just *can't*! I need to wake up now. Kara you need to *wake* up!"

"You're dead, Miss."

Kara opened her eyes. The word *dead* echoed in her ears like some sick joke. The weight of his words started to pull her under. She fought against the overwhelming feeling of panic.

"I'm not dead!" she hissed, "I'm right here, you stupid BABOON!"

"...Chimpanzee!" Spat Chimp 5M51. "Think what you must," he said, as he lifted his chin. "But think about this. Can you remember the events before this elevator?"

Kara floundered, trying desperately to remember. Bits and pieces flashed inside her brain: a white light ...metal ... darkness ...

The bus.

Kara dropped to her knees. The city bus had hit her...pulverized her core and crushed her like a tomato. But then she remembered something else, something that didn't make any sense. It was coming back to her now, like a faded memory sharpening into a clear picture. It flashed before her eyes...she saw an arm reach out and touch her during the bus crash. Someone had tried to save her...

"See? You're dead," said the chimp matter-of-factly, and Kara detected a hint of amusement in his voice, as though he enjoyed watching her struggle in misery and confusion.

As she pulled herself together she pressed her hand against the left side of her chest, she couldn't feel a heartbeat. She pressed down on her rib cage. Nothing. She clasped her wrist. No pulse. No beating. No movement at all.

"See. No beating. No heart...you're dead," declared the chimp again. Kara felt herself wanting to punch him.

But before she could make sense of what was happening, she was thrown off balance as the elevator stopped abruptly.

"Level One. Orientation!" The chimp announced.

"Wait!" Kara pushed herself away from the elevator wall and wobbled up to the chimp. "I don't understand. What's Orientation?"

With his finger still on the button, he turned his head. "Orientation is where all the new GAs are categorized."

Kara stared stupidly into chimp 5M51's yellow eyes. "What are GAs?"

"Guardian Angels."

"Huh?"

Kara heard the swish of doors opening. A hint of a smile reached the chimp's lips. He raised his arm and pressed his hand on her back. Then she flew out the elevator.

KIM RICHARDSON

About the Author

Kim Richardson is the author of the SOUL GUARDIANS series. She was born in a small town in Northern Quebec, Canada, and studied in the field of 3D Animation. As an Animation Supervisor for a VFX company, Kim worked on big Hollywood films and stayed in the field of animation for 14 years. Since then, she has retired from the VFX world and settled in the country where she writes fulltime.

To learn more about the author, please visit:

www.kimrichardsonbooks.com

Printed in Germany
by Amazon Distribution
GmbH, Leipzig